# TURNING LEAVES

## Pamela Oldfield

This first world edition published in Great Britain 2004 by
SEVERN HOUSE PUBLISHERS LTD of
9–15 High Street, Sutton, Surrey SM1 1DF.
This first world edition published in the USA 2005 by
SEVERN HOUSE PUBLISHERS INC of
595 Madison Avenue, New York, N.Y. 10022.

British Library Cataloguing in Publication Data

Oldfield, Pamela
    Turning Leaves
    1.  Communication in marriage  -  Fiction
    2.  Older people  -  Fiction
    I.  Title
    823.9'14 [F]

    ISBN 0-7278-6158-1

"*Telling Leanne*" and "*Fallout*" were first published in *You Magazine.*

# Contents

Ghost Story                                    1

Strawberry Fair                               12

Emmeline                                      22

Telling Leanne                               29

Number 18                                    41

Sylvia's Downfall                            49

Fairy-Tale Ending                            56

Seriously Weird                              71

Sacking Mizz Stewart                         79

Final Solution                               90

Flying Leap                                  101

The Stalker                                  112

Minutes of the Last Meeting                  121

Growing Up                                   129

The Power of Love                            139

Unforgiven                                   147

The Cheeseboard                              156

The Morning After                            167

A Real Gentleman                             182

What Goes Around Comes Around                190

Compromise                                   199

Fallout                                      208

# Ghost Story

It all came about by chance. Or was it chance? Looking back, I sometimes wonder if it was 'meant'. Anyway, one evening we asked our nearest neighbours round. A spur of the moment thing. Lottie, otherwise known as Charlotte, hates to provide what she laughingly refers to as 'dinner at eight' and prefers to do things off the cuff.

'Want to come for supper?' she asked. 'Tonight. Pot luck as usual.'

They jumped at the chance. Bill and Meg never refuse food. They're a sweet couple about the same age as us and we're early forties. They married young and their two daughters were late teens, so they didn't need a babysitter. We had no family. Just one of those things. We tried various things but then gave up. I could see the anguish Lottie was going through and called a halt. We have each other and it's perfectly possible to be happy without a family. Lottie's got two sisters and their children spend a lot of time with us. They love it here.

Our homes are situated along the cliffs in Fairlight near Hastings. We live in the house where I grew up. I'm an only child and I'd only ever known one place I could call home. When my parents died they left it to me and I knew I could never sell it. Lottie argued at first but then gave in. I think she realized how important it was to me although she didn't know why and I couldn't tell her.

'I'll make a very superior cottage pie,' she announced. 'Easy-peasy.'

In the kitchen later that evening Lottie said, 'You do realize it's Hallowe'en.'

I hadn't. 'So what?' I said. 'Thinking of going trick-or-treating?'
I knew the answer to that. We both hated the idea.

'Of course not but we could do *some*thing.'

'Such as?'

'Something spooky, creepy, scary . . . You name it, we could do it.'

We thought about it as she opened the oven door and slid the cottage pie into the oven. She believes in slow cooking. I love cottage pie. Lottie always makes more than enough so we can finish it up the following day. My job would be the salads and Lottie would make masses of garlic bread. Cheese, biscuits and grapes to follow. Dead easy. She straightened up and pushed back her hair – the frizzy mop of ginger hair had been what first attracted me to her across a crowded room. It shone like a beacon and although she isn't conventionally pretty, she has large golden-brown eyes that give her an animal look which is very sexy. To me, anyway.

'We could eat by the light of the moon,' I suggested. 'Curtains pulled well back. That would be spooky.'

'Mmm . . .? I don't think so. We'd get food all over the place. Big veto moonlit supper.'

'You have no romance in your soul, Lottie!'

She began to chop garlic then glanced up. 'What about candlelight and we've got those incense sticks?'

'Candlelight's fine by me.'

We've got central heating but we turn it down in the evening and light the fire. Firelight and candlelight would be spooky enough.

'And we could tell ghost stories!' I said.

I don't why I said it. The words just rushed out and it was too late to take them back. I was immediately terrified. What on earth had prompted me to say such a thing?

Lottie was looking at me, eyes gleaming with excitement. 'Sometimes you're positively brilliant,' she told me. 'Ghost stories by candlelight!'

I stared at her wordlessly. Too late. The deed was done. I shivered.

She was waiting for me to elaborate, so I said, 'Hallowe'en and all that!'

To me it sounded feeble but she seemed not to notice the slight tremor in my voice.

'Perfect time and place,' she agreed. 'But do we know any ghost stories?'

*I* did but all I said was: 'We'll think of something. I'll ring Bill and Meg and warn them what is required.'

She grinned. 'You know what they say – there's no such thing as a free meal!'

As I went in search of the mobile I thought seriously of back-pedalling. The trouble was I could see by Lottie's delighted expression that she loved the idea and if I tried to change her mind she would insist on knowing why. I couldn't explain because I still couldn't talk about it. I had hugged my secret for so many years that it had become a part of me. Something precious that must never be shared. Never exposed to the scepticism of outsiders.

In the lounge I stood with the phone in my hand, appalled at what I had done.

'But perhaps the time has come,' I whispered. I had always felt bad about keeping it from Charlotte. When we married we had agreed no secrets and she trusted me. I took a deep breath and dialled Bill's number. Part of me hoped they would have another engagement they'd forgotten about and then it would all be off. But they didn't.

Later that afternoon Lottie asked, 'What's up, Hugh?'

Very quick on the uptake, my ever-loving wife.

'Nothing.'

'You seem worried.'

'About what?' I tried to sound innocent.

'How should I know? You tell me.'

'I'm not worried. Satisfied?'

She gave me one of her looks but let it pass.

Hours later we were all seated round the table. The fire blazed cheerfully and there were candles everwhere. We had decided to eat first and save the ghost stories until we had drunk a few glasses of wine. Dutch courage, if you like. I was desperately trying to think of an alternative ghost story but my mind remained a blank.

Meanwhile we just chatted. We get on very well as a foursome. Bill works for a private maintenance firm and can turn his hand to almost anything. He helped us when we built the conservatory. Meg's a florist with a small shop in the nearby town. Lottie's an agency nurse in Hastings and I design garden layouts. We're never short of something to talk about and when it comes to politics we argue like mad.

When we'd finished the meal Bill and I loaded the dishwasher and the girls made coffee and opened the chocolate mints. We were very full and I had drunk more than usual. We all slumped into the sofas and I tried to relax. I still hadn't been able to think of a ghost story that I wanted to tell – only one that I wanted to keep to myself.

Meg said, 'Who's going to start?'

There were no volunteers.

Bill said, 'We could roll dice and the lowest score is first and so on. Highest score goes last.'

It was agreed and Lottie found some dice. We rolled. Three, six, eight and eleven. I was going last. I breathed a sigh of relief. The burning logs sent flickering shadows into every corner of the room and the candles glowed softly. I could see Lottie was enjoying herself and tried to believe that I was doing the right thing.

Lottie went first. Her story was one she had read years ago when she was ten and it had frightened her half to death!

'It was in one of my storybooks, given to me by a well-meaning aunt,' she explained. 'I was about eight when I read it and it gave me nightmares for ages afterwards.'

The story was about a haunted picture that brought bad luck to everyone who owned it. Before the curse was recognized as such, one owner had died. Eventually one of the owners suspected that there was something evil about it and burned it. The curse disappeared.

'And they all lived happily ever after!'

I must say she told it very well and earned herself a round of applause.

'Except you,' said Meg. 'You had nightmares!'

Laughing, Lottie agreed.

Then it was Bill's turn and he explained that his story was one he'd written years earlier to enter in a competition.

'I was twenty-two and couldn't write for toffee,' he told us. 'But the prize was a lawnmower and Meg and I had just bought our first flat – on the ground floor with a garden. We were the proud owner of a neglected lawn but very hard-up. I was so sure I was going to win the mower.'

Meg grinned. 'He didn't win, by the way!'

We soon saw why. The tale involved a haunted mill pond and a ghostly black dog that lived in its murky depths. The owner of the mill was an eccentric old man who collected books on black magic. The story was impossibly complicated and we were soon reduced to hysterics although Bill insisted that it was not meant to be funny. There was also a mad vicar, an evil witch and a beautiful maiden who eventually turned into the dog which then hurled itself off a handy cliff. We laughed so much my sides ached.

Lottie wiped her eyes. 'Have you ever heard the phrase "overkill", Bill?'

Bill emptied his glass. 'It scared you though, didn't it?'

Which set us off laughing again. I said quickly that I thought he had ruined the mood and should we forget the rest of the stories? I suggested watching a video but was howled down.

Meg said, 'That's not fair. It's my turn and I'm going to read it.'

'Read it? That's cheating!' Lottie appealed to the rest of us.

'It's that or nothing!' she insisted. 'Please yourselves!'

It was written by someone many years ago when ghost stories were very much in vogue and it was truly spooky. We listened in a respectful silence. I'd heard it before but Meg read it brilliantly and breathed new life into the old tale.

5

Lottie withdrew to make fresh coffee and then it was my turn. All eyes turned to me. 'I . . . I don't know . . .' I stammered, suddenly panicking.

There was a chorus of protests and Lottie gave me another of her looks.

'You must!' cried Meg. 'It was your idea in the first place! You can't duck out now.'

Lottie looked at me. 'What's wrong, Hugh?'

'Nothing. I mean, I do have a story but . . . but nobody will believe it.'

Bill poured himself another coffee. 'We don't have to *believe* it. We just have to be entertained by it. Nobody believed mine, so why should we believe yours?'

Meg popped a mint into her mouth and mumbled, 'Oh get on with it, Hugh! It's only a bit of fun.'

I still hesitated. In a way, now that the moment had come, part of me wanted to tell it. 'It's a first-person story,' I warned. 'That's the way I have to tell it. Take it or leave it.'

Bill said, 'First person? You're not saying this is a true story . . . or are you?'

Meg laughed delightedly. 'Can't you see what he's doing? The crafty devil?! He's building up atmosphere! Softening up the audience!'

Lottie was watching me. 'Do you want to tell it, darling? You don't have to.'

Bill said, 'Read it if you can't tell it.'

'It's not that exactly . . .' My heart began to beat erratically under their scrutiny.

'Who's the author?' Lottie asked.

'I am.'

Now I had all their interest.

Bill said, 'You sly old dog! You've written a story! Has it been published?'

We had reached the point of no return. They were all looking at me expectantly, so, fortified with another glass of red wine, I began.

'*. . . It was my birthday, the fifth of August and I was still a*

6

*boy – fourteen years old . . .'* I took a deep breath. Lottie reached out and took my hand in hers, '. . . *and not expected to reach fifteen. The doctors had kept me alive for a year longer than anyone expected and my parents could no longer pretend. And neither could I. Leukaemia is a killer unless it is caught early and even then, it can't always be treated successfully . . .'*

I paused. My voice, shaky at first, was growing firmer. I couldn't look at the others but I knew from their silence that they were already intrigued. A first-person telling is always so intimate. They were wondering, a little uneasy, not knowing what to expect or quite how to react. I went on.

'. . . *I had accepted my fate some months before that day and I was very calm. I was on the beach alone. Just the sound of the waves and the gulls screaming overhead. I had no brothers or sisters but I did have friends. Sometimes, however, I wanted no one's company but my own because I had things to think about that other kids couldn't share. I glanced up at the bungalow and my mother waved from the window, so I knew she'd been watching me as I wandered along the beach, picking up shells. I waved back. I knew what heartache it was for her and my father and I worried about them . . .'*

I took a deep breath and Meg said softly, 'Something tells me this doesn't have a happy ending!'

Bill said, 'Shh! Don't interrupt him.'

'. . . *I would be at peace, whatever that meant, but they would be left to grieve. I couldn't think of any way to save them from that. I kicked an old shoe into the water and followed it with a few pebbles. Then I noticed a girl coming towards me and for a moment I considered turning back before she reached me. I looked very odd with my bald head, thin frame and pale gaunt face and I knew I would see pity in her eyes. It always happened when I met someone for the first time. I was so obviously desperately ill. Instead of showing horror, however, this girl's face was alight with a radiant smile. Her smooth hair was long and dark and her eyes were grey. She was barefoot and wore a long dress which floated around her as she moved.*

7

*"Hi there!" she cried and half ran to cover the remaining distance between us. I thought she'd be carrying her shoes but her hands were empty. She arrived breathless and waited for me to speak.*

*"Hi there!" I echoed, feeling rather stupid. I wasn't used to girls. Still thought of them as silly creatures who later on would somehow set about breaking men's hearts.*

*She wasn't in the least shy. "You don't recognize me," she said, "but I know you! You're Hugh Davies. My name's Moyna."*

*"Nice name." It was all I could think of. Too late I realized I could have said "Pleased to meet you" or something like that. Something a bit more mature.*

*Moyna looked about my age but she was very self-confident. "I've seen you around," she told me with a sly smile. "I bet you haven't seen me!"*

*"I don't think so. Should I have?"*

*"You should have," she laughed, "but things went a bit haywire, so you couldn't. Anyway, happy birthday, Hugh!"*

*Now I was really confused. I hated riddles. I didn't think I'd ever met her before but presumably I had or how did she know me? And she knew it was my birthday. It was weird . . .'*

Lottie leaned closer. 'Are you sure you're OK?' she whispered. I nodded. She offered a second cup of coffee but no one was interested. Meg and Bill were still staring at me, waiting for the rest of the story. By now I think they all suspected that the story was more than just a ghostly tale. I took a deep breath and continued.

'. . . *"I have to sit down," I told her abruptly and managed to make it as far as the large rock where I always rested. My legs were trembling with the effort of standing so long but I didn't want her to think me a wimp. Because of the illness I wasn't eating well and I didn't sleep at night. My energy was ebbing away fast.*

*Moyna sat down beside me as though it was the most natural thing in the world. "I'm sorry you've been so alone," she said softly. "I didn't want it that way – but I was never far away from you."*

*I was tired and growing irritated. She knew something I didn't know but why did she have to be so mysterious? Before I could say something I might have regretted, she stood up and turned slowly round as though she were modelling an outfit on a catwalk.*

*"Look at me, Hugh. What do you see? Anything you recognize?"*

*There was something vaguely familiar about her but I was beginning to feel unwell. I knew the symptoms. "I . . . I have to go home now," I stammered. "I have to lie down."*

*I stood up but she caught my hand. "Wait! I brought you something. A birthday present."*

*Before I could guess what she intended she threw her arms around me in a hug. Girls didn't often hug me. Actually they never did, so I didn't struggle. I stood stock still and felt her warmth flow into my poor thin body. She pressed closer, her face against mine, her hands stroking my back. It was so wonderful, so . . . unearthly, that I closed my eyes. I wanted it to last and last . . . After what seemed like for ever, I felt her draw away and she kissed my cheek. A kiss so light I wondered afterwards if I'd imagined it.*

*"Goodbye, Hugh!"*

*Slowly I opened my eyes. She had slipped away. I searched the beach in both directions but there was no sign of her. Dazed but happy I made my way slowly up the wooden steps to the bungalow.*

*Mum saw me coming and caught me as I collapsed . . .'*

There was silence for a moment.

Meg said, 'Did he die?'

Bill said, 'Of course he did. The girl was Death coming to claim him!'

Lottie said nothing but she was watching me with those lovely golden-brown eyes. Now I couldn't stop. I quite desperately needed to tell it all.

'. . . *My mother gave me hot milk with honey and time to rest and recover. I told her what had happened and she listened carefully. Then, with one arm round me, she helped*

9

*me along the road to the nearby churchyard. There was a small grave tucked away in one corner. Although the grass was long and full of stinging nettles, the grass on the tiny grave had been neatly clipped and there were fresh flowers in a small holder.*

*Moyna Ann Davies*
*Died at birth – 5th August 1959*
*Beloved Daughter and Sister*

*I was slow to take it in. Then, shocked, I looked at my mother. "Does this mean I was a twin?"*

*She nodded. "There were complications . . . I don't know why we didn't tell you when you you were old enough to understand. I suppose because you became ill. We thought you'd be upset and kept delaying it. And now . . . she's come to you."*

*"But . . . but how?" I dropped heavily to my knees beside the stone and ran my fingers across the chiselled words.*

*"I don't know, Hugh. I really don't understand. Your father might be able to explain it."*

*He couldn't. That evening we all cried for the little soul that was lost but I still didn't know what to think. What was the present she had given me? A kiss? A hug? That wonderful hug was present enough but somehow I felt there was more to it than a sisterly embrace.*

*That night I slept deeply for the first time for months and I woke feeling refreshed. I was hungry. I ate porridge with milk and brown sugar while Mum fussed round me, thrilled with the change in me.*

*Three months later I was discharged from the hospital, totally free of all signs of the leukaemia. No one outside the family could understand it and we couldn't bear to talk about it. We agreed to keep Moyna's birthday present a secret . . .'*

Bill said, 'Wow!' and exchanged a glance with Meg.

She said, 'That's the most wonderful thing I've ever heard. It was you, wasn't it?'

I nodded. Lottie was staring at me reproachfully and I knew what she was thinking.

'I tried to tell you,' I told her. 'Many times. I wanted you to know but I couldn't do it. I thought that if you didn't believe me it might break the spell. I might somehow become ill again.' I shrugged. 'I'm sorry.' I blinked frantically as tears threatened. After so long the relief was unbelievable.

Lottie slid an arm round my shoulders and pressed close. 'So that's why you won't move away from this bungalow. Now I understand. You're afraid of losing touch with your sister!' She kissed me and hugged me while I wept.

For once Meg and Bill were lost for words. There was a long silence and Bill rallied. 'My God, Hugh. That's the ghost story to beat all ghost stories!'

He was right, of course.

Ghost stories . . . As Charlotte had said – there's a time and place . . .

# Strawberry Fair

There were five of us that Thursday morning. Mr Trimbull called us his regulars and we were exactly that. Pickers who picked anything in the fields between Rye and Hastings. Strawberries, blackcurrants, raspberries – even apples. We looked on ourselves as a team and we moved from farm to farm as the fruit came into season. Picking strawberries was back-breaking work. Some of them stood over the rows and bent down to the fruit. Others like me, knelt on something soft, like an old rubber hot-water bottle, and shuffled along. It's hard however you do it, but you get used to it.

We enjoyed the company and the money came in useful. This year for Kath the money was for her kid's school uniform. At eleven her son Michael was leaving the village school and transferring to the secondary school in Rye. Green cap, green blazer. For Lou and May, sisters, it was for their week's holiday in Cornwall at the end of September. For old Mrs March it was for coal for the winter.

For me it was money we saved for the car we were going to buy one day. Me and Tom, that is. My husband. He was caretaker at the secondary school and I was proud of him. Not because he was a school caretaker although it was a worthwhile job but because he was also an amateur actor and from time to time I'd see him on stage at the village hall and he'd have his photo in the local paper. At twenty-five he was young enough to play various leading parts and he had a wonderful memory for lines. Me, I can't even remember birthdays!

On this particular morning we were picking strawberries at Lunsfell Farm. It was nine thirty. We didn't pick any earlier because you have to let the dew dry on the fruit. We worked in adjacent rows so we could chat and because it kept us up to speed. Nobody wanted to be last to reach the end of their row.

The sun was hot for June and I began to sing although I knew it would drive Lou mad.

'*As I was going to Strawberry Fair,*
*Singing, singing, buttercups and daisies,*
*I met a maiden taking her wares, fol-de-dee . . .*'

Lou said, 'Pack it in, Sally!'

I grinned. 'Sorry!' I never did get further than the first three lines before she complained.

'You're not a bit sorry!' she grumbled.

She hates the old ditty for some reason. Says it's arty rubbish.

I popped a large ripe strawberry into my mouth and bit into it. I love strawberries. Trimbull, the farmer, lets us eat as many as we like while we're picking. He knows we'll sneak some anyway but he reckons that we'll get fed up with them after a day or so and give up on them. Most of the women do, but not me. We pick into large cardboard trugs and then take them to the end of the rows to be collected by Trimbull's son and taken into the weighing shed. That's how they know how much to pay us. It's by the hour but if you pick extra weight you get a small bonus.

Kath said, 'So are we going to see your Tom in a play this year?'

I nodded. '*The Glass Menagerie.* You know – all those little glass animals. That's the title. He's got the lead again and I'm helping him learn the words by reading all the other parts. He plays this Welsh chap who's committed a murder and he keeps whistling a certain tune and that's the clue that helps the police to catch him. Bette Sanders is in it and Errol Tookey. The usual lot.'

I can't act for toffee but I help with the costumes. Making them and helping the cast on and off with them when they have quick changes between the scenes.

13

Mrs March turned to Kath and said, 'Your Michael gone to camp then?'

She nodded. 'A long weekend. He loves it. Camp fire and sing-songs and whatever they do.'

May grinned. 'Dib, dib, dib!'

'That's not scouts, that's cubs! Fat lot you know about it.'

Suddenly their words registered and I stopped picking. 'Gone to camp? It's not half-term yet.'

'Of course it is.'

They went on picking but as the words sank in I went hot and cold. Tom had gone off at the usual time. He hadn't said it was half-term – so where was he if he wasn't at the school checking the boilers for the hot water and cleaning the windows or suchlike? Like a fool I said, 'You sure?'

Sue said, 'Sure as eggs is eggs! My two are with my mum.'

Then they all stared at me. I must have gone pale because Lou said, 'Are you OK, Sal?'

I sat back heavily on to Kath's row and felt strawberry juice seep through my shorts. 'No, I'm not OK. I think I'm going to faint!' I really thought I would. It was the shock of knowing that Tom had deliberately deceived me for the first time ever – at least to my knowledge. He had let me think it was work as usual and had gone off on his bike with his usual cheery wave. I started to shake. We had been living together for three years and I had never loved anyone else. In time we planned to get married but nothing was cast in stone.

Lou said, 'Didn't Tom tell you?'

I didn't answer and they looked at each other and then at me. I asked them, 'Is something going on? Tell me!'

They assured me that they didn't know anything and I believed them. Especially Kath, whose husband had left her for another woman years ago. She would have warned me. I know she would.

Now she said, 'You'd best get after him, Sal!'

Before I could answer she called up to Trimbull and said I was feeling faint and would have to go home. He grumbled but I said if I could I'd go back after lunch and he agreed.

As I walked home I felt rather sick but it was fright more than anything I'd eaten. Where, I wondered, had Tom gone? Who was he with? What were they doing? By the time I reached the cottage my legs were shaking and I made myself a cup of tea, added two sugars for energy and reached for the biscuits. I was on my third chocolate digestive when I tumbled to it. It had to be Bette Sanders, his leading lady.

'Got you!' I muttered. At least I could soon check *her* out because she and her husband Flynn lived less than half a mile away.

The Sanderses lived in the end house of a row of three fairly modern buildings. Ten minutes later I was standing outside the house wondering what to do next. If I simply knocked and asked to speak to my husband she would probably deny he was there and I could hardly force my way in. I would have to be more subtle than that. I suddenly remembered that a small alley ran past the back of the houses for the dustbins, so I could walk past the back and take a peek. I didn't want to find him there but if I didn't I wouldn't know where else to look. Crossing my fingers, I sauntered casually to the third house and turned into the alley.

Long before I reached the Sanderses' place I heard them laughing together. Closing my eyes, I was confused by a rush of unfamiliar bitterness. Here was Tom 'playing away' while I was supposed to be working in the fields for the money to buy our first car. I thought of Kath and for the first time I understood what she had gone through.

Then I saw them through a gap in the hedge. They were sitting close together on a tartan rug and in front of them there was a dish of crisps, two glasses and a bottle of wine. How very elegant! How utterly *tasteful*! I felt a great surge of anger. I wanted to burst through the hedge, screaming at them – but mostly at Tom because I loved him and had trusted him. I wanted to stamp on their stupid crisps and empty the wine over the marigolds in her nasty little flower bed. Just in time I saw how foolish I would look if I let them see how hurt and angry I was. No doubt they would get together afterwards and laugh about me. I'd be 'Poor old Sally!' and Bette would pass the story round the village. Instead, I turned around and walked back the way I had come, thinking hard.

Tom came home at the usual time and I tried to appear normal. Dinner was ready and we chatted as usual. I asked Tom about school and he was very cool. He invented several incidents – one about a badly behaved child and another about a row he had had with the headmaster. He certainly could act! I was trying hard but he obviously sensed something was wrong. After a while he said, 'Are you OK?'

'Not particularly,' I said. 'I nearly fainted at Trimbull's this morning and had to come home. I expect it was the sun.'

He nodded, not really listening. Then he said, 'Oh by the way, we've got an extra rehearsal tonight. John's not too happy about the way things are shaping up. From eight to about ten.'

I nodded without speaking because I didn't believe him for one moment. But I would find out. I would ring John after Tom had left and ask him what time he expected the rehearsal to end. I was recovering from the initial shock and my courage was returning. Also an idea was forming in my brain – a plan of campaign, for want of a better term. At ten to eight, as Tom left for the so-called rehearsal, he said, 'Oh by the way, tomorrow is half-term. We've also got the Monday and Tuesday off. I thought we could have a day out somewhere.'

I tried to sound grateful but I wondered if this would mean 'accidentally' meeting up with the Sanderses. It's amazing how suspicious you become at such times. As soon as he'd gone I rang John Sowsbury, the director of the dramatic society. He's a very decent man in his fifties who was once a professional actor although he was never famous.

'Tonight?' he echoed in reply to my question. 'Not tonight, Sally. Tell him he's got his wires crossed!'

'Thanks, John. I'll catch him before he leaves.'

By this time I had perfected my plan and was eager to put

it into action. Actually I was eager to do anything rather than sit at home being miserable. I desperately wanted to talk to my mother but I knew she would worry – and she would never forgive Tom! Mothers never do. And that would muddy the waters for the future and I wanted to avoid that.

I went upstairs and had a quick shower and put on lots of perfume. Then I dressed carefully in my new short skirt, a frilly off-the-shoulder top and my best dangly earrings which my ever-loving husband had given me for my birthday. Finally I applied glamorous make-up – glossy lipstick, blusher, eyeliner, the lot! I did look rather dishy by the time I'd finished and it gave me some much needed confidence.

Downstairs, I went to the fridge and took out some strawberries which I had brought home the previous day with the intention of making a fruit trifle. I lined a small carton with a paper serviette and filled it with the luscious berries. Then I set off for the Sanderses' house.

Flynn answered my knock and he stared at me in surprise. He was fair with sleepy grey eyes and what magazines call a 'generous' mouth. He was wearing shorts and sandals and a terrible faded shirt that had once been Hawaiian. After studying me in some surprise he glanced up and down the road as though I might have a support group hidden away. Before he could say anything, however, I started on my spiel.

'Hi! I'm Tom's wife. Tom as in Dramatic Society.' I smiled brightly.

He frowned. 'Do I know you?' He looking warily at the strawberries.

'I think we met at the village hall once or twice. Tom and Bette are often on stage together. I'm behind the scenes and you're in the audience.'

He began to nod. 'Perhaps we met at the after-show party!'

'Probably.' I didn't remember seeing him but he didn't need to know that. 'I brought us some strawberries,' I went on chattily. 'I thought while they're at this extra rehearsal you and I are both alone. Seemed silly. Why not get together?'

'Really? We-ell . . . I don't know.'

Poor Flynn. I thought he was going to refuse, so I said quickly, 'I need to talk to you. Actually I need your help.'

He was intrigued. 'My help? Well, you'd better come on in.'

Once inside his lounge I gave him the strawberries. 'They might need a bit of sugar.'

The room was what I'd call homely. A polished wood floor, a wood-burning stove, a frayed carpet and lumpy sofas. But it was clean and smelled of lavender polish. There were early roses on the windowsill and the horse brasses had been recently polished. I was glad Flynn hadn't turned up on our doorstep unannounced.

He nodded towards an armchair which was covered by a brightly coloured throw and I sat down, crossing my legs carefully and smiling to lull his suspicions. When he returned he had shared the strawberries between two dishes and had added a scoop of ice cream to each. Good sign, I told myself. At least he was entering into the spirit of the thing. I allowed him to enjoy a couple of mouthfuls in the nervous silence that followed and then dropped my bombshell.

'They're not at an extra rehearsal, Flynn. There isn't one. I checked with the director. But they are together. Bette and Tom.'

He spluttered as a strawberry went down the wrong way. 'Together? Now?'

'They were also together on your tartan rug this afternoon when I came looking for my husband.'

'What?' His jaw had dropped.

'I didn't know if you knew what was going on but I thought – I hoped – that between us we could nip the romance in the bud.'

At first he pretended not to believe me but eventually the truth emerged. Bette had done something similar two years ago and they had come close to a divorce. 'She's too attractive for her own good!' he said gloomily.

I let that pass without comment. I *had* originally thought

18

Bette attractive but my feelings had recently undergone a sudden change. Now I considered her long fair hair totally unfashionable and thought that her pert nose might have been surgically enhanced. But I didn't say so. Flynn was obviously shattered by my unwelcome news. I patted his knee reassuringly. 'We mustn't panic, Flynn. We can nip the romance in the bud. Now listen . . .'

I told him to go on eating while I explained my plan. Then we talked it over for nearly twenty minutes and when we'd finished we'd agreed on what the military call 'joint action'.

Bette returned at twenty past ten, her high-heeled shoes clattering on the brick path. She let herself in and came into the lounge, calling airily to Flynn that she was home. When she entered the lounge her face was flushed with excitement but almost immediately the radiance faded as she took in the scene. Flynn and I were close together on the sofa. He had changed into chinos and his best shirt and his feet were bare. I was sitting with my feet tucked under me and I had tousled my hair and mussed my lipstick. My off-the-shoulder top was dangerously low and I was attempting that 'satisfied' look that cats have after cream.

Flynn said, 'Hi, darling,' but smiled at me.

I said, 'Oh Bette! I thought you'd be later than this. Never mind.' And smiled at her.

She hid her shock with an effort. 'Sally! I didn't expect to find you here. Nice surprise.' She tossed the *Glass Menagerie* script on to the table and gave Flynn a frosty look.

I said, 'How did it go, Bette?'

She fell for it. 'How did what go?'

'The extra rehearsal.'

'Oh!' The blush said it all. 'It was fine. Yes. Good.' Her gaze took in the two coffee cups, the liqueur glasses and the bottle of port which Flynn had opened specially. 'You seem to have enjoyed yourselves.'

Flynn said, 'We certainly have.'

I laughed gaily. 'Next time it's my turn. Flynn's coming to our house.'

'Next time?'

'Whenever you have an extra rehearsal. No point in the abandoned spouses spending the evening alone. I knew you wouldn't mind. We left you a few strawberries. They're in the fridge.' Slowly, with exaggerated reluctance, I straightened my legs and stood up. 'I expect Tom will be wondering where I am.'

Flynn insisted on seeing me to the door.

'You were terrific!' I whispered.

'So were you.'

'I think we both deserve an Oscar!'

To my surprise he pulled me close and gave me a clumsy kiss. I kissed him back. It was strange being kissed by another man after so long. But nice.

He said, 'We'll play it by ear. Let me know what happens your end!'

Loudly I said, 'See you next time, then, Flynn.'

I walked home at a leisurely pace. I was still worried but I felt stronger and not so afraid. I guessed that Bette was longing to phone Tom but she couldn't because Flynn was there.

Tom opened the door, trying to hide his relief. 'Where have you been? I was worried sick. No note or anything. Honestly, Sal! You're so thoughtless!' As I stepped into the lighted hall he saw what I was wearing and blinked. 'What on earth . . .?'

I said, 'Did you find the strawberries? There was some cream in the small jug. I've been to Bette's place. Spent the evening with Flynn. He's a really nice chap. How did the rehearsal go?'

'It was OK. What do you mean, you were with Flynn?'

I gave him a straight look. 'I rang John Sowsbury and he said there wasn't a rehearsal. And why didn't you tell me it was half-term? And why did you spend all day with Bette Sanders on a tartan rug in her garden?'

He sat down, horribly shocked, and I almost felt sorry for

him. Then I reminded myself about the strawberry field and the shock *he* had given *me*.

Tom stammered, 'You and . . . and Flynn!'

'You and Bette!' I mimicked, heading for the stairs. I turned. 'I shan't ask you any questions, Tom, and I shan't answer any of yours. Just don't think you can ever make a fool of me and get away with it.'

I went upstairs singing softly under my breath.

*'Ri-fol, ri-fol, tol-de-riddle-li-do,*
*Ri-fol, ri-fol, tol-de-riddle-dee!'*

# Emmeline

I let out my breath in a long sigh. The bougainvillea was in bloom, fiery red against the white wall. In the fierce sun, a white oleander glowed against the orange trees. The Algarve in Portugal is full of such scenes.

My hostess, Paula, appeared at my shoulder.

'Wonderful, isn't it,' she said, refilling my glass with the local red wine.

I turned from the window. Paula's smile was eager and I felt guilty. Drinks by the pool, barbecues under the stars, a carefree lifestyle. Of course it sounded idyllic and to some people it was. But I had never been a 'party animal'. Married for nearly thirty years, Steve and I had shared quiet pleasures. We read and compared books, listened to music together, pottered about in the garden and took our holidays in the small village of Santa Barbara de Nexe, a few miles inland from Olhao. We had dreamed of retiring to Portugal but now I was alone. How could I make the move without him? I wondered. I had never been very confident.

Paula tossed back a lock of dark hair. 'The garden, I mean. It's a perfect climate. You really should move out here, Geraldine,' she urged. 'You'd love it. I've never regretted my move and nor have any of the others.'

She gave my arm an encouraging pat and drifted away.

'You must be Geraldine,' said another voice. 'I'm Daphne. Try one of Paula's specialities.' She held out a plate. Seeing my expression, she said, 'Blinis. Tiny pancake things topped with prawns. They're delicious.'

I popped one into my mouth. They *were*. So this was Paula's

speciality. I felt a rush of nervousness. Did I have any specialities to offer? Would I be able to compete? I had a momen-
tary vision of myself panicking in the kitchen as friends
descended upon my villa, intent on partying. Then I tried to
visualize myself standing nonchalantly by the pool making
smart conversation. Daphne was tanned and her glorious red
hair was tied back with a red ribbon. She looked enviably
perfect and totally at home.

Daphne went on. 'Jenny says your husband died a while
back. I'm so sorry – but it isn't the end of the world, you
know. This is a wonderful place for women alone. Some of
us are divorced, some widowed. A few are still married or
with partners. We've all had to make a fresh start.' She smiled.
'Life goes on, Geraldine. Your husband would have wanted
you to be happy.'

I know she meant well. They all did. So why wasn't I reassured?

She said, 'I hear you're staying at Jenny's place.'

Jenny's place, otherwise known as Villa Romana, was part
of a modern complex built on a hillside near St Bras. Jenny
had insisted that I stay there for a few weeks while she was
in London. Her theory was that I would find the peace I was
looking for. Villa Romana was beautiful with marble floors,
spacious rooms and views to die for but I rattled around, lonely
and guiltily homesick, unnerved by my echoing footsteps. It
made me want to rush back to the UK and my cluttered
Victorian terraced house in Blackheath. There I'm surrounded
by my happy memories. I'm not at all the adventurous sort.

Yet today, standing beside Paula's pool and feeling like an
alien, I wanted to be seduced. Without Steve I had nothing to
keep me in England, for we had never been blessed with children. All I had to do was sell the house, choose a villa and
move into it. It sounded so easy and yet I was still hesitating.

'There's plenty to do here.' Determined, Daphne went on,
helping herself to a blini. 'There's a shop that sells English
books and videos – and not a million miles away there's a
cinema showing English films. You can swim to your heart's

content and keep fit – and we entertain a lot. We're also involved with charities. We have a sanctuary for worn-out donkeys . . .' Seeing my expression, she finally faltered and smiled. 'You're not convinced.'

I said quickly, 'Actually, I'm looking at some properties this afternoon.'

'Oh! Brilliant!'

After a long pause I said, 'I passed a woman yesterday outside the old farmhouse. Wearing a long red dress, hair scraped back in a straggly bun.'

The implied question surprised me, coming unbidden from a shadowy corner of my mind, for at the time I had given the stranger no more than a passing glance.

'You mean Emmeline.' Daphne rolled her eyes. 'She's quite alone on that farm, you know. She's your typical English eccentric. Bit of a mystery really. Disappears now and again for a few days at a time. God knows how she manages. It's very primitive although there is a bore hole, so she doesn't have to buy water. There was no electricity until they built our villas and were able to link in her farm.'

'Doesn't she ever come to these parties?'

'Good Lord, no! She'd hate it. I told you, she's a loner. We gave up on poor Emmeline ages ago.'

So Emmeline was a loner. I felt a rush of sympathy for her but then checked myself. Emmeline didn't need sympathy. She might be a loner – even a little eccentric – but in my mind I saw again her confident stride and calm, thoughtful expression. Now that I thought about her I saw that Emmeline was a woman at peace with herself.

As soon I could decently do so I said my 'goodbyes' and drove myself back to Villa Romana. I spent the next twenty-four hours inspecting white-walled villas, vibrant with red and purple flowers and huge cactus plants. Some had roof-gardens, others boasted a small vineyard or an olive grove. If I sold our home I could buy a substantial property or maybe something smaller, leaving me spare money to play with.

Tuesday night I lay awake for hours but failed to come to a decision. Wednesday I drove into Olhao and shopped for groceries. On the way back to the villa I was overcome by a wave of homesickness. What on earth was I doing in Portugal? I could never live alone in a foreign country.

'I want to go home,' I whispered.

Tears filled my eyes and blurred my vision and I slowed down. As I turned the corner a donkey cart appeared suddenly ahead of me and I was forced to wrench the wheel over. The car veered off the road and hit a cork tree. I was badly shaken but unhurt. Leaning my head on the steering wheel, I began to cry in earnest, for the first time since Steve's funeral.

I was startled by a tap on the car window. Mortified, I dabbed at my eyes, took a deep breath and looked up. It was Emmeline, wearing the same red dress. Close to, she looked older – perhaps late fifties. Her face, devoid of make-up, was pale, her eyes huge. Without saying a word, she opened the car door and helped me out. Still without speaking we made our way slowly along the road towards her farmhouse.

Hens pecked around the dusty yard, two goats grazed nearby and washing fluttered between two almond trees. A nondescript dog rushed to greet us, barking a noisy welcome.

Emmeline smiled. 'Henry, *please!*' The dog fell back, abashed.

Her kitchen was simply furnished. The floor was brick, saucepans hung on one wall and something savoury was cooking on the stove.

'Sit down,' she said. Pouring two drinks, she handed one to me. 'Fig wine.'

With a brief smile she went outside and I sank back in the chair. I sipped the wine, closed my eyes and was surprised to find myself relaxing.

Returning moments later, Emmeline said, 'Eat with us.'

Instinctively I glanced round. Was she including the dog?

Laughing, she looked younger. 'Carlos sometimes shares my cooking,' she said enigmatically. 'He gets homesick.'

She didn't explain.

Carlos arrived a little later, ducking his head as he came through the doorway. Younger than Emmeline, he was a sturdy man in jeans, a faded shirt and trainers. While he washed his hands, Emmeline laid knives, forks and plates and cut thick slices from a flat brown loaf.

'It's kid,' she told me as Carlos carried the heavy casserole dish to the table. 'It's Carlos's favourite.' She refilled our glasses and poured one for Carlos.

He said something I couldn't understand.

'Carlos made the fig wine,' she translated.

She explained that his father used to own the farm. He left it to Carlos but he didn't want to be a farmer. He worked in Faro in a travel agency. 'Carlos sold it to me but he likes to call in from time to time.'

A wide smile lit his swarthy features and he gave me a shy glance. While Emmeline served the sweet dark meat I noticed how thin her hands were. As we ate, Carlos's dark eyes watched me curiously, wondering probably about the pathetic stranger with red-rimmed eyes and a blotchy face.

Abruptly they spoke to each other in rapid Portuguese.

Emmeline turned to me. 'Carlos has rescued your car.'

It was dented but driveable, she explained. He would fetch a friend to take it back to the rental people and bring me another. 'That would be best,' she said.

Neither asked for my approval.

At the end of the week I flew back to London, still thinking from time to time about Emmeline. Two months passed. I remembered her voice. 'Henry, *please!*' I signed up to yoga classes. I took one day at a time. Regular postcards arrived from Jenny.

'. . . *Lazing and swimming and enjoying the sun. Daphne, Paula and the others came for a barbecue . . .*'

I remembered the two goats contentedly nibbling the grass. I had my hair restyled and joined a local history group. Jenny phoned occasionally but Emmeline was never mentioned.

Then one day the news came that she was dead. The funeral was Saturday. I flew out to Faro.

Sitting on the patio, an hour before the funeral, Jenny filled in the details.

'Leukaemia. She knew she had it, apparently. Some chap found her propped against a tree. He thought she was asleep.' Jenny went on. 'It seems she was an artist. Quite a good one. None of us had a clue! She sold to a small gallery in Portimao.' Jenny glanced at her watch and stood up. 'I do so hate funerals.'

The small church was half empty but just before the service started five smartly dressed strangers arrived by taxi.

Jenny raised her eyebrows. 'They must be the arty people from Portimao. I wish now I'd bought one of Emmeline's paintings.'

I remembered her thin hands ladling out the tender kid meat. Carlos was in the church looking stricken. On the way out we shook hands wordlessly.

I was back in London when the solicitor's letter came. Emmeline had left me one of her paintings and he suggested I collect it next time I was in the Algarve.

'Emmeline,' I whispered. She seemed to be haunting me.

What would happen to her farmhouse? I wondered. Who would care for her excitable Henry? Who would feed the goats and the chickens? I wrote to the solicitor promising that I would collect the painting next time I was in the area.

Months passed. Jenny urged me to fly out for another break.

'I've seen a wonderful villa for you,' she urged. 'A stone's throw from Villa Romano.'

My courage failed me. I couldn't go – but I couldn't stay either. Blackheath had lost its charm and the thought of spending my last years there frightened me.

One night I dreamed of Emmeline. She was walking along the road beside the farm, striding out with her hair blowing in the wind. As I watched her enviously she turned, smiled her brief smile and waved to me.

The next morning I sat bolt upright in bed. I knew exactly what I had to do. Suddenly I could see the way forward. I could see a life for myself in Portugal. I would milk goats,

27

feed hens. I would plant onions and beans and pick lemons and oranges from my own trees. I would find recipes for flat brown bread and kid casserole. I would hang Emmeline's painting on the wall – and I would learn Portuguese.

I slipped from the bed and hurried to the phone.

When Jenny answered I asked, 'What happened to Emmeline's farmhouse?'

'She left it to a Portuguese chap. He's put it back on the market.'

'Is it still available?' I held my breath. Suddenly her answer was very important.

'As far as I know. Why do you ask?'

I took a deep breath. 'I want to make an offer for it . . .' I began.

Jenny tried to talk me out of it but I insisted. When at length I put the phone down I was smiling. I picked up Steve's photograph and hugged it. He would come with me in my heart and Emmeline would be there in spirit. How could I be lonely? I smiled at Steve's likeness, at peace with myself.

'You'd have liked Emmeline,' I told him.

# Telling Leanne

Ten to seven. Dawn glanced at her watch, steeling herself for the conversation that would start the moment her sister picked up the phone. And she would, of course, because Dawn rang her every Friday at the same time. Her sister, Leanne, had insisted that if Dawn was determined to hide herself away in the middle of nowhere in darkest Kent, then she should at least keep in touch regularly with her only close relative. Their mother was in a home with early Alzheimer's and her father had left the family years ago.

Leanne, a committed town dweller, had been quite certain that Dawn would regret her move from the London flat-share in Peckham.

'Being crossed in love is no reason to desert all your friends. And a rented bungalow on the outskirts of Apsley Marsh! For heaven's sake, Dawn! You must be mad! Who will you talk to, for heaven's sake? The *villagers*? They'll either be tramping around in green wellies or . . . or riding to hounds if they're rich enough! You won't fit in anywhere. You're a townie.'

'Of course I will! Just because I was born in London . . .'

'Village life is different. Villages don't even have pavements and . . . and with the cutbacks they're lucky to have one bus a day!'

'I'll get myself a little car.' At least she could thank Tim for that. He had taught her to drive.

'You'll hate it, Dawnie.'

But Dawn had gone ahead with her plans, unable to explain that London without Tim had lost its magic and that the constant attempts of her friends to 'fix her up' with another man was not the answer to her problem. Privacy and seclusion – they were what she needed and she had found it. Time to come to terms with the loss of someone she loved and to recover from the shock of his betrayal.

Tim had been the third inhabitant of the flat-share. He had joined Dawn and Stella after the first year when they found the rent too much for two to bear. Six months later Stella had left to take up a job in Florida, leaving Tim and Dawn to advertise for a third occupant. Somehow they never did.

Dawn allowed herself a faint smile as she reached for the telephone. Each week she had scraped the barrel for snippets of news with which to regale Leanne. A quick precis of a book she had found on the mobile library, details of the argument she had had with the window cleaner over the corners or the proliferation of molehills in the lawn. Leanne, of course, had made it. Five years married to the dishy Ian, living in a small but fashionable flat conversion overlooking the Thames. Her life revolved around theatres, dinner parties, birthday trips on the river with trendy friends, and holidays in Bermuda.

Dawn had found the village people friendly and her red Fiat a joy. The countryside soothed her anguished spirit and she was beginning to enjoy herself in a quiet way. News, however, was thin on the ground and Leanne had gloated. Now, however, Dawn had something exciting to tell her sister – but she was still holding back. Because somehow, she knew, Leanne might spoil it for her with a well chosen word or a subtle inflexion.

'Just do it!' Dawn told herself and punched in the numbers.

'Dawnie! Is that you?'

Leanne always called her Dawnie and it always made her feel that she had just come last in the sack-race. She had been named after her mother's rich aunt in the hope that she would leave her something but she died impoverished and Dawn was stuck with the name.

'Yes, it's me. Who were you expecting? George W. Bush? It's seven o'clock and it's Friday.'

Leanne laughed. She was nine years older than Dawn and a bit of a high-flier with a wardrobe to match. Now she asked,

'How are things down on the farm?' and before Dawn could answer added, 'Any interesting men on the horizon?'

Dawn counted to ten. Let it go, she told herself. 'Another letter from Brad Pitt!'

That was one of their jokes. She took a deep breath. News time! 'Actually I've got a dinner date. A bit of gracious living.'

'You're invited out to dinner? How kind of someone.'

Meaning that you'd have to be kind to want Dawnie at your table. Dawn took another breath. Do not rise to the bait, she told herself sternly.

'Isn't it kind,' she agreed with a light laugh. Closing her eyes, she clutched the phone to her chest and glanced at herself in the mirror. The Cheshire cat! 'I don't know if you've heard of Mara Sholte. She's a chat-show host among other—'

'*Mara Sholte!*'

'You've heard of her?' Dawn tried to sound innocent. The little country bumpkin.

'Of course I have!' Leanne had been caught off guard. 'Everybody knows . . . You're going to dinner with Mara Sholte?'

'Yes. She has a cottage about a mile from here. Don't you remember I told you when she bought it. The old smithy. They converted it. Her and her husband, Dan. Now it's finished they're throwing a dinner party . . . Are you still there, Leanne?'

'Yes.'

'I thought we'd been cut off.' Dawn grinned. 'It's taken them ages to convert it – it's a second home.'

'Well, it would be! People like Mara Sholte can afford more than one property. They've got that huge house in Hampstead where they had that security alert last year *and* a place in Spain. How come they've asked you? Do you know them?'

'I soon will!' she laughed. 'They've decided they want to get to know the local people – the villagers – now that they have more time. I'm one of their nearest neighbours.'

There was another silence. Then Leanne said, 'What on earth will you wear?'

'I'll find something. They said come casual. Nobody dresses up much in the country.'

'So who's coming to this casual dinner party?'

'A couple called Walters. He's called Steve and he's an actor but not very well known, and his live-in girlfriend is a scriptwriter . . . I've forgotten her name for the moment. And there's an Australian chap who's over here for a year. Staying in a motel somewhere. Mara Sholte's nephew.'

Leanne said, 'An *Aussie?* Oh no! Probably a lifeguard called Bruce!' She laughed but Dawn could tell her heart wasn't in it. Leanne was being eaten up with jealousy. 'Probably a *Baywatch* wannabee!'

'I thought *Baywatch* was California.'

'Whatever! Oh Dawn! Anyway, when is this casual dinner party? It sounds so odd, doesn't it? When we give a dinner party we expect the guests to make some sort of effort but obviously not in Apsley Marsh.'

'It's Saturday.' Dawn waited, knowing that Leanne would jump on this.

'*This* Saturday? You mean tomorrow? You didn't mention it last week. When did they ask you?'

'Wednesday.' Dawn closed her eyes. Why hadn't she lied?

'That's rather short notice isn't it? Maybe someone dropped out at the last minute.'

The same thing had occurred to Dawn but she wasn't about to admit it. 'Oh no! These media people are like that. Everything's casual with them. Everything's last-minute. Off the cuff. We met up in the village and got chatting and she just said would I like to pop along and join them for dinner.' She decided to change the subject. 'Apparently Mara's quite a good cook. I'm looking forward to it.'

Dawn could almost hear her sister's brain ticking over. Leanne had trendy friends but none of them were in Mara Sholte's league. She would hate being upstaged by her younger sister.

'Look, Dawnie, why not come up tomorrow and we'll find

you something to wear. There can't be much where you are. We could dive into Harrods – or have a look along Oxford Street. I can see you in something—'

'Thanks but no,' Dawn told her hurriedly. 'There's no need to fuss. They're not dressy people when they're not on the box. When I last spoke to her in the post office she looked like a hippie. Old suede jacket with a mangy old fringe . . . She looked wonderful in it.' She thought enviously that if *she* had been wearing it she'd have looked shabby.

'Well, she would,' Leanne explained. 'Londoners have flair. Well, please yourself, Dawn. Don't say I didn't make the offer.'

Adroitly Dawn steered the conversation away from the dinner party and brought it to a close but Leanne had the last word.

'Enjoy yourself with the luvvies,' she said and put the receiver down.

Dawn replaced the phone and sat for a moment struggling with the familiar loss of confidence inspired by talking to Leanne. She acknowledged to herself that she probably *was* a last-minute replacement, but did it matter? She was going and she should make up her mind to enjoy it.

'It'll be great!' she said. 'Go for it, Dawn!'

As she headed back to the kitchen to empty the dishwasher she suddenly found it in her heart to forgive Leanne. She smiled. It took a lot to make her sister jealous.

Saturday arrived and after an hour or more trying on every garment she possessed, Dawn settled for newish chinos and a plain black T-shirt worn with several gold chains. She swept up her hair and caught it in a black ribbon and set off to walk to The Old Smithy. Mara welcomed her with a kiss and showed her round. A view to the roof through ceiling beams, a dramatic free-standing log fire, flagstones with thick rugs and white walls hung with original paintings. The kitchen was to die for. Dawn could imagine herself telling Leanne.

*Very stylish, the conversion. You'd be impressed. Somehow*

*they've kept the best of the original smithy but it has this modern feeling. Wonderful. The sort of thing you see in magazines ...*

An hour and a half later, when the meal was finally under way, things were not going as smoothly as Dawn had expected. The Walterses were hardly speaking to each other and Dawn suspected they had quarrelled earlier in the day. Steve Walters was tall and slim and reminded her of John Travolta. His girlfriend's name was Natalie but everyone called her Nat. She was petite with a trace of a foreign accent and Dawn decided she would tell Leanne she was Russian. It would add an exotic touch to the account. Mara, artificially bright, seemed to be drinking rather a lot and Dan talked incessantly, mainly about himself but with frequent references to well-known colleagues. Was this flow of words his usual style or was he trying to fill the silences? she wondered.

To be fair, they each tried in turn to chat with her and Dawn struggled to sparkle but, unnerved by the atmosphere, failed dismally. Alan, the Australian nephew, was younger than she had expected, with shoulder-length hair bleached by the sun and a generous sprinkling of freckles. He was going to be in the UK for a year studying at Manchester University. He obviously shared her current unease but made no attempt to help things along. Perhaps because he was family. He glanced once or twice at his watch as though counting down the hours until he could decently escape.

The food arrived on huge platters from which everybody helped themselves. First a platter of seafood with a vast salad, then an enormous dish of creamy chicken curry with a bewildering number of side dishes.

*Very Jamie Oliver, the food. Casual but sophisticated and utterly delicious ...*

After another awkward silence the Australian turned to Dawn.

'So you're a photographer.' The Aussie drawl was noticeable.

Mara smiled at Dawn. 'And a very good one, I'm sure.'

All eyes were suddenly on Dawn, who lowered the forkful of food she was about to put in her mouth.

'Yes ... in a small way. I'm hoping to make my living from it one day.'

Steve said, 'I've been offered a job with a touring company headed off to South Africa in a few months' time. A wonderful opportunity but Nat doesn't want me to take it. Scared of being left on her own!'

Nat threw him a poisonous look.

Mara said, 'Maybe she doesn't trust you!' and Dan sniggered.

Dawn's stomach knotted fearfully but Alan ignored them. He said, 'Tell me about it. Your photography, I mean.'

Thankful for the distraction, Dawn explained her current project. 'It's for the Tourist Board. For all the foreigners coming across. Now that we've got the tunnel as well as the ferries. They're commissioning a book of photographs about the coastal area. Folkestone, Dover, Littlestone ... I'm including interesting people as well as views. Fishermen, farmers, craftsmen ...'

'Artists and writers?'

She nodded. 'Exactly.' She couldn't tell him that the deal hadn't been finalized yet.

*They were very interested in my photography. Asked a lot of questions ...*

'Isn't it lonely – working on your own?' Alan looked as if he really wanted to know.

It was but she shook her head emphatically. She could have said she'd felt lonely all her life but she didn't want him to know that either.

Mara was leaning over the table with a bottle of red wine. 'Top-up?' she asked and Dawn said, 'Please.' Maybe a little more alcohol would help.

Suddenly Mara's elbow caught the wine bottle and knocked it over. A thin stream of red wine spilled on to the table and ran unerringly on to Nat's lap.

'For God's sake, Mara!' She jumped to her feet and began to scrub at the wine with her serviette. 'You stupid cow!'

Steve rolled his eyes and said, 'Can't take her anywhere!'

Eyes down, thought Dawn, and concentrated so firmly on her poppadom that it shattered in all directions. Meet no one's eye, she told herself and began to scoop the crumbs into her hand.

Mara, ignoring Nat's outburst, refilled Dawn's glass. Dawn thanked her, took a large gulp. It went down the wrong way and she spluttered inelegantly. Dan said 'Oops!' and patted her back.

Nat glared at Mara. 'You did that on purpose!'

Alan caught Dawn's eye. 'It'll all end in tears!'

Steve said, 'Why on earth should she?'

Nat sat down heavily, her eyes brimming with tears. 'Because she's been all over you ever since Cannes! D'you think I couldn't see what was going on?'

Dan muttered, 'Jesus!' and shook his head wearily.

Dawn thrust another forkful of curry into her mouth. She wanted to burst into tears herself. How was this going to translate when she rang Leanne?

Steve said, 'Shut up, Nat. You're making a fool of yourself. Nothing's been going on. I keep telling you.'

*They obviously know each other very well . . . The Walterses were a lovely couple . . .*

So I was right, thought Dawn, slightly mollified by this knowledge. They *had* quarrelled earlier. She pushed back her place and smiled brightly at Mara.

'That was absolutely delicious. Thank you.'

Everyone looked at her.

Dan said, 'Thank me. All that slaving over a hot stove!'

'Like hell you have!'

Dawn shrugged. 'Well . . . whoever!'

In a haughty silence Mara collected the plates and platters and removed them to a nearby trolley, which she then wheeled into the adjoining kitchen.

There she made a great deal of noise before returning to

rejoin them at the table. Dan leaned towards her and whispered, 'The cheeseboard, darling!'

'Get it yourself! They're your guests too!' Her beautiful eyes were narrowed and there was an angry flush in her cheeks.

Dawn heard herself say cheerily, 'Can *I* help? Just tell me where everything is.'

Dan said, 'Certainly not! We don't expect our dinner guests to serve the meal – do we, Mara?'

Mara appeared not to have heard. She had poured a small heap of salt on to the table and was stirring it with a perfectly manicured fingernail. Dan threw down his serviette and stood up. He went out into the kitchen and came back a moment later, stony faced. He whispered something to his wife, who whispered something in return.

He turned to his guests. 'I'm afraid we'll have to forgo the cheese as Mara is too lazy to unwrap it!'

Nat's 'My God!' had a triumphant ring to it.

Dawn finished her wine and stole a quick look at Alan. Was it her imagination or was he pale beneath the freckles? His thin hands seemed to be trembling.

Nat said, 'Mara, you're a total bitch!'

Mara's face crumpled. Tears coursed down her cheeks, ruining her expensive make-up.

Dan said, 'Oh shit!'

Mara jumped to her feet, sending her chair backwards on to the floor.

'I'm going to bed,' she announced between sobs. 'So you can all piss off!' She groped her way blindly across the room.

Alan said, 'Shouldn't someone help her. I mean, those stairs . . .'

Dawn followed his glance and saw his point. Mara was drunk and the original wooden stairs were narrow and twisting.

Dan shrugged. 'It won't be the first time.'

Nobody moved. They listened to Mara's stumbling ascent and heard the bedroom door slam.

Dan said, 'Goodnight, dear heart!'

The silence lengthened.

Nat rubbed again at the skirt of her dress. To Dawn she said, 'This is new. First time on!' She sighed. 'And it cost the earth.'

'Perhaps you could have it cleaned. I expect you're insured.'

'The insurance?' She brightened. 'Oh! Right! Clever you!'

Dan said, 'Right then, lads and lassies! Coffee and chocs?' He rubbed his hands together in mock heartiness. 'Port? A liqueur? Steve, you know where they are.' He disappeared into the kitchen, whistling.

Alan stood up. 'Not for me, thanks, but it's been a lovely evening.'

Nat stared at him. 'It's been a bloody awful evening and you know it!'

Taken aback, Alan turned to Dawn. 'I could give you a lift if you're ready to go home.'

She hesitated fatally.

Nat said, 'No she's not ready. She's going to stick it out like the rest of us. Aren't you, Dawn?'

Ever the coward, Dawn nodded. Alan, committed, saw himself out. For a few moments they all listened to his attempts to start his car, then regarded each other helplessly.

Dan said, 'He's got trouble with that old banger. I did warn him.'

The coffee duly arrived. With it came a basket of grapes, mint chocs and something approaching the party spirit. It was gone eleven when Dawn made her excuses and left. The Walterses were staying until Monday morning. Dan saw her to the door.

Outside she shivered. A huge hunter's moon hung in the sky, occasionally obscured by drifting clouds, and the wind had dropped. She walked home along the moonlit road, grateful for the cool night air on what she thought of as her 'fevered brow'. Breathing deeply, she was unsure whether to laugh or cry.

'I've had a wonderful evening,' she muttered, 'but this wasn't it!'

In a state of emotional exhaustion she let herself in and closed the door behind her. So much for the luvvies. So much for gracious living. Whatever was she going to tell Leanne?

Friday came at last. Seven o'clock . . . Five past . . .
Dawn dialled her sister's number then abruptly cancelled it. She couldn't do it. She couldn't tell Leanne what had happened but doubted she could lie convincingly. She had spent hours throughout the week trying to decide how to play it and still wasn't sure. Maybe the best thing was to pretend Mara had been taken ill and the whole thing had been put on hold.

She muttered, 'Make up your mind, you idiot! This is really pathetic!' and stared at the phone. 'I'll lie! I'll lie with great conviction. I can do it!'

A rehearsal seemed a good idea. 'Leanne! How's everything? . . . The what? The dinner party? Oh that was great . . .' She gave Leanne a chance to ask her eager questions. Leanne would be curious. She may even have tried to ring Dawn on the Sunday but Dawn had left the receiver off. 'Glamorous but in a low-key sort of way . . . Fun actually . . . Nice people. Sweet . . .'

Was she really going to say that?

'Oh Lord!' A new thought struck her. Leanne would want to know about the *Baywatch* wannabe. Which brought her to another problem. Alan hadn't been in touch. She had somehow expected him to ring to share the horrors of the evening. Maybe to laugh at the whole ghastly business. He only had to ask Mara for her phone number. As the only unattached woman Dawn had hoped he would show a little interest and he *had* asked about the photography.

Ten past seven . . . Quarter past . . . If she didn't ring soon Leanne would probably ring *her*!

*R-r-ring.*

Her heart jumped – but it was the doorbell. On the doorstep she found Alan, smiling nervously.

'Oh!'

'If it's inconvenient . . .' He looked at her uncertainly.

So he had showed up at last. Delighted to see him, Dawn's

resentment faded quickly and she held open the door. 'Come on in.'

He wiped his shoes on the mat and followed her into the small lounge. Suddenly Dawn realized that if Leanne were to ring now there was no way she could lie to her. Not with Alan listening. She felt cold and then hot and sat down abruptly. This was getting ridiculous.

He sat down on the sofa. 'I wanted to give you a bell earlier but I had trouble with the old car. Bit of a nightmare trying to get spare parts.' He let his gaze wander round the room and Dawn wished it was tidier. The phone rang and they both looked at it.

At last Alan said, 'Aren't you going to answer it?'

'No . . . That is I . . .' She swallowed hard. 'No. I'm not. It's only my sister.' The phone continued its trill. 'She'll wonder where I am.'

He raised his eyebrows. 'That bad?'

'It's a long story.' She laughed and they listened to it until it fell silent. Relieved she said, 'Can I make you some coffee?'

'I thought we'd maybe grab a few tinnies somewhere now I've got the car back. Chew over the other night!' He grinned. 'Sorry about me Auntie Mara! Isn't she something?'

'You don't have to apologize. It wasn't your fault.'

'Might even treat you to a bag of crisps!'

'Now you're talking!' Dawn rolled her eyes. 'Wasn't it *awful*! I'm sorry I didn't leave with you. I should have done.'

Alan's freckles seemed to have multiplied and his eyes were bluer than she remembered. As she locked the front door behind them the phone rang again.

'I can wait,' he offered.

'No! Let it ring. I'll get in touch tomorrow.'

Perched next to him in the passenger seat of the ancient Morris Minor, Dawn began to relax. Together, she and Alan would see the funny side of the dinner party. A couple of beers and they would reduce the disaster in Luvvieland to a hilarious memory. As the car lurched forward, she smiled contentedly.

Tomorrow she would ring Leanne and tell her how it was.

# Number 18

It's funny the things you see in my line of work. Caring, that is. The Limes is a small nursing home as nursing homes go. It stands on a clifftop overlooking the sea – not that many of our residents ever look at it but it's there if they ever do. It was once a very imposing house set in pretty grounds but now it's mostly grass with a few shrubs. Inside it's quite cosy with twenty-three bedrooms and various dayrooms. We're not a big staff – six qualified and three young women who are waiting to go to college or uni and want to earn a bit before they start. There are two men who push the wheelchairs and carry things and run people to and from hospital when necessary.

We all get along somehow. On a good day, that is. On a bad day we get a bit snappy and moan about just about everything but we get over it. There must be worse jobs than looking after the elderly. We'll be elderly ourselves one day and might end up somewhere similar. Nobody wants to be a burden. Most of our people are exactly that and simply couldn't be nursed properly at home.

The unfortunate relatives come to visit, looking guilty because they abandoned their responsibility, and they bring us tins of biscuits at Christmas and sometimes the odd bottle of sherry, although we're not supposed to accept anything like that – but who's to know? Most of our residents don't know what's going on, poor souls. They don't know the date or the name of the Prime Minister and they'd be no good as witnesses to an accident!

Poor old Miss Stookey is in an even worse state. She's lost

41

all her language but keeps up a long conversation made up of totally unintelligible sounds. She smiles and nods.

'As long as she's happy,' her husband says hopefully. He comes in every day for an hour. We chat to him and make him a cup of tea and I think he's grateful for a bit of company.

Old Mr Finney is writing his memoirs – or thinks he is. His daughter brings him notebook after notebook and he scribbles away as happy as a sandboy. He writes the same thing every day, starting with the date he was born and where they lived and he underlines the fact that his father was a schoolteacher. He never gets further than his first birthday and he's been here three and a half years.

Most of them are women and they aren't really mobile, so they sit round in the dayroom and watch cartoons. We've tried them with the news and *Mastermind* and *Only Fools and Horses* but they prefer the cartoons. The only resident who goes outside is Mr Cornwell, who loves gardening and he potters round with a watering can caring for the window boxes. He never says a word to anyone but he hums a lot.

The only one we can have a conversation with is dear old Mr Warren in number 18. Mr William Warren. A real sweetie. Been with us for seven years, so we must be doing something right! Ninety-eight and still enjoys a small dry sherry before his lunch. (His niece smuggles a bottle in once a fortnight and we turn a blind eye.) And talking about lunch – he eats like a horse even though he's so tiny. I don't know where he puts it all. Hollow legs! That's what my mother used to say, bless her. Not that she's still with us but she had a saying for everything.

Number 18 is one of the nicest rooms. It's on the corner of the building and slightly larger than most with a built-in wardrobe, sink and vanity unit. I describe it to him occasionally because he forgets and his vision's going. Whenever I mention the sink and vanity unit he smiles.

'Vanity unit's just right for you,' I tell him, laughing. 'Men are vainer than women!'

'We've got more to be vain about!' he says, quick as a flash.

Number 18 has a view over the park and you can just catch a glimpse of the sea. Not that Mr Warren bothers with views.

'I've seen it all,' he tells me and it's true, he has.

Niagara Falls, the catacombs and Las Vegas. The Tower of London, the Bayeux Tapestry, Ayers Rock . . . You name it and he's seen it. He was once very rich and comes from landed gentry but fortune didn't smile on him and it's all gone. But he's not stuck-up and he's grateful for everything we do for him, and we do what we can because he's one of the few that still has all his marbles. So few people with whom you can have a sensible conversation.

He doesn't get around much. Not because he can't, but because he's afraid of falling once he gets to his feet.

'Don't want to die young!'

That's one of his favourite jokes. He thinks a fall will be the end of him, poor old soul, and it might well be. Sarah Stanley in number 5 broke her wrist and went into hospital for a few days. That's what we were told, but while she was in there she caught one of those dreadful bugs that eat away at you from the inside. We never saw her again.

I say Mr Warren doesn't see so well, but he won't wear his glasses. Vain as they come at ninety-eight! Not that we call him Mr Warren. Not for years now. We've finally persuaded him that William is much friendlier. We tried Will or Bill but he wouldn't go 'the extra mile', as they say. So William it is. He does have some family, thank goodness, but they never visited until recently. They wrote to him though, I'll grant them that. Actually he has quite a lot of letters. One that always smells of violets and another written on pale-yellow paper with a deckle edge.

'From one of my girlfriends!' William tells me and laughs that squeaky little laugh of his. It always makes me smile.

'Girlfriends? At your age!' I tease him sometimes. He can take a joke.

'At any age!' he grins. 'I wasn't always a doddery old fool. I've had my moments.'

When the letters come he puts his glasses on because he

doesn't want us to read them to him. Mind you, he has to use a magnifying glass, but he perseveres and the letters always put him in a good humour.

He had one son and the son has one daughter, so although the son's dead there's a fortyish granddaughter who's suddenly taken to visiting. Her name's Millicent, after William's wife who died twenty years ago. She's tall and angular with short-cropped hair. She likes to be called Millie and I suppose William enjoys her visits. Once a fortnight she descends on The Limes and brings him goodies. Once it was a cake, then chocolates. Once it was shortbread biscuits but his teeth aren't that strong and he told her so. Once it was a bottle of madeira and we had to ration William to one small glass instead of the sherry.

'How is he keeping?' Millie asks brightly, peering in at the office door.

'Very well,' I say. 'Still got a healthy appetite.'

Her smile is rather thin. I wonder about her. How come she didn't bother before he reached the age of ninety-eight? You do see some odd things in this line of work. She might be after his money for all I know.

'Does he understand everything?' she asks. 'I mean his financial affairs? Does he need any help, because I could check things for him?'

That sort of question does get me wondering.

'He's made his will, if that's what you mean,' I tell her and she's not too sure whether to be pleased or sorry because she doesn't know what's in it.

William travelled a lot when his wife was alive and he's very interesting to talk to. I like to bring him a cup of tea in the middle of the afternoon if Elsie in number 12 is asleep. If not I get tied up with her because she will keep shouting and upsets her nearest neighbours. She doesn't talk rationally since her stroke and I have to admit it's very wearing to listen to, so I read to her. That keeps her quiet for a while. One of the visitors said we should close her door but it's strictly against the rules. We need to be able to keep an eye on them, so the doors are always propped open.

If I do get in to chat to William, I can tell he's led a very pampered life. Rich parents. A pony when he was a boy. That sort of thing. Apparently he had a big house in Chester and was a great one for the horses. Once owned a racehorse called Billabob. Or maybe it was Billabong. And he and his wife came down to London regularly for the theatre and stayed at The Ritz. That sort of thing. The big house was sold when he went into sheltered accommodation, some years before he came to us. Presumably the money is now banked and paying for The Limes. Three hundred and eighty pounds a week. Eating away at the savings. I know that's what the niece is thinking.

I say, 'We're all looking forward to his hundredth birthday.'

Her face falls, then she rallies quickly and smiles. 'I'll make him a cake.'

'We do go to town on the hundreds,' I tell her. 'A party. Tiny sandwiches. Jelly and sponge cake. Of course some of the poor dears don't know what it's all about but they seem to enjoy the excitement. And, of course, we invite a local journalist and photographer.'

It's good publicity for us. Mr and Mrs Grainger who own The Limes are very keen on publicity. Keeps the public aware of us. Have to keep the beds filled. They own another nursing home about twenty miles away. It's a paying business these days with everybody living longer.

Millie is wondering about the additional expenses that William is running up.

'They're aren't many,' I tell her. 'He has a paper every day and a few sweets from the trolley. Mostly fruit jellies. He loves those . . . And the telephone, of course. That's his life-line.'

She looks surprised. 'The telephone? Who on earth does he ring? I thought he'd outlived all his friends.'

I shrug. 'If I ask he says it's one of his girlfriends!' We both laugh. 'Oh and the horses! He likes an occasional bet.'

Millie looks alarmed. 'Does he bet much? I mean does he spend a lot?'

'Wouldn't know, dear,' I tell her. Of course I *do* know but I don't tell her.

I certainly don't tell her it's more than occasional and never less than fifty pounds. No point in worrying her. What he does with his money is his own affair.

Of course, William did bring a few things with him from the sheltered accommodation. A clock. A couple of pictures. Three small bronzes – a horse, a bull and a stag. You have to allow a few personal possessions to make it feel like home. One day Millie says, 'Mum thinks we should get power of attorney. Grandfather's mind can't be that clear, not at his age.'

That set alarm bells ringing. You hear that so many times in this line of work. 'His mind's clear as a bell,' I tell her. 'Ask the doctor. She's very impressed with his condition.'

Dr Lorna Swift is on call locally for emergencies but she does also give the residents a check-up from time to time. Millie looks depressed at this news.

After she goes home I notice the bronze horse is missing.

'She was admiring it, so I gave it to her,' says William.

That's what happens, you see. We can't keep our eyes on every visitor. They often try and wheedle things out of their loved ones – I know it's not my business, but I do wonder if it's fair.

'Was it worth much?' I ask as casually as I can while I'm settling his tea tray on his table.

Squinting, he pours in milk, adds two spoonfuls of sugar and insists on managing the tea pot even though his hands are very shaky. I mop up the spilt tea and wait.

'Not really. Maybe a thousand pounds.'

I'm shocked but I don't say a word. Not my place.

The next time Millie comes she mentions the will. I knew that was coming.

'It's been dealt with,' I tell her firmly. 'He has his own solicitor, you know. Payne & Stapley. Everything's in order.'

Time passes. Months fly past and it's William's hundredth birthday. We dress him in his best suit, shirt, collar and tie.

46

We want him to look good for the photograph. Mr and Mrs Grainger are present and Dr Swift has called in on a flying visit. Millie is here in a bright-red dress and lots of glittery eye make-up. A few of the more able residents are wheeled into the dayroom, which we've decorated with a few balloons. He had seven birthday cards and these are on display on the big table where the eats are laid out. William is asked to say a few words so that the journalist can quote him in the article.

He has obviously prepared something. We all gather round as he smiles at the guests. 'Being a hundred is very satisfying,' he tells us, 'when you are in good hands . . . I want to thank the staff as well as Mr and Mrs Grainger for all their care and kindness since I first came to . . . to The Limes. Thank you for coming to share my birthday with me and . . . and have a good time.'

Loud applause. I hand him a glass of champagne and he sips it for the photographer. Then more photographs. One with the Graingers, one with the staff, one with Millie. Everyone tucks into the feast and I hear William laughing his funny squeaky laugh. I can't stop smiling because he is so happy. That's what makes this job so rewarding. You can bring a little joy into someone's life.

When it is all over I wheel him back into his room and I can see he's very tired. It's been exciting but I hope he hasn't overdone it. It's only six thirty but I help him into his pyjamas and settle him in bed for a nap.

'You'll be in the paper tomorrow,' I tell him. 'A hundred years old! That's something to be proud of.'

'I suppose it is but . . .' He sighs.

I tell him, 'I'll wake you in an hour or so with a cup of tea otherwise you won't sleep tonight.'

I'm halfway out of the door when he speaks again. 'You know . . . I don't think I want another birthday. I think I've seen enough.'

When I go back an hour later William's dead. Lying peacefully in his bed. He slipped away while I was busy elsewhere and I want to cry but I don't. A hundred years and a good life. That can't be bad. I go to the phone and call Dr Swift on her mobile. She's only been gone half an hour but she hurries back.

The funeral's three days later and Millie is there in a black suit and an enormous black hat complete with veiling. I sit at the back with the Graingers. They're good like that. Always show proper respect for the residents. When I get back to The Limes I go into number 18 and close the door behind me. It's been cleaned, ready for the new resident and it smells of Mr Muscle and Pledge polish and nothing remains of William. It's as though he didn't exist . . . but as I stand there, with my eyes closed, I swear I hear that funny squeaky laugh of his.

Two days later we hear from Payne & Stapley, the solicitors. Mrs Grainger tells us that each member of staff has been left a hundred pounds in William's will. We're not supposed to accept bequests but the Graingers always turn a blind eye to small amounts.

I say, 'I suppose the granddaughter got the rest.' Not my business, I know, but I couldn't bear not knowing. If you don't ask, you don't get. That's what my mother used to say.

Slowly Mrs Grainger's face breaks into a smile. 'Millicent was left a small bequest but the rest, just over ninety thousand pounds, was shared equally between Mr Warren's two girlfriends!'

# Sylvia's Downfall

Funny, isn't it? There's always one. In our group it's Sylvia Bryce. Nice enough woman – short curly hair, a nicely plump figure and a cultured voice that occasionally grates. She's not exactly popular, but we're civilized people and we all get along with her – but she does have delusions of grandeur. She claims her husband is something big in the City – we're not sure what exactly – and we know he drives a Porsche, because she has told us so many times. Sylvia goes to the most expensive hairdresser in the town and wears the most beautiful clothes. Elegant. Immaculate. (I sometimes think I hate her!) Somehow she inveigled her way on to the luncheon group committee and now there's no stopping her.

'His name's Leonard Platt,' she told us recently. 'We call him Leo. He's a dear, *dear* man. Surely you've heard of him. He's been a television personality for years now.'

We were trying to find a speaker for our next lunch. There are sixty of us and, tongue in cheek, we call ourselves The Ladies Who Lunch. It's a charity thing. A friendly get-together in the function room of the Wild Boar Hotel. Women only, first Tuesday of every month. The hotel does us a meal for fifteen pounds a head (which includes the cost of the room) and we pay twenty pounds and the extra goes to a charity. We take it in turn to nominate one.

Helen said, 'Leonard Platt? Never heard of him. Which channel is he on?'

Sylvia hesitated. 'It varies. He's a sort of freelance presenter ... or newsreader. He often fills in when somebody can't appear for some reason. Holidays and illness.'

'Like a supply teacher.' Helen can look terribly innocent when she wants to.

Sylvia smile thinned. 'Hardly! He's highly thought of and tremendously versatile. He once took part in a chat show as the guest and . . . and I seem to remember him helping to run a competition for children but that was much earlier, of course. Leo knows absolutely everyone. Last time I met him he was telling us this hilarious story about his meeting with Billy Connolly, who mistook him for—'

Ruthlessly interrupting her, Marion, our treasurer, returned to important matters.

'Doesn't he charge a fee?'

Our speakers are always people like the man from the local garden centre. He doesn't charge for his talk because he reckons it's good publicity. Among others we've had a woman who runs the local museum, another who talked about 'signing' for the deaf, a man who teaches meditation and a girl who ran the London marathon. None of them charged a fee. If they did we'd have nothing left for the charities.

'He won't charge us,' Sylvia told us airily, 'because he's a *personal friend* of my sister . . . and a friend of mine, of course.' She smiled. Or was it a smirk?

'But what will he talk about?' I asked.

For a moment she almost lost her cool. 'I'm not sure *exactly*. One doesn't ask, does one. Stories, maybe, about personalities. Something along those lines. Snippets of television gossip.' She laughed. 'We could call it a glimpse behind the scenes. It's sure to be fascinating and you'll all love him. Leo's a real darling. Dishy, too. I first met him at a dinner party at my sister's and he had us all in *absolute* fits. You *must* know him!'

We didn't but that month there were no other nominations, so we settled on Leonard Platt. He actually sounded rather good but we couldn't appear too impressed, because Sylvia was already insufferable.

'I'll collect him from the station in Jack's Porsche,' she offered, 'and bring him along to the Wild Boar.'

I opened my mouth to protest. Collecting speakers from the station is one of my jobs. Then I thought better of it. Obviously Sylvia felt that my ancient Capri wasn't glamorous enough and did I really care? 'Thanks,' I said. 'I'm sure he'll be impressed.'

My job is also to arrange the meals, so I checked the booking slips and ordered lunch for the fifty-three people who wanted to attend. We don't bother with starters, so I suggested ham and pineapple followed by summer pudding and cream. I like to keep it simple so there is no excuse for slow service on the part of the hotel staff. Sometimes we used to find that the first people served had finished before the later ones had started. If we didn't finish the meal in time the speaker would be late and it became one big muddle.

It was Helen's turn to choose a charity and she opted for Age Concern.

I know it's mean of me but as the days passed I began to wish it had been anyone but Sylvia who had produced Leonard Platt. She couldn't let us forget that our guest was a result of her personal connection and it went to her head.

She rang me regularly, in a state of high excitement, to make sure the arrangements were going smoothly, apparently terrified that the visit would somehow fail to live up to her expectations. I don't know how she had persuaded him to come or what he was expecting but it became obvious that our usual arrangements would not do for 'darling Leo'.

'I thought we'd have flowers on the tables for a change,' she told me breathlessly. 'Flowers add a certain elegance, don't you agree?'

'But flowers cost—'

'I'll be bringing posies from my garden. Nothing elaborate but I want him to see that he's appreciated and that we've made a special effort for him.'

'But how will he know that we don't *always* have flowers?'

There was a short silence. I could imagine her rolling her eyes and raising her perfectly shaped eyebrows. 'Don't be difficult!' she laughed. And went straight on. 'I'm going to create a fancy menu on my computer.'

51

I opened my mouth to protest that we never have menus but bit back the words. Difficult? *Moi?*

'An A4 sheet folded once so that it will stand up. Cream with a slight weave. I'm putting Leo's picture on the front and on the back a paragraph about what he's done.'

Which wasn't much as far as I could see. Finally she hinted that perhaps we should invite a local journalist and a photographer to record the event but there was so much opposition to the idea that she withdrew it with as much grace as she could manage.

When the committee met a week later she said, 'I'll bring plenty of menus so everyone can take one home *as a souvenir*! And I'm going to run a raffle – No, no!' She held up her hands. 'Let me finish! A raffle for which *I* shall provide *major* prizes. Champagne, a basket of fruit and a twenty-pound book token . . .'

It was all rather over-the-top but we couldn't fault her enthusiasm and it was easier to let her go ahead than to fight her.

When the great day arrived it was obvious that without conferring we had all made a bigger effort than usual with our appearances. Even I had succumbed to the general excitement and had fished out a linen suit. Waiting for Leo and Sylvia to arrive, we milled around admiring each other and chatting. I picked up one of Sylvia's menus and opened it.

'*Freshly baked unsalted gammon ham with sunkissed pineapple . . . A selection of seasonal garden vegetables, mashed swede, new potatoes lightly sautéed . . . A mixture of fragrant summer berries . . .*'

I grinned. Typical Sylvia oversell. I turned to the front and was pleasantly surprised. Leonard Platt appeared to be slim, young and handsome with dark hair smoothed back from a broad forehead. On the back of the menu I discovered that he was '*. . . a well-loved TV personality who had delighted viewers for many years . . . versatile . . . professional . . .*'

I was almost convinced. Perhaps we had misjudged the situation. I smoothed my linen skirt and waited eagerly for our illustrious visitor.

Time passed.

'Where on earth are they?' Helen whispered. 'I've rung Sylvia's mobile but it must be switched off.'

The manager appeared, to ask me if they should start serving as the food was ready. After some anxious consultation we decided to go ahead. Chairs clattered and the staff bustled in with trays. Faced with the prospect of an absent speaker, the committee went into a huddle to consider our alternatives. Helen suggested we asked Muriel, one of the members, if she would give an impromptu talk about her hobby, which was collecting antiques. She agreed albeit with some reluctance and we settled down to the ham and pineapple.

We had almost finished the first course when Sylvia finally arrived with our important guest. As they entered, voices faltered and cutlery remained poised.

'Do carry on!' Sylvia cried gaily. 'Leonard's so sorry but he missed the train.'

But a silence had fallen over the room – because Leonard Platt, the well-loved TV personality, looked distinctly squiffy. Thinning hair dishevelled, tie askew, he collapsed heavily on to his chair and surveyed us blearily. Sylvia sat down next to him. Everyone knew that now he *had* turned up, we had a worse problem. The committee exchanged desperate glances. Any secret triumph we might have felt at Sylvia's predicament was cancelled out by the knowledge that we had a potential disaster on our hands.

Helen, on my left, was the first to rally. 'Tell Sylvia to get some food into him,' she hissed. 'As much as possible. Second helpings of everything – and nothing more to drink!'

Sylvia was seated on my right and I managed to pass on the message. She offered to 'help him' to potatoes and mashed swede and encouraged him to 'tuck in'. She made a brave attempt to eat but the *freshly baked unsalted gammon ham* was obviously difficult to swallow and her attempt at conversation wavered unhappily. Something glistened in her eyes and I realized she was close to tears and at that moment my heart went out to her. My earlier reservations about her vanished. Now she was just another woman put on the spot by an inconsiderate man.

Helen leaned towards me. 'Poor Sylvia. I'd like to throttle him!'

I looked around the other tables. A few expressions were gleeful but most were sympathetic.

Worse was to come. Leonard Platt insisted on having three glasses of wine while leaving most of the food uneaten. At last we could no longer delay and Sylvia rose to introduce him.

'I'm sure you will bear with our very special guest,' she said, her voice artificially bright. 'He . . . he became unwell as he travelled down from London but has generously insisted that he carry on as he doesn't wish to disappoint The Ladies Who Lunch.'

Enthusiastic applause. Nearly sixty pairs of eyes fastened on him as he clambered unsteadily to his feet because four members of the staff, sensing danger, had sneaked in to share the moment and now lurked in the area of the small bar, trying to pretend they were busy.

Leo stood up with some difficulty and treated us to a lopsided grin as he swayed dangerously. He spoke haltingly for seven minutes during which time he told the same tasteless joke twice, insulted a senior politician (who shall be nameless) and told us to look out for his first novel. He hadn't actually started it, he admitted, 'Bu's gonna – gonna be a bes'seller'. He leaned forward and managed to knock over one of Sylvia's flower arrangements. She closed her eyes while Helen dabbed at the flow of water with a couple of serviettes. 'Nothing to worry about, Mr Platt!' Helen assured him. 'Do carry on.'

It was dreadful but fascinating. The truth was we daren't take our eyes off our swaying speaker in case he overbalanced and fell face down into his *fragrant summer berries*. Somehow he stayed upright. I didn't know whether to be pleased or sorry.

When he finally sat down I rose to give a short vote of thanks. Every eye was on me as I struggled through my little speech, trying desperately not to laugh.

'I know you would all like to join me in a vote of thanks to our very entertaining speaker, Leonard Platt. The life of a television presenter is a very busy one and Mr Platt has given up his time for us and for Age Concern. We thank him for coming and I hope he will choose the winning tickets for—'

A tug at my arm drew my attention to the fact that he would *not* be choosing anything as he had fallen back in his chair and appeared to be fast asleep. Instead, after a round of applause which failed to waken him, I asked Muriel to pick the tickets from the hat. While she did so Sylvia hurried out to the car park to bring the car round and Marion, with the help of the hotel manager, bundled Leo downstairs and into the Porsche as it drew up outside the front door. With their disappearance, the ladies who lunch dissolved into hysterics and Sylvia missed a scene of great hilarity. Just as well.

Age Concern sent a nice letter of thanks for their cheque, and days later the committee set about arranging the next lunch. Sylvia was rather subdued but no one mentioned Leonard Platt. We've discovered that we all like Sylvia much more since her downfall. Funny, isn't it?

# Fairy-Tale Ending

Liz's house was situated ten minutes' walk from the station and the weather forecast, 'misty and murky', had proved an understatement. I had brought an umbrella but when I opened it outside the Underground station I saw that the cat had been at it. A long tear let in the fine rain, so I thrust it into the first rubbish bin I passed and walked on. The celebration evening was not getting off to a good start but I was confident it would get better.

Liz had been my closest friend from schooldays many moons ago when she had formally awarded me the title of Friend Number One. We had kept in touch over the years. I had married at twenty and produced two children who were now living with 'significant others'. My husband, Eddie, had just come in from work when Liz phoned to invite me over to help her celebrate the new man in her life.

Unlike me, Liz is vivacious and sexy, but she has had what I can only call 'a chequered life' – a series of dramatic highs and spectacular lows. Her problem was a habit of choosing the most unsuitable men she could find. Her first husband, Matthew, had been an alcoholic who killed himself by driving into a tree and left her with a stepdaughter. The next man, Darren, had an affair with the stepdaughter, who was only seventeen at the time, and they eventually left Liz and went to live together in Malaga.

Liz went on hoping, but she was too easily charmed and fell hopelessly in love at the drop of a hat. When I tried gently to point this out she turned on me furiously, claiming that at least she had some excitement in her life whereas mine was

56

hopelessly boring. I have worried about that once or twice since but on balance I think I prefer my somewhat cosy existence. I wasn't cut out for confrontation whereas Liz thrives on it.

As I turned off the High Street into Ranham Road, where Liz lived, I remembered our most recent telephone conversation.

'You'll love him, Chrissie. He's such a darling! *And* good-looking. *And* rich. Well, very comfortably off anyway. His name's Andrew and he's not attached! Can you believe it? My luck's changed with a vengeance! Remember that fairy tale?' She'd laughed.

It had been a childhood joke. Her fairy-tale ending was to marry a rich man and live happily after in a big house. Now Andrew was striding on stage as Prince Charming.

I was glad for her. 'She deserves some good luck,' I'd told Eddie.

'You make your own luck!' he'd answered with an enigmatic smile. He has mixed feelings about Liz and has always claimed that she's an integral part of the Chaos Theory!

Today I was due at seven o'clock (a Saturday) to meet the new man and to celebrate the fact that they were going to move in together into a large house called The Briars near the top of Windmill Hill. I would sleep at Ranham Road overnight and return home on Sunday in time to share lunch with Eddie. As the rain came down harder I half ran to number 70 and pressed the bell. It was one of a long row of terraced houses, gloomier than usual in the March rain. A newish Volvo was parked beside Liz's small Fiat. I shivered as I waited but I was looking forward to the evening. I had gone to a lot of trouble to look good, partly for my own satisfaction but also so as not to let Liz down. I know how she boasts about her friends. I was wearing high-heeled boots, a new velvet skirt and a matching cardigan patterned with sequins. I didn't want to underestimate the occasion.

A man opened the door. He wore trainers, grey tracksuit bottoms and a shapeless sweatshirt – and managed to look fabulous! Tall, slim, curly dark hair and bright blue eyes. With his designer stubble he looked like a male model. For once, I thought, Liz had not exaggerated. I might even have been bowled over, if he hadn't looked so bad-tempered.

'What?' he demanded.

I blinked. Hardly Prince Charming. I said, 'You must be Andrew. I'm Chrissie.'

He turned and shouted, 'Someone called Chrissie!' Then he disappeared, leaving me on the doorstep feeling like a complete lemon. Liz answered him but I couldn't make out what she said though I did hear the fabulous Andrew say, 'Get rid of her!'

My expectations for the celebration dinner went into free fall but I stepped inside and called, 'Liz! It's me!' I closed the front door behind me and made my way along the passage. Glancing in at the dining room, I saw a table thick with dust and two half-burnt Christmas candles which still trailed golden strands. The truth hit me with considerable force. Either I had muddled the date or they had forgotten the invitation. Either way I was not expected.

Liz came down the stairs, smoothing back her tousled hair and trying to look welcoming. She was in a baggy sweater and leggings, her face was drawn with anxiety and her eyes were red-rimmed.

'Chrissie! It must be the twelfth. I'm so sorry.'

'It doesn't matter.' I decided I could still turn round and get back to the station and home again before ten o'clock. 'I don't need to stay.'

Despite my wetness, we clung together for a moment and I knew she was wondering how to salvage something from the wreckage.

I said, 'We could make it some other time. Honestly, Liz.'

I pulled her favourite chocolate brazils from my pocket, handed them to her and whispered, 'Have these to cheer yourself up!'

'Oh Chrissie!' Her face crumpled but she held back tears. 'You've come all this way. I can make up a bed. Come and meet Andrew.' Seeing my hesitation, she whispered, 'Please, Chrissie.'

Wavering, I decided I would have to stay. In her voice I detected the familiar signs of stress and unhappiness. Was this the end of another fairy tale or a temporary blip? Liz helped me take off my mac, shook it a little and hung it up on the row of coat hooks. With an attempt at brightness she said, 'It's nothing, really. We'll be OK.'

I nodded. 'Teething troubles?'

'Something like that . . . I'll make us all a coffee and we'll chat. Go in and talk to Andrew.' She pushed me towards the tiny lounge and disappeared into the kitchen. I found Andrew with what looked a glass of whisky in his hand. He was standing staring out at the rainswept garden. For the first time I realized that he was much younger than Liz. She was mid forties – a few years younger than me. He looked thirtyish and fit with it.

I said, 'Filthy weather. They got the forecast right for once.' Hardly original but I hadn't yet recovered from his initial welcome.

He turned to face me, making no effort to pretend that I wasn't an inconvenient intrusion. Taking in my celebration outfit, he said, 'Trust Liz to screw things up. D'you want one?' He held up the glass.

'No, thank you. Liz is making coffee.'

'She drinks too much caffeine. No wonder she's hyper!' He emptied the remains of the whisky in one gulp and stared at me. 'Memory like a sieve, our Lizzie.'

'No, it's my fault,' I protested. 'I should have rung to check that it was still OK.'

Liz came in with the tray and glanced nervously towards Andrew, who said, 'Poor Chrissie's all tarted up and nowhere to go!'

He gave a mocking laugh and I wondered what had happened to cause the row. Perhaps Liz would confide in me if she got the chance.

I said, 'Why don't I take us all out for a pizza? Birthday treat.'

Andrew rolled his eyes. 'Because you've been invited to dinner and you shall have one. Fancy beans on toast?'

Liz gave us an apology for a smile and poured three coffees. She and I sat sipping ours. Andrew ignored his and poured himself another whisky. With an attempt at humour I raised my coffee cup and said, 'Here's to us chickens!'

At last Liz smiled. She raised her cup and Andrew shook his head at the obvious stupidity of women and muttered, 'God!'

I said, 'The Briars sounds wonderful. I expect you're looking forward to the move.'

The Briars, I had been told, was a five-bedroomed house in an acre of superb garden with a view over the heath. They were buying it together. Compared to number 70 Ranham Road it would be palatial.

Brightening, Liz jumped to her feet. 'I'll find the photos.'

As though these words were part of a mood-enhancing spell, Andrew suddenly took an interest. 'I have a friend who's an estate agent,' he offered in a more neutral tone. 'Geoff Wilde. We go back a long way. I told him exactly what we needed and he came up with the goods. Only took him two weeks.'

'You were lucky.'

'I knew Geoff would come up with the goods.' He was thawing rapidly. 'We looked at three but he knew which one we'd go for. It's got everything. En suite bathrooms, a games room, would you believe, and room to build a swimming pool if we ever want one.' He smiled.

It was a charming, boyish smile that lit up his face and suddenly I could see the charm that had won Liz's heart and I began to think that they *could* be happy.

As though he had read my thoughts he raised his glass. 'The Briars!'

The photographs arrived and Liz suggested that Andrew show them to me while she prepared something to eat.

'Let me give you a hand,' I said, hoping for a quiet word, but Andrew shook his head before Liz could answer.

'She'll be much better on her own,' he assured me. 'Lizzie

goes to pieces if there's somebody in her kitchen. Come and sit next to me.' He patted the sofa beside him and I dutifully moved across to sit beside him. Liz took the hint and disappeared into the kitchen and I was conscious of her footsteps, to and fro between the kitchen and the dining room. I hoped for her sake she had something tucked away in the freezer but I doubted it.

For the next quarter of an hour Andrew and I sat mulling over the photographs. The sight of the house brought about a dramatic change of mood and he became quite expansive. The Briars was perfect in every way. Prestigious, even. A dream house.

'This is the third bedroom. We shall use it as a guest room . . .'

'Very nice! I like the archway.'

'It's tastefully done, isn't it . . . and this is a view along the landing. We shall need some decent pictures for that. Make a sort of gallery . . .'

I said, 'You'll need some ancestors painted in oils!' and he laughed. He was undoubtedly a very attractive man. Good on you, Liz! I thought.

'This is the garden seen from the French windows . . . we thought we'd have a sunken area there with roses – all one colour . . .'

Liz had come in and was standing behind me. 'Sunken area with roses? What are you talking about? I thought the pool was going there.'

A strange expression flashed across his face, unseen by Liz but clear to me. Then he grinned at me conspiratorially and said, 'Oops!' To Liz he said, 'Sorry, darling. You're right. We did agree the pool.'

Liz took the photo and studied it. 'Roses would look quite nice there but where could we have the pool?'

'It's all about compromise,' he said, taking back the photograph. 'You worry about the meal, Lizzie love. We're only halfway through the snaps.'

I sat back and grinned at Liz. 'I can see you swanning

61

around in that house. I'm sure you'll both be very happy. Will I be invited to visit?'

Andrew said, 'Most certainly. We'll give a big party, won't we, Liz! Invite everyone. Champagne flowing in the fountains!' He laughed and tapped his head. 'Remind me to add fountains to the list! We'll throw it in June. We could have a marquee – there's plenty of room on the lawn. And we'll have smoked salmon and salads, strawberries and cream and an enormous cheese platter. A good time will be had by all.' He reached over and pressed Liz's hand and she returned his smile. Was the friction now over? With relief I concluded it was.

Half an hour later we sat down to eat. Liz had done her best with what she had found. A large bowl of savoury rice, cheddar cheese, a small plate of cold lamb and a bowl of pickled beetroot. There was also a dish of still warm hardboiled eggs. We all joked about the selection and Andrew was charming and witty throughout the meal. He found a couple of bottles of wine and from the way he behaved around the house I could see he was familiar with it. So they were living together. I wondered where his place was.

I raised my glass and said, 'Here's to both of you and to your future happiness!'

Liz beamed at me and I was just congratulating myself that the celebration was all systems go when a mobile phone bleeped.

Andrew said, 'That's mine!' and dived back into the lounge, leaving us alone. I was opening my mouth to say something nice about Andrew when I realized that Liz was trying to overhear Andrew's conversation and I remained silent.

She looked anxious until she remembered my presence and then she looked guilty. 'Sometimes I answer it and whoever it is hangs up.'

I noted a certain tension in the way she spoke but before I could ask her anything, Andrew came back into the room wearing a leather jacket. His face was etched with worry.

'It was the hospital. My father's had a heart attack. He's

in intensive care . . . Where are my damned keys?' He was searching distractedly for them.

Liz said, 'Oh darling, I'm sorry. Shall I come with you?'

I said, 'Do, Liz! I'll be fine here until you—'

He said, 'No! You two stay here. It might be a long night.'

'But you've been drinking, darling. I could drive you.'

'For God's sake don't fuss, Lizzie!'

He found the keys on the mantelpiece and gave her a quick kiss. She went with him to the door and I heard a whispered conversation, then a car door slammed and he drove away with squealing tyres.

'He'll drive too fast. He'll be stopped by the police . . .' She sat down, reached for her wine and emptied the glass.

I swallowed a mouthful of beetroot and tried to think of something helpful to say but before I managed it Liz burst into tears and ran out of the room. After a decent interval I went after her and found her in the bathroom, sitting on the edge of the bath, mopping her eyes. We went back downstairs to the dining room and tried to carry on with the meal. After a little prompting, the sad story emerged.

Liz suspected that Andrew might still be married. If so the odd phone calls were probably from his wife. If not, somebody, male or female, was keeping tabs on him. Either way, she was worried.

'I want to trust him, Chrissie. Of course I do but . . .'

'Is that what the row was about? I take it you had had a row before I arrived.'

She nodded. 'It started yesterday. That's what put tonight out of my mind. It's over the house. Well, it's about money basically.'

I listened with growing dismay.

'Obviously I haven't got as much money as Andrew – he's got this wonderful job in the City to do with insurance. He's some sort of investigator. You know how so many people make false claims? They set fire to their own business if it's failing – that sort of thing. So-o, I've put this house on the market and found a buyer. Andrew needs his money to add to mine to clinch The Briars but it's all tied up in some sort of offshore trust and they're being so slow.'

I closed by eyes to hide my dismay. Here comes the sticking point, I thought unhappily.

'The vendor's solicitor needs a cheque by tomorrow to prove good faith – just part of the money – and Andrew wants me to use the money my aunt left me. But if I do and if I go ahead with this house sale and Andrew's money doesn't come through we'll lose The Briars and I'll have no home!'

'Why can't you move in with Andrew? Doesn't he have a flat or something?'

'Apparently not. He was staying with a friend when we met . . . or so he says.'

Those last few words rang warning bells.

'So how much,' I asked, 'does Andrew need from you?'

'Thirty thousand.'

Instinctively I winced.

'I know it sounds a lot but when you consider the price of the house – six hundred thousand – it's peanuts. I have ten thousand from my aunt plus a few Premium Bonds but . . .' She looked at me and I could see that more tears were on the way. 'All I want is to move into The Briars and be happy with Andrew. I *know* we will be. You think I can't judge men and I know I've made mistakes before but this time I *know* we're right for each other. I do, Chrissie! He adores me. He really does. He carries one of my letters in his wallet so he can read it while we're apart!' She gave me a watery smile.

'That's lovely,' I said, aiming for conviction and failing. I wanted to advise her to hang fire on the cheque but I know her moods and if she sprang to his defence she and I would quarrel and I felt she needed me. Maybe I was overreacting. Maybe Andrew was a sweet man who would do the right thing by her. Perhaps, perish the thought, I was *jealous*.

Moments later the phone rang again and I couldn't help hearing Liz's end of the conversation.

'Oh no! Darling! Of course you must stay with him . . . D'you want me to . . . No, I'll be fine. Chrissie's here. We'll amuse ourselves until you get home . . . Your wallet? Oh dear. Yes I'll find it and bring it to you. Bye, love.'

She came back into the lounge looking more depressed than ever. 'He's left his wallet, so I'm going to run it over to him. The hospital's only a few minutes away in the car. You don't mind, do you? I won't stay there. He thinks he left it by the bed . . .' She ran upstairs and returned with it open in her hand. 'Look! Here's my letter! I'll show you!'

She pulled a folded sheet from the wallet and opened it up with an expectant smile on her face. Suddenly the smile faded to be replaced by a look of shock. She muttered, 'Oh God! No! . . .' Wordlessly she handed me the letter and sank down on to the sofa.

I didn't recognize the handwriting and I know Liz's almost as well as I know my own. It began:

*Dearest Andy,*

*I can't wait for you to get back from Morocco. It's been a very, very, very long week without you. The estate agent rang twice and seems rather impatient. The vendors are anxious to exchange contracts (but not half as anxious as I am for us to move into our new home!!!) . . .*

I looked at her. 'Morocco? What does it mean?' I thought I knew what it meant but I didn't want to be the one to utter the fateful words.

'What's the date on it?' She snatched it back. 'Two weeks ago!' Carefully she began to refold the letter and I watched in disbelief as she eased it back into the wallet. 'He won't know I've seen it,' she told me, white faced and trembling. 'I won't say anything.'

'Who was it from?'

'Probably his mother.' She couldn't meet my eyes.

'*It's been a very, very, very long week without you*?' I quoted. 'Liz?'

Her mouth tightened. 'OK. Have it your way. It's not his mother. Are you satisfied?' She glared at me.

'Liz, *please*! She's longing for them to move into their new home . . .?'

Liz took a long deep breath. 'OK. He's stringing this poor woman along but that's not my problem. That's hers. He and I are going to be together and this . . . this Paula . . .' Her voice faltered.

I said, 'Paula and how many others?' I knew it would hurt but I couldn't sit there and let this wretched man fleece her of thirty thousand pounds. 'If you still trust him, tell him you saw the letter – it fell out of the wallet – and ask him to explain. All very civilized and he can put your mind at rest.'

She covered her face with her hands. 'I can't,' she said at last.

I had a brainwave. 'Then . . . ring this Paula! Ask *her*? Tell her the truth. If she's his mother or his sister you'll know and you can stop worrying and go ahead with the wedding and the house and I'll be the first to offer my congratulations.'

'I can't,' she repeated. 'I trust him.'

I hardened my heart. 'So when did he go on this trip to Morocco?'

There was a long angry silence. Then she said, 'He'll be wondering where I am.'

I pointed to the phone. 'Prove it, Liz. Prove that you trust him. Ring Paula . . . or shall I ring her?'

'*No!* You stop meddling, Chrissie. It's none of your business.'

'You make it my business,' I reminded her sharply. 'Whose door did you come knocking on when Matthew died? Mine, Liz. Whose telephone was ringing night after night when Darren left you? Mine, Liz. And who helped you to pick up the pieces? I did. So don't pull that shit about it's none of your business! You *always* make it my business! I'm always there for you, Liz, and I still am!'

She glared at me, sullen-faced, then jumped to her feet. 'Ring her then – before I change my mind!' She pulled out the letter and handed it to me and I found the telephone number. For a moment I hesitated. I didn't know what I was going to say because Liz had called my bluff. But if I didn't make the call I knew she would never do it.

A woman's voice said, 'Andrew! You're back! Did you have a good trip?' Presumably Paula.

I almost panicked. Should I pretend to be the police making enquiries . . . or pretend I had found the wallet? I decided to pretend I was another woman but *not* Liz.

She said, 'Darling? Are you there?'

I said, 'Who is this? I wanted to speak to Andrew.'

'I'm his fiancée, Paula Garrett. Who are *you*?'

I let a few seconds pass. I daren't look at Liz who was hovering close beside me, listening in. 'I'm Meg . . . Meg Warren. You say you're his *fiancée*? There must be some mistake. Andrew and I are going to be married shortly. We're buying a house together . . . Hullo? Are you still there?'

I felt a great wave of compassion for Paula Garrett but better she should find out now rather than later when she'd parted with her money.

She said, 'I take it this is a joke.' Her voice shook. 'If so it's not funny.'

I took a deep breath. 'I'm sorry, Paula, but it isn't a joke. I've just written a cheque for a large sum of money for a down payment on a house. Andrew and I have been engaged for three months. My Andrew Patten works in the City.'

There was another long silence then she said, 'Mine travels abroad for his firm. He's a sales manager. Power tools. It can't be the same man. I'm sorry . . .'

'Wait!' I told her. 'I'm thinking we should both make a few enquiries just in case. These things do happen. In case you need to get in touch with me—'

The phone went dead. I replaced the receiver and turned to put my arms around Liz. She was dry eyed but trembling. I couldn't think of anything to say. After a moment she pulled away and made a grab for her mac. I persuaded her to have a coffee first and calm down but while I was in the kitchen I heard the front door slam and ran out in time to see her driving away. She had taken the wallet and the letter and I imagined

67

that she was going to tackle Andrew. Then I remembered that his father was desperately ill with a heart attack. Suppose she made a terrible scene in the hospital?

At that minute the phone rang again and it was Paula Garrett. I was suddenly cold. Liz's words came back to me. I had meddled and I would have to deal with the consequences.

Paula Garrett said, 'I used "ring back". I have to talk to you because I've been checking up and no one called Meg Warren lives at your number – so what's going on? If you don't give me a decent explanation I'm going to phone the police.'

Her decision to speak to the police forced me to a decision. I would confess to the Meg Warren lie and start with a clean slate. I explained briefly why I had lied to her but I didn't give her Liz's full name and she didn't think to ask for it. I had no idea what Liz was doing or saying at the hospital or what she would want to do when she got back. 'I just came over to meet Andrew,' I told Paula. 'We were supposed to be celebrating. This has all happened very suddenly but something is definitely wrong.'

There was a short silence but when she spoke again her voice was tight with repressed fear. 'I've given him eight thousand pounds . . . For a house called The Briars. I borrowed it from my father. We went to see round it. It's not a scam. It's a real property.'

'I know. I've seen the photographs they took.' I remembered suddenly what Andrew had said about the sunken rose garden. That had been *their* plan for it. His and Paula's. He had slipped up badly but somehow got away with it. I heard her voice break and then she was sobbing. I said, 'Shall I ask my friend to call you when she comes back from the hospital?'

She said, 'Yes. We have to sort this out before I ring my father and we go to the police. That cheating bastard is not going to get away with this.' Then she hung up.

I had lost my appetite. I cleared the table and loaded the dishwasher, then made myself another coffee. More than anything I wanted to go home but that was out of the question. Time passed. Finally I heard a car draw up and I rushed to the door.

Liz was alone. Her face was white and drawn. 'Don't ask!' she muttered bitterly. She sat staring into space for a quarter of an hour, then it all came out.

'Andrew was waiting for me outside the hospital. He wouldn't answer me. I was holding out the letter as I crossed the car park, shouting about this Paula, He just snatched the wallet, ran to his car and drove away. I didn't know what to do, so I went inside and enquired after his father but they said a man had been admitted with a heart attack but the name wasn't Patten and they aren't allowed to give out details except to relatives.' She looked at me. 'I'll never see him again, will I? Andrew, I mean. I know I won't.'

I told her about Paula Garrett. 'You should speak to her,' I said. 'She's already lost eight thousand pounds.'

Liz covered her face with her hands. 'I've lost Andrew!'

'She's going to involve the police, Liz. You have to talk to her.'

Reluctantly she took my advice and they talked on the phone for more than an hour. Then Liz spoke to Paula's father and it was arranged that all three would meet at a police station the next morning.

The next morning, after a sleepless night, I decided to leave them to it.

Liz had Paula and her father by way of moral support and didn't need me to stay on, so I went home. Eddie listened to me sympathetically but I knew what he was thinking. It was an accident waiting to happen

Time passed and Liz kept me informed with an occasional brief phone call. The police traced Andrew by way of his father. Over the following weeks the truth emerged. His real name was Andrew Bridges but he used several aliases. He mostly preyed on vulnerable women but he had once had a custodial sentence of three years for embezzlement. He had no job but *did* have a wife whom he had abandoned somewhere in Scotland.

It took some months before they brought him to trial but when they did he was found guilty of serious fraud and sent down for five years. During that time relations between myself and Liz were a little strained. I felt that illogically she held me partly responsible for the fiasco and feared it might be the end of our friendship.

A year later, however, out of the blue, I got an invitation to her wedding. She was going to marry the detective who had been in charge of the fraud case. DCI Lesley Carter was a genuinely nice widower. He and Liz have been happily married now for two years and live in a modest house in Ealing with his ten-year-old daughter, Sue.

Not exactly the fairy tale, perhaps, but near enough.

# Seriously Weird

'Myra! Come in, dear! Long time no see.' Jess gave me a quick peck, closed the front door, helped me off with my coat and led me into the sitting room, which was as grand as I remembered. Thick carpet, leather suite, a chandelier and flowers everywhere. And a huge mirror over the fireplace. Her parents had left her a lot of money and she'd put it all into property. Very wise, I should think, with property prices always rising. Even our bungalow is worth ten times what we paid for it.

The others were already there – Jim and Sarah and the two sisters from across the way – Janice and Laura.

They all jumped to their feet to greet me and I felt so pleased I had agreed to come. It was two years since my husband died and I hadn't wanted to face the world without him. Only our daughter had kept me sane. You have to carry on living if you have children.

'Come and sit by the fire,' said Jim. 'Warm yourself up. It's a rough old night.'

I said, 'They did promise us gales.'

Minutes later I had a glass of sherry in my hand and was sipping it cautiously – it does sometimes upset my stomach but I was determined to enjoy the evening.

Jess asked me about Trish, my daughter. She'd been so upset by John's death and we'd all worried about her.

'She's fine,' I said. 'She's lying on her bed doing her home-work—'

'With one eye on the telly, I'll bet!' Janice laughed. 'How do they do it, kids today? Concentrate, I mean. My mother made us work in silence.'

'If it's not the telly, it's videos or gameboys or whatever they call them.'

'Well, at least it's not boys!' Janice laughed. 'That's what really turns the hair grey!'

Not hers though. She'd been rinsing her hair for years and would probably never go grey. At the moment she's a strange reddish colour but last Christmas it was dull orange although she called it 'summer gold'.

'I try to keep an eye on what Trish watches,' I said. 'She's got a thing about vampires at the moment. Dreams about them. Vampires, Frankenstein monsters, ghouls and ghosties. Mind you, it's her own fault. She always has loved horror stories. Horror and the supernatural.' I shuddered. 'John said once she should have been a boy. I said to her only last week, "No wonder you have nightmares!" But when does a teenage girl ever listen to her mother?'

Jess is a wonderful cook. Not hearty casseroles and chunky pies which I aspire to but *fancy* things. *En croute* things. And strange desserts like syllabubs and things in filo pastry. I'm not nearly so adventurous. Probably because John preferred sensible cooking, as he called it. I like Jamie Oliver's cooking because he just seems to throw things together and they come out all right. And Nigella makes it look easy. I was really looking forward to one of Jess's fabulous dinners. In fact I'd been starving myself all day.

An hour later we had just sat down at the dinner table and I could see the home-made salmon paté and a basket of thin-cut toast. I was just helping myself to a slice when the phone rang. Jess groaned and went out into the hall and we all heard her say, 'Yes, your mother's here,' and that she would fetch me. I apologized and left the table feeling none too pleased. I'd left Trish a plateful of ham sandwiches, a large slice of chocolate cake and a couple of cans of Coca Cola. Her choice.

'Bad luck, Myra!' said Jim. He must be eighty if he's a day but no one has ever asked him. He's terribly pernickety and that's probably why he's never married but he's kindly enough. 'Make it quick or we'll have eaten it all!'

I went to the phone, feeling really put out.

'What is it?' I didn't mean to snap but I did. 'I've only been here half an hour or so. We're just starting our—'

'Mum, I'm scared!' said Trish. 'Something is happening. Something seriously weird. I want you to come home.'

'Come home? I've only just arrived! It wouldn't be fair. Jess has gone to all this trouble and I'm not going to break up the party.'

'I mean it, Mum. There's something creepy going on. Please come home.'

I closed my eyes. My first evening out for ages. Why did she have to do this? Did she, deep down, resent me trying to have a life of my own? 'Stop messing me about, Trish,' I said crossly. 'I'm not having my evening out spoiled. I'll be home about eleven. You finish your homework and—'

'There's something tapping at the window.'

'A branch of the pear tree, I expect.'

'But you had Mr Cross round last month to cut it all back.'

That was true. I hesitated. I knew it couldn't be anything much. In fact it couldn't be anything at all except her imagination. And she wasn't a child any longer. Fourteen in two months' time.

She said, 'It sounds like someone knocking on the window.'

I gritted my teeth. Mustn't shout at her in case the others heard me. But she was being ridiculous. I realized that this was some sort of prank – a practical joke. Or else she was trying to spoil my evening and I didn't think she would do that. Unless Claire was with her. That girl was a nasty piece of work. She lived across the street and they spent a lot of time together.

I said, 'Is Claire with you?' Claire might have put her up to it. It's the sort of thing she would do.

'Claire? No. Why should she be?'

'I don't know. You might have asked her over.'

'Well, I haven't . . . Should I open the curtains? To see who it is?'

'But your bedroom's upstairs. Whoever it is would have to be about fifteen feet high! Look, if you're feeling scared play some cheerful music . . . or do your homework downstairs in the lounge with Goldie. She loves a bit of company.' Goldie's the dog. She's not allowed in the bedrooms, poor old thing. I waited but Trish didn't answer. I frowned suddenly. 'What's that noise?'

'I told you, Mum. There's someone knocking on the window!'

Jess appeared from the dining room. 'Come on, Myra. You're missing out. I've just made some fresh toast.'

I gave up. I told Trish I'd call back in ten minutes when I'd finished my starter. I told the others what was going on and they laughed but Laura said, 'You have to blame the television people. It's all violence these days. Sex and violence. No wonder our kids are mixed up. And this "trick or treat" that has come over from America. Very unpleasant.'

'Trish isn't mixed up,' I said, a little too quickly. 'She just has a vivid imagination.'

'Perhaps she'll be a writer,' Jess suggested. 'A famous novelist!'

'It would have to be horror stories then,' I said and we all laughed.

We got on to the subject of films then and from there to books and then we were into the main course, which was duck pan-fried with apples, and I suddenly realized I hadn't rung Trish back. I'll do it between the main course and the dessert, I thought, but then the phone rang and it was Trish again.

I grabbed the phone and said, 'Now don't start this nonsense again, Trish! It's not funny.'

'He wants to come in, Mum,' she said. 'The vampire. He's outside the window and he wants to come in.'

For a moment a shudder ran down my spine. She said it in such a spooky way but then I realized what she was up to. 'It's not Hallowe'en!' I told her. 'Have you finished your homework?'

'No . . . but Mum, he looks so sad.'

'Have you had your supper?'

'No. I have to let him in.'

I wanted to shake her. I was sure by this time that Claire was with her. Probably listening in on the extension. But I'd had the sherry and a glass of red wine, I was beginning to relax and enjoy my evening and I would not let them ruin it for me. 'Where are you?'

'In my room.'

I counted to ten. 'Look, I'll give Mr Carter next door a ring and ask him to pop round and look round the house, outside and in. So no more about vampires, if you don't mind!' Before she could protest I said, 'See you later.' And blew her a kiss. I knew she'd hate that. She doesn't like me to treat her like a child.

I put the phone down and rang Mr Carter. He wasn't in but his mother said she'd give him the message. She was expecting him home any minute, she said, and she'd send him round before he took his coat off.

I'm ashamed to say I didn't give Trish another thought after that. She and Mr Carter were great pals and I knew he'd set her mind at ease. We finished the meal and were tucking into the chocolates with our coffee when there was a knock at the front door.

Jess went and she came back as white as a sheet. 'It's the police for you, Myra. There's been a – a sort of accident.'

Before she had finished I was out of my chair and into the passage and there was a young constable and a policewoman.

'What?' I shouted. 'What's happened? Is it Trish? Oh no! Not Trish!'

He said, 'We had a call from a Mr Carter, your neighbour. He said he's—'

'But Trish! Is she all right? She is, isn't she? Oh God!'

Jess grabbed my arm. I think she thought I would fall and I did feel faint but I had to know about my lovely daughter.

The policewoman said, 'We'll take you in the car to the hospital. Mr Carter's waiting there. Your daughter's going to be all right.'

I grabbed my coat and rushed out of the house, leaving the others on the doorstep. I don't think I even said 'Goodbye' but I knew Jess would understand.

Mr Carter was watching for me from the doorway to the casualty ward. He looked anxious and he was smoking. He'd only recently given up. Oh God, I thought. It must be bad news. I ran towards him, shocked and afraid.

'Don't tell me . . . She's not . . .?' I couldn't get the words out.

'No, no! There's no change. They say she'll be all right.'

I wanted to see her straight away but a nurse said the doctor was with her and I must wait a few minutes. The policewoman went in search of a cup of tea for me and I asked Mr Carter what had happened.

'I got home about ten,' he told me, 'and Mum asked me to go round and check for you. There was no sight of anyone in the garden – except Goldie.'

'I suppose Trish let her out,' I said. 'But it's unusual that late in the evening. She's a lazy old thing.'

'Goldie was very excited, though. Barking and whimpering and jumping up and down.'

I stared. 'Goldie?' I couldn't imagine it.

'So I knocked on the front door but no one came, so I thought Trish must have her music up loud although I couldn't hear anything. I tried the kitchen door and it was open. The house was dead quiet – so I called out and there was no sign of her, so I went upstairs and . . . and she was lying on the bed. The window was wide open and leaves blowing in all over the place.' He put his hands over his face. 'It was awful. I thought . . . she was so terribly pale. I – I thought she was dead!'

I patted his arm. 'Poor you. I'm so sorry. But go on.'

'I touched her and she was very cold. My first thought . . . Forgive me, but I thought she'd OD'd. Taken something. Pills. Drugs. You know . . .'

Before I could recover from this terrible idea a nurse fetched me to a cubicle at the far end of the ward. Inside the green curtains, Trish was on a trolley. The doctor looked very young and was obviously worried. He introduced himself as Dr Reeves. I was almost afraid to look at Trish after what Mr Carter had told me. When I did, my heart sank. She was lying on her side and looked like a corpse. Or a stone statue. Her skin was grey and shiny with sweat and her eyes were closed. Something colourless was being fed into the back of her hand but she looked . . . strangely serene. No sign of an accident. No bruises. No blood.

'Trish!' I leaned over and kissed her and she was so cold. I couldn't believe she was still alive. Seeing my expression, the doctor said, 'She's in deep shock, Mrs Denny, from a massive loss of blood, but she's still with us. And it's not drugs. Nor an overdose. Put that out of your mind.'

'Loss of blood?' I stared at him.

'According to all the signs. She has a very weak and rapid pulse.'

I squeezed Trish's hand, willing her to give some sign but there was nothing. I blinked back tears and swallowed hard. 'So what is it? What's happened to her?'

He frowned. 'I'll be honest, Mrs Denny. I don't really know. The symptoms don't add up. Frankly, I've never seen anything quite like this before.'

I stared at my beautiful daughter and I could feel my heart racing painfully inside my chest. 'But she's not going to die?'

'I certainly hope not. When the tests come back we'll know her blood group and then we'll give her a blood transfusion.' He smiled. 'She'll soon be on the road back.'

'It's not a heart attack, is it? My mother and my aunt—'

'Oh no! If we thought that, she'd be in intensive care . . . The puzzle is that the symptoms point to a massive blood loss but your neighbour says that's impossible. He'd have seen it.'

I patted her hand. 'Trish! *Trish!* Listen to me. It's Mum. Open your eyes. Wake up. *Wake up!*' Nothing. Not a glimmer. I had another thought. 'Is she in a coma?'

The policewoman brought the promised cup of tea but I

shook my head and she retreated with it. The doctor pulled up a chair for me and I sat down.

'No, it's not a coma. I do know what it's *not*. I'm just not sure what it *is*! Unless you keep any exotic pets. A snake, perhaps?'

I shuddered and shook my head. I can't bear snakes.

'Mr Carter says the window was open,' I told him. 'Maybe a snake got into the bedroom – but it's upstairs.'

He shrugged. 'Highly unlikely, then.'

'A squirrel might have got in – or a bat. Why do you ask about snakes?'

'There were two puncture wounds in her neck about an inch and a half apart apart.'

It didn't make any sense.

I went in search of Mr Carter to thank him for calling the ambulance and being there for her. I told him to go home but he insisted on staying.

'I'll hang on for you. I've rung Mother and told her not to wait up. Taxis are expensive.'

'They're saying she lost a lot of blood. Did you see any blood anywhere in the house? The bathroom, maybe?'

He shook his head. The policeman had also made a pretty thorough search while they were waiting for the ambulance. There was no sign of a break-in, either. I went back to Trish and sat down again, trying to puzzle out what had happened. Somehow I couldn't imagine a snake climbing up the wall to her window – but nor could I imagine a squirrel or a bat getting in and attacking her. The doctor was right. It was puzzling but at least she was going to be all right. But puncture marks in the neck?

On the way home in the car I looked across at Mr Carter. 'I've racked my brains but I haven't the foggiest!'

He shrugged.

Puncture marks! You tell me!

# Sacking Mizz Stewart

Gerald sat down at his desk and a long, resentful sigh escaped him.

'Damn the woman!'

Gerald Foster was a burly man in his early forties. He had once almost married but his bride-to-be had changed her mind, literally at the eleventh hour, and the service, due to start at twelve, had been cancelled. Until then he had been reasonably ambitious but the incident had badly dented his confidence. He had been office manager at the time, newly appointed, but now seven years later, he was still office manager. His career ladder was rather short and if he'd been a woman, people would have been talking about glass ceilings and saying how unfair it was. Because he was a man, Gerald thought, nobody cared. Probably nobody even noticed that his progress up the ladder had ground to an ignominious halt.

'Damn Mrs Stewart!' he muttered. He couldn't blame her for his failures but he could blame her for ruining his Monday morning. He liked to ease himself gently back into work after the weekend but today he was faced with the unpleasant task of sacking one of his employees.

Mrs Stewart was a 'returner'. He groaned. He should have had more sense. This was one of the few times he'd got things wrong and that irked him. He'd only taken the woman to satisfy the Chamber of Commerce, who had appealed to his better nature. One of their many initiatives for which funds were available was to help place into work people who had been away from the workplace for years and now wanted to return. Most of them were women who had finished bringing up a family. He'd joined the Chamber of Commerce with high hopes but nothing useful had come from the association. Small firms like Drake & Wesley existed on a shoestring and he suspected they always would.

He glanced at his watch. Five to ten on Monday morning. He tried to remember how much notice Mrs Stewart would have to work – or was she still on probation? He really ought to know these details but where on earth was her file? Pulling open a few drawers, he looked for it but without much hope of finding it. Samantha would know. Samantha had been with them for eight years and she could probably run the place single-handed if the need arose. He frowned. Samantha had told him not to take on a returner when the idea was first mooted. Cheeky little madam! He'd told her to mind her own business – but not in those exact words.

'Just trying to warn you,' she'd said with her usual shrug. 'My dad took on a returner – a chap of fifty-something – and he was useless. Lost sight of the work ethic. That's what my dad said.'

It rankled that she'd been proved right.

Was Samantha due for a rise? He couldn't remember that, either. He presumed she would eventually get married and leave to have a baby. It would be a mixed blessing.

Another glance at his watch. Ten o'clock. The moment he'd been dreading. He couldn't put it off any longer. Picking up a paper clip, he fiddled with it, forced it open then tossed it into the waste basket.

'Get on with it, Gerald,' he muttered. 'It's not the end of the world. You have to sack Mrs Stewart. That's all.' He felt terrible and a small muscle fluttered in his eyelid. He rubbed it and blinked rapidly until it stopped.

He buzzed Samantha and she materialized, genie-like, in the doorway. Twenty-four, pert, pretty and skinny with it.

He said, 'Sit down, please.'

She obeyed, tossed back her short dark hair, crossed her legs and glanced approvingly at her silver nailpolish. He hated her nails. Sometimes they were dark purple and sometimes an evil black. Once she had painstakingly painted them red, white and blue! Gerald tried not to look at her legs, long and stick-like in their fine black stockings. They made him wince. She wore unflattering black shoes with enormous clumpy heels which reminded him of horses' hooves. Gerald sometimes wondered what modern girls ate. Or didn't eat. There was a disease that afflicted modern women. Perhaps she suffered from it. If so he ought to feel sorry for her but he didn't.

'Samantha!' He forced a smile. 'A quick word in your shell-like.'

She perched on the edge of the chair. The firm had three such colt-like creatures working for them. With a stretch of his imagination Gerald could sometimes see them skittering round in a field, whinnying and tossing their neat little manes.

'So . . .' he began. 'About Mrs Stewart . . . How's she been making out? Any improvements?'

Samantha said, '*Ms* Stewart. She asked us to call her Ms.' She picked idly at one of her nails. 'Being divorced and everything. Trying to be trendy, I suppose.'

'Mizz Stewart? I see.' He didn't, of course, but he wasn't going to tell Samantha. So Mrs Stewart was divorced. Poor soul. He knew from bitter experience that it wasn't much fun recovering from something like that. Rejection was a bitter pill to swallow. So the poor woman had been left on her own. Presumably that's why she was a returner. Why hadn't he known that? he wondered. 'I couldn't find her file,' he said accusingly.

With a heavy sigh she crossed to a filing cabinet, riffled through the top drawer and handed him two sheets of paper. One pink, one white. The white one looked like a letter. She returned to her seat and watched him with a bored expression.

'Thank you, Samantha . . . So has she improved at all?'

If she had, he wouldn't sack her. He'd warn her about the need to 'pull up her socks' and then give her another chance. Sacking people could be a dangerous business. Everyone in the firm knew that his predecessor, Donald Wayne, had come

81

a terrible purler when he sacked Mandy Price. It was now the stuff of legends.

Wayne and Mandy had been having an affair although his wife knew nothing about it. When the two lovers finally quar-relled Mandy threatened to tell his wife and in a panic Wayne sacked her. She promptly sued him for wrongful dismissal and won a large amount of compensation from the firm. Head Office were not best pleased and Wayne was 'eased out' of the job and disappeared. It was rumoured he was not even in London. Samantha had suggested darkest Siberia.

Gerald took a deep breath. No chance of anything like that happening, he reassured himself. A simple case of not being up to the job and Samantha would back him up.

'Ms Stewart's OK really.' Samantha recrossed her legs. It was common knowledge that Samantha had a new 'fella' every three months. Apparently she lost interest very quickly. Gerald wondered what a man would have to do to keep her happy.

'What do you mean, she's OK?' He regarded her indig-nantly. 'I thought you said Mrs Stewart – Mizz Stewart was slow.' Had this wretched girl put him through agonies of mind without good cause? 'A week ago you told me she wasn't pulling her weight and that she wasn't getting through a fair share of the work. Now you say she's OK really. Which is it?'

She shrugged. 'It's not that she doesn't pull her weight. Not exactly. I mean, not deliberately. She works all the time. It gets on your nerves. You know? You can't have a chat with her.'

With a jerk of her head she flicked her hair back from her face, exposing the sharp cheekbones. Were they normal? he wondered. Her collarbones were also very visible.

She went on. 'She's slow on the keyboard. I know she went on that course to learn IT skills and she does understand the computer but it hasn't helped her speed. At the end of the day, she often stays late to get stuff finished. Charlie's always on about her.'

Charlie was the caretaker, an awkward, miserable man who seemed to thrive on conflict and enjoyed a good moan. It was his job to lock up and check the offices when all the staff had gone home. Gerald kept out of his way as much as possible. Not that he was afraid of the caretaker, he reminded himself hastily. He could give as good as he got and Charlie would never get the better of *him*.

Gerald rolled his eyes. So it wasn't going to be as straightforward as he had expected. 'So you're saying that Mrs Stewart actually works very hard.'

'Yes, she does. And longer hours. You know? Comes in early most mornings. Quarter of an hour, twenty minutes. She always pretends the traffic was easier than she expected but it's obvious what she's up to. She's hoping we won't put two and two together.'

Gerald frowned, intrigued. He had learned to lean on staff who skived off early, spent ages in the toilets or hung about in the back yard having a smoke. Overwork was a new one on him.

He glanced at Samantha, who was fiddling impatiently with her biro, signalling a desire to get back to her colleagues. He glanced at one of the white sheets – Mrs Stewart's meagre dossier. He read it quickly. So she was forty. His own age, in fact, give or take a few years. Would he have known? Yes. There was an air about her. She had lived a little. Suffered a little. It showed in the lines around her eyes. No children. He wondered why. Perhaps the marriage had broken up before they got round to a family. Or maybe she couldn't have children, like his sister.

He frowned. 'So she works very hard but still doesn't pull her weight.'

'In a nutshell!' Samantha glanced at the wall clock. 'It's like there's four of us but we're only getting the work done for three and a half.'

He turned to the second sheet. It seemed Mrs Stewart was back in the workplace after an absence of fifteen years. Previously a secretary and a doctor's receptionist. The doctor's reference described her as 'hard working, punctual and totally reliable.'

Samantha recrossed her legs. Not that she was trying to impress him. That would have been something, but Gerald had no illusions about the way the girls regarded him. Since the senior partner had retired, Gerald was the oldest man in the office. A 42-year-old dinosaur. They never called him Gerald although he had more than once hinted that he wouldn't object . . .

But he set a lot of store by Samantha's opinion. She had been with the firm longer than any of the others and she was a hundred per cent efficient. If she had time to gossip it was because she was fast with the work.

He sighed. It was a difficult call. 'You don't think if we gave her a little longer . . . ?' he suggested.

Samantha's mouth tightened. 'She jammed up the printer yesterday.'

'She did? Oh dear.'

'Emma wasted twenty minutes unjamming it.' Samantha fiddled with her hair. 'And Friday she screwed up one of Chris's tapes. Played it on "RECORD" by mistake and wiped off three of his letters. Chris wasn't best pleased. You know. He couldn't remember what he'd said in them.'

Gerald frowned. There was always that hint in her voice when she mentioned Chris. A subtle suggestion of intimacy. Chris was the junior partner. Thirtyish. Single. Good looking. Cropped hair. The girls adored him and he knew it.

'So you don't think she deserves a second chance?'

'Not really. I mean, it's not fair on the rest of us. The partners give *us* the tapes rather than her because they know they'll be done quicker.' To let him see how bored she was, Samantha reached down and adjusted her black tights, smoothing them up carefully over each ankle.

Gerald had suspected for some time that she and Chris might sleep together. If so they probably talked about *him*. The thought was unsettling. They would have nothing good to say about him. He imagined them laughing at him, mimicking his voice, criticizing his ties and despising his

Sierra. He felt he ought to think about changing it but his mother thought it would be a waste of money.

'There's nothing wrong with that car, Gerald,' she'd insisted. 'And the warranty's still valid. Change for the sake of change, that's you! Your poor father would turn in his grave. He took a great pride in his cars and always maintained them properly. He kept them for years . . .' And on and on!

Sighing, he returned to the current problem and nodded. 'Well, that's settled then. *Mizz* Stewart has to go. And we'll re-advertise next week. I'll leave you to see to that. Thank you, Samantha.'

'Thank *you*, Mr Foster.' With a small mocking smile she withdrew.

Gerald shook his head. Perhaps she *was* suffering from an eating disorder. He ought to feel sorry for her. He buzzed Mrs Stewart.

'Not Mrs! Mizz,' he reminded himself.

She came in, looking distinctly nervous. Almost pretty, she had auburn hair and a freckled face. Her skirt reached primly to her knees and her white blouse was obviously new. The long cardigan was obviously *not* – the second button down, on a loose thread, was about to fall off. She looked like someone from an old movie, he thought, vaguely irritated. Had she really been here six weeks?

Indicating the chair recently vacated by Samantha, he said, 'Well now, Mizz Stewart. How are things?'

'Fine.' She smiled brightly. 'I'm getting the hang of everything at last.'

'Ah . . . Not finding it too difficult then?'

When she didn't answer, he said, 'Good.'

They stared at each other. He found himself wondering where she lived. *How* she lived.

She said, 'I'm sorry I was late.'

'Late? Were you? Traffic, was it?'

'No. A woman was mugged in the car park, just a few yards from the ticket machine where I was standing. A young man – a young *thug* – snatched her handbag and then pushed her

85

over!' Her eyes had widened and he noticed that they were grey-blue. 'There was no need for him to push her. He'd already got the bag. She was a big woman and she fell heavily. Her knees were hurt and she couldn't stand. It wasn't life-threatening but I could see she was badly shaken. Shivering with shock. I thought someone ought to wait with her until the ambulance arrived.'

'Did they get him?'

'I don't know. I came on here. I like to make an early start – to get on with things.' She gave him another bright smile. 'I like to think it's all coming together.'

Did she live alone? he wondered and mentally reviewed her file. There was nothing in her file about a live-in lover. But there wouldn't be.

He took a deep breath. 'The fact is, Mrs – I mean *Mizz* Stewart, that Samantha feels . . .' Alarm showed in her eyes. 'Not that she's *blaming* you. No, no. You mustn't think that.'

'I – I know I'm not up to speed yet.'

Unable to bear her expression, Gerald stared unhappily into the waste basket at the broken paper clip. How on earth could he sweeten the pill? The telephone rang and he snatched it up eagerly. 'Yes, dear?' He put his hand over the receiver. 'Excuse me, please. It's my mother. She's probably lost her pills.' He returned to the telephone. 'They're probably in your other handbag. The brown one . . . You had it with you when came over to my place . . . Yes, dear . . . Of course. See you later.'

Replacing the receiver, he turned once more to the woman in front of him. You have to sack her, he thought. For heaven's sake, get on with it!

She was regarding him earnestly. 'Make the most of your mother, Mr Foster.' She swallowed. 'You never stop missing them when they die and nothing is ever quite the same.'

For a long moment neither spoke. Gerald was staring at her hands. Sensible hands. Browner than might be expected in the middle of December.

He said, 'Have you had a holiday this year?'

Surprised, she nodded. 'I spent a few weeks with my sister

Paula in Alicante. She lives there. Now my mother's dead Paula wants me to join her. Maybe I will. If things don't work out here I mean. In this country.'

She was wearing a pearl necklace, the white gleaming softly against her skin. If he sacked her she would go to Alicante. Gerald was vaguely aware of a sense of impending loss.

Suddenly she sat up straighter and took a deep breath. 'Look, Mr Foster, let's be honest. I think we both know what you're trying to say. You can't keep me on.' She tried to smile. 'I'd hoped to pick up speed but I'm finding the work rather daunting. I have to admit that it isn't what I expected when I applied. You advertised for a secretary but I am actually a member of a typing pool. Working from tapes with earphones is boring although I do my best.'

Surprised, Gerald tried to rally his thoughts in his defence. 'I think you must have been thinking of a *personal* secretary, Mrs – *Mizz* Stewart.'

She was undeterred by the interruption. 'I expected to be taking letters in shorthand – my dictation's pretty good. I thought I'd be answering the telephone, talking to people, making diary engagements . . . that's what I did when I was last at work and I loved it. Since then I realize things have changed. That's inevitable but I won't pretend I'm not disappointed . . .' She smiled suddenly. 'But I'll go quietly, Mr Foster.'

'Ah! You've heard the story!' She was making it easy for him.

She swallowed and the pearls moved against her throat and in that moment Gerald realized that he didn't want her to leave. He had allowed that wretched Samantha to influence him. Who was calling the tune here – Samantha or Gerald Foster?

'Mizz Stewart, I'm actually not thinking along those lines at all,' he told her. 'Speed isn't everything and I'm a great admirer of dedication. Samantha says you work very hard. I've been thinking for some time now that I need a personal assistant.' Was he really saying all this? Was he quite mad? Would Head Office agree? 'Would you be willing to consider that?' His mind was racing. Without her salary as a full-time typist, they could probably afford a part-time PA. He would put it to the powers that be. He could make out a decent case if he put his mind to it.

To his relief Mrs Stewart's face brightened immediately.

'I certainly would consider it – but wouldn't Samantha want the job?'

'Only if it were full-time and it wouldn't be.' He felt pleased with himself. 'It would be around fifteen hours a week. Three full days. Say Mondays, Wednesdays and Fridays.'

'I could be flexible about that. I have other work, working from home.' She blushed faintly. 'Telephoning people.'

He assumed an expression of mock horror. 'Not double glazing!'

'Conservatories!' She laughed. 'Actually I do quite well at it. I like talking to people – except the ones who slam down the phone on me.'

They both laughed.

Gerald said, 'You can phone me anytime and I promise to listen!'

'You might end up with a conservatory!'

'I live in an upstairs flat!'

'There might be difficulties!'

He would point out that Mizz Stewart would be taking some of the work on to her shoulders so that the load on the others would be lighter. And with someone in charge of the office in his absence, he would be able to travel and follow up certain sales opportunities. Might even take in a few conferences. His mind raced. He might even screw up enough courage to *speak* at some of them! He grinned suddenly.

She asked, 'What is it?'

'Just thinking. So what do you say? I'd have to clear it with the big boss but I don't foresee any problems. The thing is, Mizz Stewart, our staffing at present is a little unbalanced. I'd like to have a more mature person, like yourself. Youngsters can be rather scatterbrained. An older member of staff would help steady them.'

'You make me sound positively elderly.'

'Oh no! You're a long, *long* way from being elderly.'

Now she looked embarrassed. Gerald stood up and held out his hand.

'Good. That's settled then. Stay on as you are until the arrangements are finalized. Please send Samantha in as you go out.'

After the door had closed, Gerald rested his elbows on the desk and covered his face with his hands. He was smiling broadly and his heart was racing. He hadn't sacked Mizz Stewart and it felt wonderful. So how long would he have to wait before he could take her out for a drink – or ask her round to Sunday lunch at his mother's? The door opened.

'Ah! Samantha.' He smiled at her. 'A quick word . . .'

# Final Solution

The first thing George thought about on waking was his excuse for the day. What was he going to do with his time that would exclude him from accompanying his wife Marie on yet another shopping trip? As he lay beside her in the king-sized bed under his expensive duvet, he thought, not for the first time, that this was not what he had expected from his retirement. It was certainly not what he deserved after thirty-five years in the Army. He had worked his way up to the rank of colonel and had looked forward to a pleasant retirement pottering in the garden, playing golf with his friends and holidaying in cottages in parts of England that he and Marie had never previously visited. Unfortunately Marie refused point blank to put the cat into a cattery for a week, so this last dream had been shattered.

Now George considered his options for the day. He could say he had to go to the library to take his books back and choose three more – but that wouldn't take up enough of the day. He could pretend he had a dental appointment but that was risky. Marie might remember that the last one was less than two months ago.

Beside him Marie stirred, rubbed her pretty brown eyes and sat up. She was an attractive woman who had never run to fat and whose hair, expertly coloured on a regular basis, was still a soft shade of auburn. Men admired Marie and envied him and he knew he ought to be grateful. True, she had produced no children for him to boast about but she had been honest about that from the start. She was simply not the motherly type, she told him.

She now looked at him. 'You awake, dear? I thought we'd pop into Debenhams this morning and have a—'

'Not this morning, Marie.' He thought frantically. 'I don't feel up to it, to tell you the truth.'

'Not up to it? Oh George!' The brown eyes opened wide in alarm. 'Aren't you well?'

'I'm not ill, dear. I simply don't fancy wandering round Debenhams for hours and spending money just for the sake of it.' As the soon as the words were out he knew they were a mistake. The excuse was too flimsy and he had effectively accused her of wasting money.

Marie said, 'Spending for the sake of it? George Duke! That's a terrible thing to say! When did I *ever* spend money for the sake of spending?'

He swung his legs over the side of the bed. 'I'm going to take those last books back to the library. While I'm there I'll browse through the periodicals. Probably be back around twelve.'

'You haven't read them.'

'What?'

'You haven't read the library books. I know you haven't.'

'I couldn't get into them. You know what I'm like. If it doesn't grab me by page thirty I'm not—'

'We'll go to Debenhams *after* lunch. You'll feel better by then. We don't have to buy anything. Just stroll around the store and have a coffee and a Danish.'

'You go, dear. I told you, I don't feel up to it.' Now he really didn't feel up to it because there was a dull ache developing at the back of his head.

'You know I hate to go alone, George.' She pouted prettily, widening her eyes. At one time this expression had softened his heart but over long years he had become immune to it. 'I thought you promised me we'd spend more time together after you retired. You did, George. You know you did.'

'We *do*, Marie. We spend *all* our time together. Twenty-four hours a day!'

Before she could counter this comment he hurried into the

bathroom and shut the door with a little more force than was strictly necessary. Cleaning his teeth a few moments later, he searched his reflection for signs of the iron will which had served him well as a colonel. The men had nicknamed him the Iron Duke and feared his wrath. Marie was made of sterner stuff. Had he lost all his strength of purpose? 'Don't give in, George,' he advised. 'You've stuck your neck out this morning but you can ride out the storm!'

Downstairs in the kitchen Marie served up an elegant breakfast as recommended in most of the many magazines she read. He knew that she prided herself on giving him nourishing food attractively presented. With Marie it had become something of an art form. In the centre of the table there was a small glass vase containing three late roses and the serviettes had been rolled and pushed through silver-plated rings. Muesli with added banana, yoghurt, toast with home-made marmalade and tea with lemon.

She also monitored his eating habits, counting every calorie and pointing out how slim he was.

'You are the same size, George, as you were when I first met you!'

He yearned for the occasional meat and dumpling or a suet pudding but these were never served. George glanced at her across the table. She had tied back her hair with a frilly pink band which matched the pink satin housecoat which matched the pink satin pyjamas. After breakfast she would spend the best part of an hour in the bathroom with her favourite toys – shower gel, scented deodorant sprays, talcum powder, face creams, lipstick, perfume . . . The result would be beautiful. Only George knew that the soft feminine exterior hid a steely centre.

An hour later, sitting in the library, he stared at page fifteen of the *National Geographic*, and thought back over the years. The best years. The years when he mattered. Life in the military had been his whole world. The challenges, the excitement, the camaraderie of the men and, of course, the respect due to him for his experience and judgement. He could have gone on for another five years but Marie had insisted he owed some time to her. Her life, she pointed out with some justification, had been spent in the company of other soldiers' wives and her home life constantly disrupted by George's various overseas postings. Only the cat had given her undivided loyalty and affection, she told him plaintively, on more than one occasion. Which was why the latest cat, a fluffy tabby by the name of Sandy, was pampered and fussed over. Chicken liver, turkey fillets, braised beef and creamy rice were always on the menu and the poor animal was sadly overweight. Overweight and underfoot. That was one of George's jokes, for Sandy had an uncanny knack of being in the way and had tripped both George and Marie at different times.

He turned to page sixteen, stared at a photograph of a trumpeting elephant, then tossed it aside and picked up the second magazine. He had chosen them at random and found that his second choice was *The Good Book Guide*. As he flicked through it an idea came to him. It stole quietly into his mind until he suddenly recognized it as a brainwave. He would tell Marie he was writing a book! A novel. A very long novel needing hours of research and even more hours shut away on his own hunched over his computer! To actually produce a novel was out of the question, of course, and he understood that, but it would take years to prove that he was not a writer – long years in which he could steal some time for himself away from the cloying clutches of his devoted wife.

Ten minutes later he was in Boots buying a ream of typing paper and a book on 'How To Write A Bestseller'. Then on into Curry's to buy suitable up-to-the-minute software. He must be seen to be doing it professionally in a way that would brook no arguments. Who knows, he thought with rising excitement. He might even *write* the damned thing.

Half an hour later he was home again, converting the spare room into a study. Marie stood in the doorway, almost wringing her hands with dismay.

'What on earth's got into you, George? You can't write for toffee! You never even write a letter let alone a novel.'

'I've written thousands of reports and dossiers! I'm not exactly illiterate, dear.'

'Reports and dossiers aren't *fiction*, darling. They're factual. As in facts.' She wrinkled her brow. 'You need romance in fiction and . . . and passion and dialogue and description. Your reports were simply facts arranged in a logical, cohesive way. A novel . . . Well, it has to play on people emotions. Quite a different animal.'

He gave her a quick smile. 'We won't know if I can write until I try, Marie. We might both be surprised. It will have to be a detective novel because that's what I read . . . A murder story!' He was almost beginning to believe it.

'And what will I do while you're closeted up here with your novel? Sit alone downstairs? Hardly togetherness, George.' She gave a long sigh. 'I came up to tell you that lunch is ready.'

Over a lovingly made spinach quiche tastefully arranged on a plate with a side salad consisting of thinly sliced apple, cucumber and grated carrot, George told his wife that he was *not* going to Debenhams with her. He was prepared for further argument but to his surprise she gave a small shrug.

'Then I'll go on my own, dear.' Her brave smile would have convinced most men but George was her husband and knew how manipulative she could be when she chose. There was a reason for her acquiescence but he could not imagine what it might be, so he hid his relief and put it out of his mind. The shopping centre was only ten minutes' walk away and the weather was fine. His wife couldn't possibly come to any harm. 'Don't miss out on the coffee and Danish,' he told her.

She rolled eyes. 'What? Sit alone in a restaurant, George? That's very risky, isn't it? I might be accosted by a strange man!'

For a fleeting moment George imagined the scene and was shocked to realize how appealing the idea was to him. Suppose she met someone, had an affair and left him . . . Very uncharitable of you, George! He found a cushion for the chair to make him the right height for the keyboard and opened the typing paper. 'It's much cheaper by the ream,' he told her.

She nodded. 'I'll do my best without you, George, but you know how I am. I always need your advice. Still, if you won't come with me . . .'

Promptly at two thirty she came upstairs to say goodbye.

'You're sure you won't change your mind, darling?'

He waved an impatient hand. 'Must make a start while the idea's fresh in my mind.' Listening to her retreating footsteps, he thrust a fist into the air and grinned. Then impulsively he crossed to the window to watch her as she set off along the street. He thought she would turn to look back at the house but she didn't. On the windowsill Sandy purred, blinking green eyes at him and George realized he was glad of his company. He would read out a sentence here and there for the cat's approval! Grinning, he settled back on his cushion and searched his mind for a title. A working title, he corrected himself. He would no doubt come up with a better one later on, once he knew what the story was about . . .

When he next glanced at the clock he was amazed to see that it was after four and Marie hadn't returned. Frowning, he looked along the road and was relieved to see her turn the corner, carrying a large plastic carrier bag. A familiar bag. A Debenhams' bag.

'Oh no! What has she bought now?'

His first instinct was to rush downstairs and ask but instead, recalling his new guise as a writer, he sat down again. He waited for her, hands poised creatively over the keyboard until it dawned on him that she wasn't coming up to show him her latest purchase. Reluctantly he abandoned his pose and went downstairs.

Marie was in the kitchen, making coffee. She turned to him with an excited smile. 'Look in the bag, George!'

He opened it and pulled out a fur coat. Or rather a coat which he hoped was *imitation* fur. His stomach knotted anxiously. Holding it up, he saw the sleek sheen on the dark-chestnut pelt.

'I hope you don't mind, George,' she began. 'I fell in love with it and I felt sure that if you'd been with me you'd have said buy it. I know it was expensive but it can be my birthday and Christmas presents for the next five years!'

At these words all George's hopes vanished, leaving him shaken and speechless. It was a mink coat!

Marie rushed on. 'I'll model it for you when I've made the coffee. You always promised me a fur coat.'

He was trying to work out what the coat cost and suddenly he needed to sit down. His heart began to thump in his chest and he felt slightly dizzy. Five years of birthday presents and . . . Surely not. He usually spent a few hundred for each. Did that mean that the coat cost somewhere around four thousand pounds? That was monstrous!

'How much?' he stammered. *'How much?'*

But Marie was pulling on the coat, spinning round, clutching it to her and swinging it open with dramatic flourishes. 'Look!' she cried. 'Marilyn Monroe!' She pursed her lips and sang, *'Boo boopy doo!'* in a breathy imitation of the star. Leaning towards him, she sang, *'Happy birthday, Mr President . . .'* and laughed at George's expression.

Desperation seized him. How could he undo this? If she had written a cheque he could cancel it before the banks closed. Tomorrow they would take the coat back.

He took a deep breath. 'How did you pay for it?'

'Credit card, of course. Amex.'

His heart raced again and he felt a sweat break out on his forehead. 'You know damn well we can't afford a coat like this.'

'I did wonder, George, but I was rather carried away. I'm sorry, dear. I feel so silly. I suppose I didn't listen. You're usually there to advise me. Oh, I do wish you had come along with me.' She blinked and her trembling mouth was almost convincing.

'What on earth possessed you?' But even as he framed the

question he knew the answer. Marie had done it on purpose. This was her revenge.

Her face crumpled. Tearfully she pulled off the coat and tossed it over the back of the chair. 'It's your own fault, George. You know how confused I get when I'm on my own. I always make mistakes.' She reached into her pocket for an embroidered handkerchief and dabbed delicately at her eyes. 'Say you forgive me, George. I was so nervous . . . I was muddled. You'll have to take it back for me. I can't face them. Or we could go together and you could deal with it.' She looked at him with brimming eyes. 'I think they take advantage when they see a woman alone . . .'

That night George lay in bed, breathing heavily and trying to control his rapid pulse. Marie would be the death of him, he fumed. She had always been sly but this time she had gone too far. Perhaps he should divorce her . . . The idea grew as he considered his options but at last he dismissed it as unworkable. She would put on a wonderful act – the wronged wife – and he would lose everything he had worked for. Marie would be awarded half of everything and they would each live out their days in a cheap flat.

He turned over, hot and restless, his mind in turmoil. Maybe he would disappear. He could take out the money – all of it – and flee to the Bahamas under another name. But then he might lose his pension . . . After a while this idea also lost its appeal. So should he murder her . . .?

He sat up in bed, excited by the idea, and looked at the clock. Quarter to two. He glanced at Marie, her face innocent in repose. *Could* he murder her? At that moment, with so much anger in his heart, he knew he could strangle her with his bare hands if he thought he could get away it. Would anyone believe him capable of murder? Possibly not. Everyone knew what a devoted couple they were. Always together.

He leaped out of bed. He would make himself a coffee and work on the idea. The problem was how to avoid being caught.

At the top of the stairs he nearly fell over Sandy and cursed mildly as he picked the animal up and carried him downstairs.

'I'm going to murder your mistress,' he whispered into the furry ear. 'But you'll be OK. I'll look after you. Poor old fatty!'

He sat at the kitchen table, hardly believing that he was really going to do it. Probably he wouldn't but if he did, how would he tackle it? He thought about all the films they'd watched together, side by side on the sofa.

'How the hell do I do it?'

Tampering with the wife's car brakes was a popular solution but unfortunately Marie didn't drive. George sipped his coffee while Sandy, perched on a nearby stool, blinked knowingly. He could pretend they had been burgled while he was out and suggest that Marie must have disturbed the intruder. That often worked. Or he could take her to Beachy Head and push her off and claim she stumbled or was blown over in a gale. Perhaps he could take her for 'a nice long drive in the country', strangle her and hide the body where it would never be found. He would claim that she had wandered off with her camera and never come back and report her missing. If they did find her body later the police would assume she had been attacked. He frowned. Marie didn't own a camera and had never taken a photograph in her life. Would anyone remember that?

'Hmm . . .' He finished his coffee and yawned. 'Difficult!' Sandy began to purr. George decided that he would put the cat on a diet the moment Marie had gone. 'Boiled fish and a bowl of water. You'll thank me for it,' he told the cat. He got up, washed up his cup and put it away, folded the teacloth and returned it to the peg inside the cupboard door. He was on his way to the stairs when Sandy leaped out in front of him and tripped him up. Slowly George sat up and discovered that no bones were broken. He stared at the cat. Images were forming in his brain. Sandy sitting on the top stair. Marie stumbling over him . . .

'Perfect!' he whispered. 'What a clever cat you are!'

\*     \*     \*

98

A week later the ambulance pulled up outside the house followed by a police car, siren wailing mournfully. George, horror-stricken, watched as his wife was wheeled out on a stretcher and gently loaded into the ambulance. George struggled with his tears as he spoke to the young policewoman. 'It was the cat!' he told her, his voice hoarse with shock and grief. 'Sandy . . . Marie doted on that cat . . .'

'And you say the cat tripped her?' She wrote busily in her notebook.

George nodded. 'It was an accident waiting to happen. He was always sleeping at the top of the stairs. We used to warn each other about him. "George! Mind the cat!" she used to say. Poor Marie. I can't quite believe this has happened.'

The policewoman touched his sleeve in a small gesture of sympathy. 'I know it's a tragedy, Mr Duke, but you mustn't blame the cat. It wouldn't be fair.'

'Oh no! Because my wife adored Sandy. It's so ironic . . .'

That evening the police checked with the neighbours 'just in case'.

Mr Brooks said they were a devoted couple. Never a cross word.

Mrs da Silva, on the other side, said, 'Colonel Duke? That's what he liked to be called. Army men love their titles, don't they? As for Marie, he adored her. Never let her out of his sight! Not even to go shopping and it's only round the corner!'

On the other side of the road old Mr Partridge laughed at the very idea of anything being wrong between the two. 'I used to see them, day after day. Arm in arm. "Off to the shops?" I'd say and she would smile and give me a little wave. Wonderful woman, Mrs Duke. Classy but delicate. Know what I mean?'

The police were satisfied. The case was closed.

Three years passed and somehow George found himself sitting at a table in W.H. Smith's in Bromley with a pile of novels to his right and a queue of eager fans to his left. The press were there and so was his agent, a pretty woman with soft blonde hair, and another younger woman whose job it was to refill the champagne glasses. It was the seventh and last signing. George had put his foot down. No more signings. No more interviews. And definitely no more chat shows. He was longing to get home and press ahead with his next novel.

He glanced up, smiling. His very first book had been a runaway success and he was almost sorry Marie couldn't be there to share the excitement with him. He glanced up at the stack of books with a rush of pleasure. The jacket was striking in red and gold with his name and the title in large letters. *Final Solution* by George Duke.

# Flying Leap

Taking a deep breath, Kate pushed open the door and stepped into a gloomy passage lit at the street end by an overhead lightbowl which was dirty and full of flies.

'I will succeed,' she muttered. 'I *will* succeed.'

Ahead of her, to the left, she saw a small office and made her way towards it. As she expected, there was an elderly inscription on the glass panel of the door.

STAGE-DOOR KEEPER.

Sitting below a tarnished lightbulb, an elderly man in shirtsleeves was huddled over a copy of the *Daily Mail*. Kate straightened her back, forced a smile and tapped on the door. With a show of reluctance, the stage-door keeper slowly lowered the paper. He was small and thin with sparse brown hair and he looked about seventy. He appeared to blend in with his surroundings like a chameleon – his flesh and clothes the same dull ochre of the painted walls. For a moment he regarded her disapprovingly over the top of his spectacles and Kate's carefully prepared introduction fled from her mind.

At last he said irritably, 'Well, what d'you want?'

'I'm . . . I've come to . . .' Her throat was dry but her hands, clutching the book, were damp.

'If you're the understudy you're to—'

'No, I'm not the understudy.' Abruptly, her lines returned to her. 'I'm here to see . . . that is, to visit Marie Mackee.'

'Marie only sees people by appointment. She likes to get away early.' He raised the newspaper.

'But I wrote to her. She's expecting me. Look.' Holding

up her copy of Marie Mackee's recently published autobiography, Kate struggled to keep her voice steady, to keep the strain from showing. Tonight was a test of her new-found confidence, the direct result of the first four sessions of her assertiveness training. Or AT as Linda, the tutor, referred to it. There were two more sessions to come. Four two-hour classes in a shabby village hall with seven dejected women who for various reasons felt the need to become stronger and more in control of their lives.

They had been a true cross section of humanity and Kate believed she had learned a lot from them. Dinah, a recovering alcoholic; Sue, whose children had been taken into care when she went to prison for shoplifting; a woman in her fifties who had been widowed and couldn't find another job after years away from the workplace . . . Even Linda, who was tutoring the course, had suffered a hostile, very abusive, neighbour who had totally broken her spirit over a matter of years. Kate was determined to recover from her husband's betrayal and a difficult divorce. Alone for the first time in her life, she needed to learn to stand on her own two feet.

Linda had asked them all to set themselves a challenge. This visit backstage was Kate's. She had travelled up by train, found her way to the theatre and was about to meet Marie Mackee, the actress, and ask her to sign her autobiography. So far, so good, thought Kate.

'Don't expect too much,' Linda had warned them. 'It takes time but you'll make it. Trust me.'

The meeting with Marie Mackee was daunting but Kate was determined not to fail.

This grubby little man is not going to defeat me, she told herself firmly. She said, 'I've just been to see the play. It was brilliant!' She gave him a positive smile but in reality her trite praise was false. It was a new play about loss, according to the programme, and Kate had been thoroughly depressed by it. The conversation in the row in front of her had convinced her that she hadn't understood the subtleties of the play and she had escaped to the bar. There she had apparently become invisible and, giving up, had joined the queue for an over-priced ice cream.

'If you say so.' His tone was weary as he crumpled the newspaper and pushed it into the narrow space between his chair and the wall. He reached for the telephone. 'Who shall I say?'

'Mrs . . . No!' She stopped herself just in time. 'Ms Linley. Ms Kate Linley.'

Not Mrs Carr, she reminded herself. Never again. She had had to decide what to call herself once the marital ties were severed and Miss Linley, her maiden name, had not pleased her. Ms Linley had been the final choice. The Ms helped her to feel modern and independent.

The stage-door keeper rolled his eyes, punched in a couple of numbers and said, 'I've got a Ms Linley here . . .'

Kate heard the buzz of another voice.

He frowned. 'Well, she says you're expecting her. Claims to have written to you . . .'

Kate said, 'I *have* written!' It came out more sharply than she had intended because his comment sounded suspiciously like a put-down and they had been encouraged to look out for them. But had she overreacted? Was it a put-down or had she imagined it? Kate felt herself to be in a constant state of confusion.

He tutted and replaced the receiver. 'You can go along.' He waved a bony hand towards the far end of the dimly lit passage.

'Where exactly . . .?'

'If you can't find it, ask.'

As she left he was hauling up the crumpled *Daily Mail*, making heavy work of it. Yes, it had been a put-down, thought Kate. She was annoyed but pleased to have recognized it for what it was. That was important if she was going to stay in control. She had already taken one small step in the right direction by interrupting the Sunday lunch routine with her father. 'Learning to say "No" and mean it.' Repetition. Firm but pleasant repetition. That was the key, if Kate had understood Linda correctly. That had been lesson one.

As expected he had protested.

'But you always come to me for Sunday lunch, Kate. Why not this Sunday?'

'Because I've been invited to lunch by a colleague at work. Sandra. I've mentioned her before. She and her husband are having a lunch party for her birthday. I'm sorry to disappoint you but I'm looking forward to it.'

'Well, I certainly *am* disappointed.'

'I know that, Dad, and I'm sorry to disappoint you, but I'll see you the following Sunday.'

'I'm surprised at you, Kate.'

'I'm sorry you feel that way, Dad, but I am so looking forward to it and I'll be over as usual the following week.'

Reminding herself of that small success, Kate walked along the passage, her footsteps echoing. The theatre was one of London's oldest and neediest and it was obvious. Only two toilets in the ladies' room and peeling paint in evidence on many of the walls. The seats were too narrow and the sight lines far from perfect. Narrow passages and a labyrinthine layout outside the auditorium would send shudders through any self-respecting fire officer. How much would it cost to refurbish the entire building? she wondered.

The play, too, had been an unhappy choice. Three people locked in an interminable series of misunderstandings and recriminations. She had applauded as loudly as the rest of the audience but wondered secretly if her own disappointment had been shared by anyone else. If not, then what did that say about her?

She passed an elderly woman hurrying in the opposite direction and wondered if she was a member of the cast making an early escape. Since the woman averted her eyes, Kate did the same. Or perhaps the woman was eager to meet her fans outside the stage door, where a small, loyal crowd was already waiting in the misty rain.

Kate tried to remember the sophisticated phrases she had prepared for her brief meeting with Marie Mackee. No need to sound like a woman crushed by divorce although that was what she was. Or had been before the sessions. Now, according to Linda, she was one of a vast group of strong women making new lives for themselves. Setting themselves targets. Stepping back into the mainstream of life with heads held high. Within the confines of the village hall, Kate had been seduced by the smooth reassurances and the rallying calls and the determined attempts to raise self-esteem. Linda had sounded very convincing. Here, alone, it was very different. Chilly and uncompromisingly alien. Kate had agonized over what to wear for an evening at the theatre and had settled for the ubiquitous black trousers and top under a light raincoat but felt very much a country cousin as soon as she set foot in the theatre. The woman next to her sported a little red dress with ribbon straps and a stole that looked very expensive. Her male escort had been equally well dressed.

Now, turning a corner in the passage, Kate whispered the first of her lines.

'I'm Kate Linley. I wrote to you. I'd very much like your autograph.'

Damn! She'd forgotten the line about how brilliant the play was. Not that she'd been able to concentrate properly, overshadowed as she was by the looming challenge which awaited her when the final curtain came down. However, the reviewers had said it was brilliant and they should know.

Two young women passed her, heading out, and one of them flashed Kate a smile. Aha! Things are looking up. She felt vaguely reassured. She passed several doors but none had the star's name on it and at last she was forced to ask someone. She chose a man who might and might not be the male lead and who looked as though he expected to be recognized but Kate had forgotten to bring her long-distance glasses, so had not seen any of the players very clearly. She followed his directions and quickly found herself outside the right door. Now all she had to do was knock.

She took a few deep breaths and forced a cheerful smile. Her plan was to breeze in as if visiting stars in their dressing rooms was something she did all the time. Not that she and

Jeff had ever been theatregoers and even if they *had* she certainly could no longer afford it. The flat in Faversham ate into her salary, leaving little to spare for luxuries. She thought of the house on which she had lavished so much attention and which was now being shared by Jeff and his new wife.

At once Linda's rather strident voice came back to her with the familiar warning. 'Don't look back, ladies. Look forward. You are going to take a flying leap into the unknown – a new future. A new life! It won't come to you. You have to go out and make it happen. You all have deep reserves on which you can draw.'

At the time, Kate had felt an immediate rush of courage. Today it had deserted her but she straightened her back and knocked on the door.

A voice called, 'Hang on just a minute!'

Probably still changing out of her costume, thought Kate. Or halfway through removing her stage make-up. The minutes ticked away but at last a voice called, 'Come on in!' and Kate opened the door and stepped into the brightly lit room. Marie was reflected in a huge wall mirror circled with small light bulbs. Removed from the stage, she seemed smaller and, without her make-up, distinctly less glamorous. Round the edge a dozen or more cards, presumably to wish her luck, were tucked behind the glass. On the dressing table, pots, jars and tubes of colour mingled with brushes and tubs of cotton-wool buds.

Marie Mackee was staring at Kate, waiting. She looked bored, thought Kate, beginning to panic.

'Hi! I'm Kate Linley.' Her voice sounded cracked. 'I wrote to you. I'd very . . . Oh no! I mean, the play was great. Wonderful.'

'Thank you.' Her expression hadn't changed.

Kate's mind became a total blank. Dazzled in more ways than one, she felt like the rabbit trapped in the glare of a car's headlights. Desperately she searched for her next line. Oh yes! She smiled the positive smile. 'I'd really appreciate it if you would sign my book. I mean your book. You've always been one of my favourites. In fact—'

She stopped abruptly. She nearly added that Jeff had always adored her. Had positively drooled over her. But no. Leave Jeff in the past where he belongs, she told herself sternly. Flying leap *forward*. 'I've read your autobiography,' she substituted. 'I loved it.'

'How very kind.' Marie held out her hand for the copy of her book, took the proffered biro and then frowned at the copy. 'A disappointing jacket,' she said. 'My name doesn't stand out enough against the background. Don't you agree?' She held it up and Kate leaned forward to consider this unexpected criticism, flattered to be asked for an opinion.

'I suppose so but I hadn't noticed.'

'People rarely do!' Marie sighed.

Marie turned over a few pages and bent her head but almost at once there was a commotion in the passage outside and Kate turned towards the door. What a rowdy lot! Perhaps they had drunk too much wine in the interval. Now, wondering what Marie had written, she turned back but at that moment the door burst open and half a dozen excited people rushed into the dressing room, borne in on a cloud of expensive perfume and aftershave. Bouquets crackled in their cellophane wraps amid shrieks of delight and Kate was surrounded by exuberant friends, waving arms and handing out hugs and kisses. Taken by surprise, she was elbowed aside and stepped back. Thus sidelined, she found herself watching the happy melee.

'Darling! You were fabulous!' cried one of the women, thrusting flowers into Marie's arms.

A middle-aged man with thinning ginger hair cried, 'Absolutely stunning, old love!'

Marie laughed. 'Not so much of the "old", Colin, if you don't mind!'

'You're going to run and run with this play. You do realize that?'

Marie's bored expression underwent a change as the compliments rained down and the flowers piled up on top of the pots and jars of make-up. Her face was radiant, her eyes sparkling in the warmth of the praise. Kate hung back, unsure what to do next. She had lost sight of the autobiography.

'Act Two is the killer!' Marie was insisting. 'Two costume changes! It's all systems go. I should be losing weight at this rate!'

A huge burst of laughter and delighted giggles followed this sally and drowned out Kate, who said, 'If I may just take my book . . .'

Nobody heard her. She stood alone behind the happy group and all but drowned in a moment of self-pity. Linda would have known what to do but Kate was torn. She wanted to get out of there as soon as possible but she wanted the autobiography back. That was her trophy. That was what she was going to produce at the next AT session. Proof that she had taken step two on the long road back to self-confidence and assertiveness.

She raised her voice. 'Excuse me but may I have the book back, please?'

One of the men, young with a mop of floppy blond hair, was kissing Marie's hand amid cries of pretended outrage and further giggles. He turned towards Kate in surprise with a trace of dismay.

He said, 'Marie darling, there's someone here . . .'

He didn't actually mention the words 'party pooper' but Kate could have sworn she heard them. The situation was slipping away. Repetition. Repetition.

She said, 'I'm off now but I'd like my book back, please.'

Blank faces turned towards her and then back to Marie.

The man translated, 'She says she wants her book?'

Instinctively the little group parted so that she could see Marie, who glanced around her, looking faintly irritated. 'Book? Which book?'

Kate thought she might well faint if she had to continue this ridulous farce. The desire to turn and run was almost overwhelming, but instead she clung fiercely to the last dregs of her dignity. She pushed forward, lifted the flowers and found the autobiography.

'This one! Thank you.' She forced a none-too-confident smile. 'I'll – well, I'll leave you to it.'

It wasn't exactly a strong line on which to exit but Kate walked out of the room and closed the door behind her – and listened. For a moment there was silence then the excited babble broke out again.

As Kate fled along the passage, past the stage-door keeper, still hunched over his newspaper, she fought back tears. Had she failed or had she won? She had done what she had set out to do, but had she done it with the right amount of panache? Had she allowed herself to become the victim or had she escaped unscathed? Would Linda have been proud of her performance?

'Perhaps,' she muttered, stepping out into the drizzle.

Shouldering her way along the crowded pavement towards the Underground station, she remembered how she had stood her ground and retrieved her book. Surely that counted for something. A few brownie points? As she went into the station someone stumbled clumsily against her and she managed not to apologize. Her spirits rose. Another small success, surely. Jeff had often laughed at her for apologizing unnecessarily, insisting that she was turning it into an art form.

On the platform she had just missed a train and shared the deserted platform with a youth in a Day-Glo pufferjacket, black T-shirt, combat trousers and dirty trainers. Ignoring him, she found the right coins and bought a bar of chocolate with fruit and nut from the machine and sat down to eat it. Comfort food or a prize for good behaviour? Well, she deserved it. Determined to be positive, she ticked off her achievements. She had bought the ticket for the play, found her way up to London, seen the play – a big disappointment – and made her trip to the star's dressing room. All without Jeff's help. She had survived the abortive meeting and would certainly put a good gloss on the whole affair when she recounted her adventure to the group.

'Got any change?'

Startled, she discovered that the youth had joined her. He

was standing in front of her, his hand thrust out. If she hadn't been feeling so wretched she would have been frightened.

'No.'

He glared. 'You haven't even looked.'

'I don't intend to.' She was suddenly angry. Mug me, she thought bitterly. Stab me. Shoot me. Shove me under the next train. Who cares?

They glared at each other for a long moment until Kate realized how young and pathetic he was. His too-big combat trousers wrinkled round his ankles, his laces trailed and his unkempt hair straggled from a greasy baseball cap.

'Here,' she said, and slapped the unopened chocolate bar into his upturned palm.

Day-Glo Puffer glared. 'I don't like chocolate.'

'Tough titty!' It was her niece's favourite comment but Kate had never expected to hear herself use it.

He gave her a disgusted look but, after a brief hesitation, apparently decided she was a lost cause and swaggered away. The almost empty train arrived, Kate found a corner seat and leaned back to examine her feelings the way Linda had suggested. Was she feeling marginally better now that she had met the challenge? Possibly . . . Probably . . . Yes. She *was* a little less anxious. Was she stronger and more in control? A cautious 'Yes'. She had faced down a sad little boy, if that counted.

'Yes! Damn it, I am stronger!' she muttered. Think positively, Linda had said. Every positive step, no matter how insignificant, is important and to be valued. Kate drew in a deep breath and let it out slowly. Roll on Thursday, when it would be her turn to stand up in front of the group. She noticed Day-Glo Puffer sitting at the far end of her carriage with his feet up on the seat opposite. She ignored him, rehearsing what she would say.

'*Last Saturday evening I popped up to London to the theatre . . .*'

She could imagine the astonished looks.

'*It was brilliant. After the show I went round to Marie*

*Mackee's dressing room to ask her to sign her autobiography.
She was very sweet. We chatted for a bit . . .'*

It was going to sound very impressive. Kate's face relaxed
into a smile as she imagined the scene. She would hold up
the book and laugh as though the entire trip had been what
Linda called 'a doddle'. She opened the autobiography and
looked for Marie Mackee's autograph. There was nothing
written there. She turned the pages. Nothing at all. Tears of
defeat and weariness filled her eyes and rolled unheeded down
her face. Fumbling for a handkerchief, she failed to find one.
The train pulled in to a station and Day-Glo Puffer got up to
leave. He caught sight of her, swaggered towards her and then
his eyes widened at the sight of her tears. Pulling the unopened
chocolate from his pocket, he tossed it into her lap without a
word and stepped down on to the platform.

After a shocked silence Kate's mouth twitched. She began
to laugh and couldn't stop. She went on laughing and crying
until she was exhausted.

Hardly a flying leap, she acknowledged, more a small jump,
but she had survived the adventure. A deep sigh escaped her
and she felt the first small stirrings of real hope.

# The Stalker

At first I rather liked him. Hal, I mean. I mentioned him casually to Mummy and she was immediately full of questions. Are you sure he's not married? Does he talk about his parents? Where does he live? And so on. I couldn't ask him outright because it would have been rude and a bit pushy but I gradually learned more about him from the others. He was twenty-three, had a girlfriend, a degree in accountancy and rich parents who spoiled him. So not at all suitable for a relationship – at least that's what Mummy said and she was right.

But I couldn't help liking him. He worked at the next desk to me, so we were often chatting and he was so easy to talk to. Very natural and always seemed to take an interest. Not only in me but all the others. One day he insisted that he knew me from somewhere.

'I do, Shirley. I know I do but I can't for the life of me think how or where. I recognize you from somewhere.'

I felt myself blushing. It was surely one of those chat-up lines you hear about. 'I don't think so,' I told him. 'I never go into pubs and clubs and I expect you do.'

He grinned. 'What never? Perhaps you should. Perhaps I'll take you out for a drink one evening after work.'

I didn't dare tell Mummy. I may be twenty but she's very protective since Daddy deserted her. Us, I should say. I sometimes pretend he only left her but of course it was both of us. Not that I can remember much about it except that she cried so much she made herself ill and she has never trusted another man since – and who can blame her?

The other girls started to tease me about Hal, saying he had his eye on me and I should watch out. I just laughed, but he did seem to take a lot of notice of me and I was secretly rather flattered. He wasn't especially handsome or clever but he had a cheerful, round face and nice blue eyes behind his spectacles. His hair was a bit odd – curly brown and cut in an old-fashioned way but his nails were neat and the back of his neck was rather attractive. To me, anyway. I don't know about the others. His name's Harry but everyone calls him Hal. And not after Prince Harry because the prince is younger than him. I wrote about him in my diary which Mummy doesn't know about. He said I ought to ask Mr Curtis for a rise because I'd been there longer than Etta who came a few months ago and earns more than I do.

'And you even had to show her the ropes, Shirl!'

'Yes, but she was new to everything. I didn't mind. I like her.'

'Maybe you do but that doesn't mean she should be paid more with less experience than you. Ask Mr Curtis for a rise! Go *on*, Shirl,' he urged.

He always calls me Shirl and I don't mind. I hate the name Shirley but Mummy has always loved the film *Shirley Valentine* so I'm rather stuck with it.

But I couldn't. Henrietta Steadman is younger than me, too, but she's very pretty and flirty and I suppose she charmed Mr Curtis into paying her more. Mummy says most men are vulnerable to a pretty face or a pair of nice legs. I'm not ugly and Mummy says I'm not plain and I know my legs are quite nice, not fat or anything, but men are so strange. You can never have a sensible conversation with them. I sometimes wish I'd had a brother because then I might understand them better.

When Hal kept on insisting that he knew me from somewhere I began to be worried. Was this becoming an obsession with him or was he trying to scare me or maybe make fun of me? I still liked him but I wished he would stop going on about it.

The next time he said he was sure he knew me from

somewhere I said sharply, 'It must have been in another life then!' but he only laughed.

'No. It was in this one,' he insisted. 'It's driving me mad but it'll come to me. Maybe you shop in Waitrose. I go in there sometimes.'

I had a vision of him shopping for himself – one chop, a small bag of oven-ready chips and a tin of baked beans, all rattling around in a big trolley and I immediately felt sorry for him. I asked Emma about the girlfriend he was supposed to have and how she knew about it. She said she saw him walking along Bank Street with a young woman and a child in a pushchair and they were both laughing and looked really happy together.

'So do they live together?' I asked.

'They all do nowadays.'

'But . . . is it his baby? I mean, are they married or something? He never talks about her.'

'Don't ask me. Ask *him*!'

But I didn't.

The girls began to tease me about Hal. They seemed to find it funny but I wished he would stop. He didn't stop, however, and at last I began to wonder if we *had* met before, because if so that would make everything all right.

One day I said, 'Maybe it was in the video shop,' because Mummy and I watch a lot of videos, mostly costume dramas because we hate sex and violence movies. At least Mummy does. I've never seen any because when we go to the cinema we choose our film very carefully. *On Golden Pond* was lovely and so was *Rainman*. But Hal shook his head. He said he didn't have time for videos because he watched a lot of sport. He also had a motorbike and he tinkered with it at the weekends.

'When do you get to ride it?' I asked.

'Not often. It's always in pieces. Bits all over the kitchen!' He laughed.

Seeing my chance, I asked, 'Doesn't your wife get fed up with it?' but he said he didn't have a wife only a mother and she *did* get fed up. So I didn't know what to think about the girlfriend.

One day he said, 'I saw you yesterday in the High Street and tooted the horn but you didn't look round.'

Well, of course I didn't. I don't expect men to toot at me in the street. Not that I'd actually *mind* if they did but it can be embarrassing. I was waiting at the crossing one day and a lorry stopped to let us across and the driver gave me the thumbs-up sign. He had his sleeves rolled up and his arms were covered with blond hairs and his face was freckled. I turned round to see who he was looking at and he said, 'It's *you*, gorgeous!' and blew me a kiss. I could feel my face burn but luckily the lights had changed and I was able to hurry across the road but the woman next to me laughed and said it looked as though my luck was in and I had to tell her I didn't know him from Adam.

Finally Hal asked me out for a drink after work and I knew it wasn't a good idea but I heard myself say 'Yes' and we went to The Black Horse at the top of the hill but I didn't know what to ask for, so he brought me some beer – it was awful, but I couldn't say anything in case I hurt his feelings.

He said, 'Cheers!' and drank at least half of it in one go. He had another one but I made mine last, and when I'd finished it I got up to go to the ladies' room and felt quite tottery. Probably because I'm not used to it. It was very noisy in the pub and it smelled of stale cigarettes but everybody seemed to be having a good time except me. I tried to relax but I was nervous. What on earth would we talk about? I could tell Hal was trying to jolly me along and eventually he told me a joke. Something about a nun. I didn't get the point of the story but laughed anyway. I was like a fish out of water in there and must have been a big disappointment to poor Hal. Afterwards I tried to remember the joke but some of the details had gone from my mind, so I couldn't put it in my diary.

He wanted to run me home in his car but he might have driven me anywhere, and anyway I didn't want Mummy to know just yet, so I said 'No'. When we got outside he gave me a quick kiss on the side of my face as though it was the most natural thing in the world. I was delighted, because that meant it had been a sort of date, but then he ruined everything by saying, 'I have this vague image of you in a swimsuit. Have you ever been in a magazine?'

I stared at him.

'I meant have you ever modelled swimwear?'

My throat went dry. All my fears flooded back. The Black Horse had been a mistake. Going for a drink had just encouraged him. Perhaps he would become really persistent and expect more from me and refuse to take 'No' for an answer. He might end up stalking me. I felt a creeping panic and began to stammer. I had to get away from him. I thanked him for the drink and said 'Goodbye' and hurried away with my heart thumping. I rushed along the street without looking back in case he was following me and even when I was inside Marks & Spencer I didn't feel able to look round for him. I bought a pair of tights and when I went back into the street there was no sign of him.

Modelling swimwear? Is this what they mean by men fantasizing? I want it to be all right but is that a normal thing to say? In a swimsuit! Rather like undressing someone with your eyes and I've heard about that. It's on the television all the time. Next day in the office he was his old cheerful self and I pretended I'd forgotten all about The Black Horse.

Then on the Saturday I was looking out of the bedroom window and nearly had a heart attack. There was Hal. His car was parked outside Mr Smith's and he, Hal I mean, was standing leaning back against it with his arms crossed. When he saw me he waved and I simply froze. He beckoned me but I backed away from the window. I almost pulled the curtains to, but that would have been rude. I went into the bathroom and locked the door and waited for him to ring the front doorbell – it would be just like him – but he didn't. Next time I looked out he was gone. It seemed so creepy I had to tell Mummy.

I went downsatirs and into the kitchen and said, 'You'll

never guess who I saw just now. Hal Finch, from the office.
He was parked outside Mr Smith's.'

She was loading the dishwasher but she stopped and turned.
'I saw someone out there from the lounge window and thought
it must be Mr Smith's nephew. So that's your Hal, is it. He
looks quite nice . . . How does he know where you live?'

'He must have asked someone at the office.' Or looked me
up in one of the files, I thought, as the back of my neck
prickled with alarm.

Mummy smiled. 'Perhaps he's taken a fancy to you.' She
went on stacking the plates and I handed her one of those
three-in-one detergent cubes which brings the glasses up so
well. She didn't appear particularly worried.

I said, 'I hope not! He's already got a girlfriend according
to Emma.'

But, of course, I didn't know what to think. It would be
nice to have someone take a fancy to me, but a stalker . . .
No. Surely not. Not Hal. But he had made those odd remarks
and he kept popping up. In my diary I wondered whether I
should tackle him about it but would that work? If he was
stalking me, he would hardly be stopped so easily but if he
*wasn't*, it would put him off me. He'd think I was neurotic.

Mummy said, 'Why don't you ask him round for Sunday
lunch? You said he lives alone. Then I could take a good look
at him.'

I was at once longing to ask him but terrified he would say
something about The Black Horse, so I suddenly blurted it all
out – about the swimwear and the pub – and to my surprise
she was quite calm about everything. She seemed to think I
was getting myself worked up about nothing.

Monday morning I was on the point of asking him about
Sunday lunch but Etta was going on about something in the
paper in Northampton. A man had been arrested for stalking
a middle-aged woman. The woman was married but the stalker
had been following her everywhere and sending her letters
and flowers and making her life a misery for nearly two years
and so she'd reported him to the police. Etta was saying that

probably the woman had been encouraging him or leading him on and she was half to blame and had brought it on herself. That gave me food for thought. Had I been sending Hal the wrong messages? Perhaps it was all my fault. I needed time to think about it, so I didn't ask him to lunch. I told Mummy I'd forgotten.

The next day Mr Curtis called me into his office and gave me another twenty-five pounds a week and I knew at once that Hal had said something to him and I went straight out and tackled him.

'Yes, I did have a word,' he admitted. 'I could see you were never going to get round to it. Curtis was really surprised but very reasonable. He just hadn't given it a thought. So how much did he give you?'

I couldn't tell him the exact figure, obviously. 'Ten pounds a week more than Etta,' I said carefully. 'That was really kind of you, Hal. Thank you.'

'Any time – but you owe me!' He raised his eyebrows and I had to laugh. Then I asked, 'Have you got a sister?' The words just came out because I *had* to know.

He had got two, apparently. 'But no girlfriend!' he added, grinning. 'And definitely no baby.'

I was mortified. 'Emma told you!' Somehow I managed a smile.

'I'm totally available,' he said. 'No strings attached!'

I have to say he's got a lovely smile and suddenly I felt a rush of courage and decided to take a chance. I wanted him to come home and sit opposite me at the table and share pork and all the trimmings and sprouts and roast potatoes. I said, 'My mother was wondering if you'd like to come to lunch on Sunday.'

The smile broadened. 'I'd love to,' he said.

At once there was a round of applause from the rest of the staff and Tim shouted, 'About bloody time!' and then everyone was laughing and Hal put his arm round me and gave me a quick hug.

Emma said, 'You've just won me five pounds!'

It seemed they'd been laying bets on whether or not Hal and I would get together before Christmas. I suppose I should have been embarrassed but I wasn't. I could see the funny side of it. Then Hal reached into his pocket and pulled out a photograph, which he handed to me. In the photograph Hal was sitting on a beach in the sun with a young woman and two small children.

'Me and my sister Alison and her kids,' he said. 'Her husband, Frank, took the picture.'

I could see a vague likeness between him and his sister. Hal was wearing shorts and a T-shirt. The children, two girls, were eating ice-cream cornets.

'Where were you?' I asked.

'Javea, in Spain. My parents have a villa there.'

I was opening my mouth to say that we rented an apartment there last summer but Hal said, 'Take a look at the people behind us.'

I looked . . . and then I stared and my mouth fell open. 'Is that *me*?'

'Isn't it?'

It was. And Mummy was beside me, wearing the sarong thing she'd bought in the local market. We were sitting under our big beach umbrella and I was wearing my green swimsuit and patting sun cream into my arm. Mummy was reading a book. *Palamino*, I remembered. She loves Danielle Steel.

Everyone was crowding round to look at the picture.

Hal said, 'I was looking through these last night and there you were! No wonder I thought we'd met. We had in a way. While you were swimming, your mother spoke to Alison and said what well-behaved children she had. Alison was over the moon about that. And your mother said you were staying at—'

'At The Miramar! Yes we were.'

'And she said you'd got some ants in the kitchen and Alison said get a spray from the supermarket.'

'We did and they disappeared like magic.'

It was an amazing coincidence. More than that, it was a miracle as far as I was concerned.

'A chance in a million!' said Emma.

Somehow I resisted the urge to kiss the photograph! Everything was falling slowly into place. This was the image of me that Hal had had in his mind. A perfectly innocent explanation. As I clung to the photograph a great weight was lifted from my mind and I started to smile and couldn't stop.

I said, 'Oh Hal!' because I felt so guilty for thinking he might be a stalker and then my throat tightened and I was holding back tears of relief. Then I realized it was only Tuesday. How on earth could I bear to wait for Sunday lunch?

# Minutes of the Last Meeting

It seems as if I've been on the Social Club committee forever but that's not to say I didn't enjoy it because I do. Or rather, did. Because I'm out of there from today, thanks to Sophie. Silly cow! I was minuting secretary. It was interesting and I got along OK with the other members most of the time until yesterday. There's Sophie. Our so-called treasurer. From the wrong side of the track, as they say. She married her rich boyfriend as soon as his scandalized family realized she was pregnant and was *not* going to 'go quietly' or 'do the sensible thing' and they now live in a big house on the outskirts of the village.

And the Colonel, poor old devil. Lives next to the tea shop in the village. He's gone to pot since his wife died – a badly trimmed moustache and overlong fingernails. That sort of thing. He doesn't eat enough and he's very thin – a case of 'can't cook, won't cook'! But it hasn't dented his arrogance. Once a colonel, always a colonel. That's what Sophie says. When his wife died I half expected him to advertise for a batman from his old regiment! He's like a creaking gate, lingering on, but at least he's still got all his marbles.

Then there's Kathleen, who lives with her widowed mother and a couple of elderly dogs. Smelly and unlovely (the dogs, not Kathleen!), they have the run of the house. Enough said! Mother and daughter were left well provided for and make the best of things. Kathleen does the garden and Mother walks the dogs twice a day, so they keep fit enough. They have a 'little treasure' who cleans for them once a week and her mother pushes a duster round the place occasionally.

Then there's Oliver. Poor Ollie – larger than life in more ways than one! He must weigh in at around eighteen stone and is getting more cantankerous with every week that passes. He has a chip on his shoulder because he was made to work in his father's butcher's shop in the village although he wanted to be an artist. He may have shown some talent, but his father considered his artistic leanings 'cissy' and promised him a comfortable life as the owner of a successful business and a man of some substance. Sadly the shop failed when his father started to drink the profits and when he died under the wheels of the twice-weekly bus to Brighton, there were debts. Oliver's a miserable devil in many ways but you can see why. I try to make allowances. I shan't miss him.

Our latest addition to the committee is Laura Leckie, a fortyish divorcee. Still thinks she's in with a chance and seems to be on the lookout for a second husband. Flutters her eyelashes and wears clothes that are too small for her attractive plump figure but I like her so far. Never judge a book by its cover. That's my motto. At least Laura's always cheerful.

Robert Meadows is a lost cause. I can't think why he agreed to come on the committee in the first place because he rarely turns up.

We have a meeting once a month to plan social events for the village and to raise cash, naturally. We've tried everything – fancy dress balls, riverside barbecues, harvest suppers, quiz nights – you name it, we've tried it but we could do with more support. We do make money, however, but not as much as we should considering that we're a large sprawling village. But we press on. I suppose none us wants to admit defeat.

I was the first to arrive at yesterday's meeting. We meet in each other's houses to save money. The village hall is twenty pounds an hour and at this time of year it's draughty. Being the minuting secretary isn't easy but I like to think I make a reasonable job of it and I thought I was appreciated – 'thought' being the operative word. It's not easy listening, contributing *and* making notes at the same time.

Oliver arrived next – he walks up (or should I say 'waddles

along') even when it's raining. I heard Kathleen telling him to shake his brolly outside and not in the hall. I doubt if Robert will show but the Colonel never misses a meeting. I think he comes for the tea and biscuits. Sophie's always last so when she arrived, we made a start . . .

I'm still mad about what happened but I've done my duty. I've conformed to requirements, you might say. I've written the minutes exactly the way they wanted them – with plenty of detail! I'd love to see their faces when they read them.

**Minutes of the meeting of the committee of the Social Club, held at 6, Newcombe Way, at 3.07 on Friday, 5th March, 2004**

*Present: Diane Maybury, Kathleen Baynes, Oliver Wesley, Colonel Mark Tarrant, Sophie West and Laura Leckie. Apology for absence from Robert Meadows, who explained that he has yet another cold.*

The meeting was held round the large table in Kathleen's lounge to the accompaniment of snores from Susie, one of her elderly dogs, who was sleeping behind the sofa. As usual Kathleen was thanked for the use of her room and said it was a pleasure.

**1) The minutes of the last meeting**. These were read but to the surprise and dismay of the minuting secretary, Diane Maybury, Sophie then observed that in her opinion the minutes were so brief *as usual* as to be almost useless. There was a brief silence before Oliver, currying favour, agreed with her that they certainly could be a lot more detailed. The minuting secretary argued that the minutes had been no shorter than usual and surely they were meant to be notes not novels. Sophie argued that minutes should be a detailed account for future reference. A lively discussion ensued. Kathleen looked worried at this point but did not say a word to support the minuting secretary, who felt totally betrayed by the unexpected attack. Laura Leckie said they seemed OK to her, but Sophie pointed out that Laura was a new member and had confessed to her when they met in the village shop on Monday that she had no experience at all in committee work, so her opinion amounted to very little. The minuting secretary then asked for a show of hands and a more detailed set of minutes was requested for the future – the only abstention being Laura Leckie who, red-faced, was glaring at Sophie.

The minuting secretary at once agreed to more detailed minutes in the future and apologized profusely for all the years during which she had obviously been failing at her job. She explained that she had not hitherto thought it necessary to consider the increasing ages of members of the committee. (If further details are required here on this point, Sophie is fifty-three although she pretends to be forty-five and the others are even older.) Naturally their memories for detail might well be faulty and the minuting secretary promised to bear that in mind in future.

Kathleen then asked Oliver if he would appreciate 'a firmer chair' as the one he had chosen had belonged to her grandmother and was not very reliable. Oliver at once saw through this offer, took offence and declined and Kathleen continued to watch the chair anxiously.

**2) Appointment of Liaison Officer for the coming year.** The Colonel excused himself and went to the bathroom. While he was gone Kathleen whispered that *he* should never be chosen again after his disastrous stint as Liaison Officer in 1999. Laura, obviously intrigued, asked what that meant and was told that he was now a little too fond of the whisky and had failed on at least two occasions to maintain the dignity of the Social Club committee. On the latter occasion he had brought the club into disrepute by arguing with a local celebrity, Lord Willmot, (who was opening our Summer Fete) and then turning the microphone off in a fit of sulks. A discussion followed.

Nobody wanted to be Liaison Officer, so Robert Meadows was proposed and seconded in his absence and elected by five votes to one. The minuting secretary pointed out that Robert was very shy and would hate it and the

Colonel said, 'Toughen him up! Do him good!' and launched into his frequently trumpeted, always boring, views on the end of conscription into the Army.

Oliver then asked loudly that his expensive red and black gold-nibbed Parker pen should be returned to him as it had been a gift from his late sister and had sentimental value. He claimed that at the previous meeting someone who should be nameless had borrowed it and had kept it. Sophie took offence, saying that *she* was the one who had borrowed it and she clearly recalled handing it back to him across the table. Kathleen said she and her mother would have found it by now if it had been left behind. Sophie explained in a loud whisper to Kathleen that if she had wanted a pen, even one encrusted with diamonds, her husband would have bought her one.

**3) Financial Report by Treasurer Sophie West**. The accounts for the past year had finally been prepared but left in the car and Sophie hurried out into the rain to fetch them looking rather embarrassed by this oversight. In her absence Oliver pointed out that this was typical and that anyway everyone knew her husband prepared the accounts as she couldn't add up to save her life. Kathleen replied that she couldn't be too bad at figures as she had once worked in a bank but Laura pointed out that bank tellers used calculators to do the adding up and Oliver said, 'I rest my case!' On her return Sophie handed round photocopied sheets and they were read in silence. As usual nobody could understand them including the minuting secretary. Oliver asked her to explain the muddle at the top of page two where several corrections had been written in red over the original figures and Sophie became very flustered and confessed that she could not remember *exactly* what had happened there but the totals agreed and surely that was all that mattered. The Colonel said, 'Well hardly, old thing!' and pressed her to try and explain. Sophie replied that she really objected to being called 'old thing' especially by the Colonel, who is seventy-five if he's a day and looks it and, anyway, 'old thing' was an ageist remark. A short silence ensued after which she tossed her expensively tinted red hair and the Colonel hurried off to the bathroom for the second time. Looking distinctly sullen, Sophie said she would ask her husband to check her figures and would give us an explanation at the next meeting.

It seems we made £385.49 at the Quiz Night including the raffle money, £161 from the Spring Dance, £290 from the Autumn Fair and £51 from an anonymous donor. Laura nudged Oliver and asked coyly if he was the 'culprit' and he said, 'I'm not saying a word!' He tapped his nose and tried to look mysterious in the hope that we would think it *was* him. But the minuting secretary suggested it was Sophie's husband who put in the £51 because he couldn't make her figures balance any other way. Sophie said that was a lie and she challenged anyone to prove it. Kathleen looked deeply worried.

**4) The club's email address.** Oliver admitted that this had proved somewhat disappointing in spite of all his early hopes. There had been thirteen email messages in the five months it had been up and running – two bordering on the obscene and eleven mostly critical of the Social Club committee. Most of the eleven came from the same person in the village – someone who should know better. Oliver refused to divulge a name but did say something about 'a brand new Jag and we all know who *that* is'. Correction. Laura did *not* know and was told in a loud whisper that it was Sophie's husband's brother, who was once accused by Oliver of cheating during a pro-am golf match and had never forgiven him. The Colonel excused himself and rushed to the bathroom for the third time. Laura wondered if he had recently eaten a strong curry but Kathleen thought it was 'waterworks'.

**5) The Spring Dance.** A letter was read out from Albert Pringle complaining that the volume of the music at the last disco was too loud for elderly ears and was keeping people away from the dances. Before this could be discussed, the

Colonel lit up a Marlborough cigarette and was immediately asked to put it out as 6 Newcombe Way was a smoke-free zone and the Colonel said, 'Since when?' and Kathleen said, 'Since Mother and I decided to give up passive smoking – and this is *our* house.' The Colonel muttered, 'Bloody women!' and Laura complained that that was a sexist remark and asked in vain for an apology. Kathleen then suggested that the Colonel might like to smoke in the garden shed but he declined as it was still raining. Sophie then pointed out that it was not raining in the garden shed but he gave her a look which would have quelled a Rottweiler. He did, however, stub out the offending cigarette. At that moment Kathleen's mother brought in a tray of Earl Grey tea and home-made biscuits – ginger munchies and almond crescents partly dipped in chocolate. They were absolutely delicious. The minuting secretary suggested we each pay something for the home-made refreshments to cover their costs as they were so much nicer than the usual shop biscuits. Oliver said, 'Surely not! A cup of tea and a couple of biscuits . . .' and Laura said, 'I think it's a good idea. What about twenty pence each?' and it was agreed. Oliver then informed us somewhat smugly that in that case we would have to change a twenty pound note, which we were unable to do. Laura offered to lend him fifty pence, saying he could settle up at the next meeting, and Sophie said, 'You'll be lucky!' The committee then forgot all about the disco and the too-loud music for elderly ears and sat around for twenty-two minutes eating, drinking, squabbling half-heartedly and wasting time.

**6) Any other business.** The Colonel told us that someone in The Red Deer pub told someone who told him that the price per hour of hiring the Village Hall has gone up to twenty-one pounds to cover an increase in oil prices. There were groans but it was agreed that, even if true, nothing could be done as the village has no other suitable venue. Laura proposed that we hold a fashion show for charity as she has a friend who runs a boutique and would be willing to arrange it. This was quickly approved despite Oliver's comment that the women in our village wouldn't recognize a fashionable garment if it fell on them from a great height. It was agreed that Laura should arrange a Saturday during June, the event to be held at the village hall. At this point Kathleen's mother came in with the missing pen which she had found on the floor after the previous meeting and Sophie said that Oliver must have dropped it *after* she had returned it to him and hinted that an apology would be in order. Oliver, always short in the manners department, muttered something unintelligible with bad grace.

The minuting secretary then announced that this would be her last meeting as she was resigning from the position and also from the committee as, after more than five years, she had become thoroughly disenchanted with the whole proceedings as well as with her fellow members. After a short, shocked silence Laura was the first to recover. She said, 'Oh I am sorry, Diane!' Kathleen said anxiously, 'Aren't you overreacting, dear?' and Oliver, carefully examining his pen, apparently for signs of misuse, said, 'Thoroughly disenchanted? Funny thing to say!' and as the Colonel headed for the bathroom the meeting was declared closed.

**The next meeting will be held at the same address (hopefully promptly) at 3.00 on Friday May 7th, 2004.**

I hope they're finally satisfied with their bloody minutes! Enough detail for everyone, I hope. I shall mail them tomorrow.

# Growing Up

Sandra was waiting for him when he got home from work and Les knew at once there was trouble brewing. He could sense it in the air – like electricity.

'I'm back!' he shouted, tossing his denim jacket on to a chair. He grinned at the baby, who was staring up at him from the baby walker. Young Ben was just like his mother – a smouldering child with a round face and dark penetrating eyes that looked right through you. The gaze was disconcerting in Sandra but worse in a toddler.

He said, 'What? I haven't done anything!' and grinned. It was their private joke. Usually Ben dissolved into a smile at this point but today he shook his head and turned his attention to the rusk clutched firmly in his podgy fist.

'You know something I don't know?'

The rusk fell in pieces on the worn carpet and Ben began to scoot himself across the floor.

Sandra called, 'I'm in here!' and he found her in the small utility area, pulling clothes from the washing machine. She glanced up, fury written large in her eyes as she held up her pink bra and a pink shirt. 'See this? How many times have I asked you not to put those red boxers in the washing basket? Now your shirt's ruined and it serves you right!' She straightened up. 'And don't you dare blame me! You are simply hopeless! No wonder your mother threw you out.'

He wanted to put his arms round her and hug her. She was lovely when she was mad. Comfortably plump and nearly forty, Sandra was Mother Earth in too-tight leggings and a floppy T-shirt that bore the legend *GET LOST!* Instead he grabbed the pink shirt and examined it.

'Nice!' he said. 'Could start a new trend.'

She pushed past him, the plastic basket of washing under her arm. 'In future you can do your own damned washing. Do you good to take care of yourself and about time. How old are you? Ten going on twenty? You're pathetic, Les. Downright pathetic!'

He trailed after her. 'I'm not pathetic. I can do things. You just do them better than I do.'

'So that's the excuse you gave your mother, is it? She did it better. Ever wondered why?' She dumped the basket on the kitchen table and began to set up the ironing board. 'It's called practice!'

She was trying not to look at him, thought Les. Because she couldn't resist him. Never had been able to from the first moment they met when he was waiting to get off the 39 bus and she was running to catch it when it stopped. Puffing and panting and wobbling in all the wrong places, several plastic carrier bags swinging dangerously. 'Come on, Jumbo! You can make it!' he'd shouted. Just a bit of fun but she'd taken it the wrong way and given him a right wallop with her free hand. Then she'd pinned him against the stairwell and lambasted him with her tongue about manners and political correctness and being accountable for your actions. She'd made him miss his stop and he'd sat down next to her to try and explain that it was just the sort of remark he and his mates said but it didn't mean anything. Not really.

'Mates?' she'd gasped. 'You've still got *mates*? How old are you, for God's sake? When are you going to grow up?'

That was when he was nineteen and still read comics and never watched the news and couldn't find a job and lived at home with his long-suffering mum.

To make up for calling her Jumbo he'd offered to carry one of the bags for her and so discovered where she lived. A ground-floor flat on a housing estate which could have been a lot worse. She hadn't asked him in, but six weeks later his mother finally sent him packing after a row and he'd ended up on Sandra's doorstep in the middle of the night, asking her if she wanted a lodger.

'One week,' she'd said, 'while you talk round one of your famous mates into lending you a sofa to kip on. One week – and in lieu of rent you can take my kid out for an hour every afternoon so I get a bit of time to myself for once.'

He'd done other jobs for that first week – helped with the shopping, hoovered, washed up. But he had never taken the kid out. That would be social suicide.

Now she said, 'Fancy a coffee?'

'Please!' He tried to put his arms round her waist but she wriggled free.

'Make it then. I'll have one too.'

Different. He hesitated.

Ben materialized suddenly in the doorway, silent and lethal in the baby walker, and ran over Les's right foot. Les didn't bother to yell because he never got any sympathy and had given up hoping. Ben chuckled, reversed and disappeared along the passage.

'That kid ought to be done for dangerous driving,' Les grumbled. Filling the kettle and spooning coffee into the mugs, he watched Sandra surreptitiously. She plugged in the iron and spread his pink shirt out on the board.

'Right! First ironing lesson,' she said, '– and don't keep calling him "that kid". He's got a name. Start with the collar.'

His alarm was growing. She had that look on her face. The expression he had seen a hundred times on his mother's face. Clouds blowing up before a storm. He sat down on a chair with the mug clasped firmly in both hands.

'Up!' she snapped. 'Get hold of the iron and do the collar. Then the sleeves on both sides and then . . .'

'What's the point? I'll never wear it pink.'

'You said you liked it. Move, Les!'

Something in her voice made him do as she suggested.

She said, 'You'll have to wear it because it's your only

shirt. Your going-to-interviews shirt. Remember? Your going-to-work shirt!'

'I'll never get a job wearing a pink shirt!' He slid the iron over the collar and water dribbled out.

'It does that sometimes. It'll dry out. Sleeves now.'

He'd never officially moved in but he'd lived with Sandra for nearly two years and after the first three months she'd let him into her bed. Since then he had somehow fallen in love with her but had never let on. Not to Sandra. He wasn't that stupid. But he'd told his mates. 'She's wonderful. A right stunner. You can't beat an older woman. Sandra's world class.' He'd laughed. 'Nearly old enough to be my mother but knows it all. She must have been a raver when she was young.'

Come to that she still was at times – when she wasn't too tired with cooking and cleaning and looking after the kid and shopping and popping round to keep an eye on her dad (who was practising to be an alkie) and doing two hours twice a week on the accounts for her brother's garage. Oh yes! Sandra knew how to party and could dress up a treat with a bit of lipstick and a squirt of perfume. He'd fallen on his feet with Sandra and he knew it. And he *was* trying to get a job, whatever she might think. He just didn't want any old job.

'Now the front,' she nagged. 'You're doing OK for a first attempt.'

'Who'll give me a job wearing a pink shirt?'

'Try a gay bar. Washing glasses and wiping tables.'

He ignored her. She could be very cutting.

'You could be a traffic warden. Nobody else wants the job. You'd look good in a uniform.'

He stopped ironing and adopted a hurt tone. 'You want to get rid of me, is that it? You'd like to have the house to yourself. I tell you this, Sandra – you'd be lonely. You're the sort that needs a bit of company.'

'I'm the sort that needs a bit of extra money. You gave me nothing so far this week and last week only a tenner and you eat like a horse!'

'You sound like my mum, you know that?'

Her ex-boyfriend, the kid's father, had done a bunk when the kid was due but his mother had nagged him until he started sending Sandra money every week and he popped in from time to time to see the baby. Kevin, his name was. *Kevin!* His parents popped in, too. They worshipped Ben. Their first and only grandchild.

Les put down the iron and pulled a few crumpled notes from the pocket of his jeans. Selecting a twenty he tossed it on to the table. 'Are we straight now?'

She stared at it, then reached for it and tucked it into her purse. 'So where did that come from?'

He shrugged. Better she didn't know he'd won it. He held up the pink shirt and she said, 'That wasn't so hard, was it?' and he thought he'd interrupted her train of thought. He should have known better. She said suddenly, 'This isn't going to last, you know, Les. I'm not doing you any favours letting you stay here. You have to grow up and it's not easy – in fact at times it's positively painful but we all survive somehow. You will too.'

'I *am* grown up, Sandra. It's not my fault if nobody—'

'There you go again, Les. Blaming the rest of the world. What don't you understand about "grow up"? You need to get a job, a place of your own, deal with responsibilities. You'll be twenty-one soon. Don't you want to be independent?'

He was appalled. 'For God's sake, Sandra! I'm doing my best! I've just learned to iron!' He grinned – the grin that she once said had won her heart, but this time it failed to work its magic. He tried something else. 'What would I do without you, Sandra? I mean . . . we're a team, aren't we? You me and the – and Ben. The terrible trio!' He rolled his eyes.

'We're not a team, Les. He says "Dada" now but you pretend not to hear him. No, don't deny it. I've *heard* you say you're not his dad.'

'Well, I'm not, am I? I can't lie to the kid. He knows his own dad.'

She fiddled with her nail polish, chipping it off with a deadly intensity. 'You never take him out. You never even *want* to take him out. Perhaps that means you never want a child of your own.'

Something icy and hard settled in his stomach. Oh no! Not that! 'If you're trying to tell me . . .' If Sandra was pregnant he would leave at once. Go home to his mother.

She saw his expression change and sighed. 'No, Les. I'm not trying to tell you anything. Except that I'm nearly forty and I want a proper family and I want another child. A brother or sister for Ben – and I don't have all the time in the world to work something out.'

He felt faint with relief. Thank you, *thank you*, God! 'Look, Sandra, you don't have to rush into anything. Let's take it a day at a time. You love me, I know you do.'

'But you don't love me. It's part of the problem.'

'I don't love you?' He stared at her with exaggerated astonishment. 'Where did you get that idea? Of course I—'

He stopped abruptly. This was dangerous ground. She might *ask* him outright and then what would he do? Admitting it would be the thin end of the wedge.

Fortunately she seemed to be thinking of something else. She said, 'Kevin called in again while you were out.'

'Well, there you are then.' Relief washed over him. 'I don't mind. I'm not the possessive sort. Broad-minded. Why shouldn't you see the baby's father?'

She seemed unconvinced, so he took a calculated risk. 'Tell you what, I've just settled up with you financially. Now I'll take the – Ben out in his stroller. To the park. How's that?' He gave her the grin and this time she wavered. Then her eyes lit up. 'You mean it?'

'Course I mean it!' He leaned over and kissed her. 'That's me, Sandra, when I make up my mind. You get him dressed while . . .' He stopped and held up his hands. 'Listen to me. *I'll* get him dressed and then *I'll* take him out. You just put your feet up and relax. Watch the telly.'

She was beaming now. 'You will take care of him, won't you? Don't let him out of your sight. You hear such terrible things.'

'Of course I'll take care of him. I promise. Brownie's honour!' He held up two fingers and said, 'Dib dib!' That always made her smile.

She kissed him. 'OK then. I'll get round to Dad's.' She looked hopeful and Les was surprised by how good it made him feel. He kissed her and she clung to him for a moment but he didn't mind that.

Fifteen minutes later he was waving from the pavement and the kid was clutching one of his many teddies and muttering cheerfully to himself. He called, 'Back at five thirty on the dot!' and blew her a kiss. He saw the old lady from next door peering at him from behind her curtain and gave her a thumbs-up sign. Let them all take note, he thought proudly. Sandra's chap is really pulling his weight.

They went to the park and he pushed Ben on the swing and went round with him on the roundabout. It was quite good fun. Then he was chatted up by a young mother whose name was Sharon. She admired Ben, so he pretended he was Ben's father and said they had another child on the way. It all sounded so good he couldn't stop grinning. She had a scrawny little girl but he said she was sweet and one way and another he thought he'd impressed the mother with his maturity.

When she'd gone he pushed the stroller into the shopping mall and gave the kid a ride on a mechanical horse but it scared him and he started to cry and had to be taken off.

Les left the mall and wandered round to his favourite pub to show the kid off to his mates but they weren't there, so he parked the stroller outside for a moment while he went into the Gents for a quick pee. When he came out he saw that Ben had fallen asleep, so he muttered, 'Nice one!' and went back inside for a pint of John Smith. He told Larry, the barman, about his adventures in the park with Ben and exaggerated the story about the young mother who'd befriended him, insisting that she fancied him and they were laughing when Jacko arrived, so he bought him a drink and then Jacko's brother-in-law turned up and Les told *them* about the park.

Then suddenly he tossed in a hint that he might pop the question to Sandra and realized that maybe he really *would* ask her.

The others stared at him. 'What, *marry* her? *Her?* You gone off your rocker?'

Jacko began to laugh. 'You? Get married? Never! Anyway, she'd never have you!'

'Do you want to bet on it?' Les glared. 'I'm not kidding. Why shouldn't I get married? Other men do!'

Jacko's brother-in-law explained that other men were stupid and Les was not. Larry said that Sandra would never have him, not in a million years. 'Because you're an idle, good-for-nothing, unreliable prat,' he explained. 'I wouldn't let you near my sister for love nor money!'

Then, to save an argument, Jacko bought a round and they began to play dice for money. Strictly against the licensing laws but Larry turned a blind eye and before long Les had won twenty-five pounds and the others called it a day. At that moment a man came in and announced that there was a woman outside with a baby in a stroller and she was threatening to tear somebody's balls off and feed them to the dogs.

'Jesus wept!' Les almost fell off the stool. 'What's the time?' he asked, his face white as a sheet.

It was quarter past six. The door opened and Sandra came in with Ben in her arms. He was red-faced and bawling and she was mad as hell. Jacko's brother-in-law melted away, muttering about someone he had to see. Jacko braved the storm for a few moments but quickly retired to the Gents. Larry rashly tried to smooth ruffled feathers but was soon reduced to a quivering wreck and began to polish glasses as though his life depended on it.

'You, Les,' Sandra cried, 'are the rottenest, most useless piece of shit I have ever known in my whole life! How could I have trusted you for a minute?' She hugged and kissed the toddler and wiped his face with her handkerchief.

Les stammered, 'I'm . . . I'm sorry. I can explain if you—'

'No, Les, you can *not* explain. Nothing you say will be good enough. Oh God, I blame myself. Why did I trust you? I must have been crazy to believe a word you said but I wanted to give you a chance. I thought you deserved one chance to prove yourself. And this is how you repay me! You leave Ben outside a pub for God knows how long where anyone could walk off with him? Do you realize how irresponsible that is? Not to say positively dangerous. Reckless! I could have lost him.' Her voice quivered. 'Some pervert might have just wheeled him away . . .' She stopped to wipe furious tears from her own face.

Ben, frightened by his mother's shrill voice, added to the noise with more screams of his own until the licensee came down from upstairs to ask what the racket was all about.

Sandra stabbed a finger in Les's chest and said, 'Ask this one! He's caused it all!' and then swept out, slamming the door behind her.

When Les summoned enough courage to go home he found his bags packed and waiting on the doorstep. Sandra refused to open the door and, by way of the letterbox, threatened to call the police if he made any kind of fuss. When he knocked on his mother's door she explained apologetically that he'd been gone nearly two years and she'd let his room to a male nurse.

Five months later Les had a room of his own over an off licence; he shared the bathroom and loo and cleaned the stairs every third week. He also had a job as a security guard in a department store where Jacko worked as a delivery man. He boasted about his independence and stayed well away from Sandra. She would be missing him, no doubt, but that was her choice.

He told himself he was happy until one day he passed a church and saw a wedding and it was Sandra getting married. *To Kevin!* She looked wonderfully shapeless in a white dress – even a little fatter round the middle. But utterly desirable. Choked by memories, Les watched confetti flutter over the happy couple.

He whispered, 'Sandra!'

Her mum was carrying Ben, who was dressed in a tiny suit with a bow tie. The kid looked ridiculous but was smiling broadly and waving a lollipop.

Sandra caught sight of Les as she was stepping into the car and winked at him. He tried to smile but his face had frozen. He was surprised how much it hurt to see her and when they drove off there were tears in his eyes and he felt crushed with misery. She'd betrayed him with the horrible Kevin! Les wanted to blame her for breaking his heart but he couldn't. She'd given him his chance and he'd blown it big time.

He hung about, watching the cheerful crowd settle into their cars as they headed off to the wedding reception.

'Could have been mine!' he muttered, shell-shocked.

Sandra had been so right. Growing up was very, *very* painful.

# The Power of Love

After Dad died, my mother seemed to lose all her confidence and I began to worry about her. As an only child I felt the responsibility once she was on her own. She was losing interest in what went on around her and couldn't be bothered to keep in touch with her friends. Her nearest neighbour, Marjorie, tackled me one day as I was getting out of the car.

'Your mum's letting things go,' she told me, genuinely concerned. 'I notice she gets up later and later and I've seen her outside in the garden in her dressing gown at gone eleven in the morning!'

I was shocked. When Dad was alive they both made a lot of effort. Their garden was a picture and Mum was always making cakes for various fund-raising schemes. You might say they bustled through life, priding themselves on keeping busy even though they were both in their seventies. Dad always changed into clean clothes in the evenings when he stopped tinkering with the car or finished the gardening. Mum always wore her felt hat when she went to the WI meetings.

'I'll try and talk to her,' I told Marjorie.

Marjorie and Mum had always been on friendly terms and I knew Marjorie was not just being nosy. I did have a word with Mum but she was very indignant and said she was old enough to know what she was doing and I wasn't to meddle. I let it go but I didn't stop worrying.

I live about five miles away from my mother and it's easy enough to pop over. I decided to keep an eye on her. I would ring her an hour or so beforehand on some excuse and when

I arrived she'd always be fully dressed and busy with something – the ironing or the dusting.

'There you are then,' said my husband. 'She's fine.'

Then one day I popped over just before midday without any warning. No one answered the bell, so I went round to the back door and it was open. Fearing the worst, I rushed in – and found her asleep in bed.

'I'm having a lie-in,' she insisted irritably when I roused her. 'I didn't sleep well last night. You should have rung me.'

'I'm sorry, Mum. I . . . I assumed you'd be up and about,' I stammered, recovering from my fright.

'Well, you assumed wrong!'

I made a pot of tea for two but all my worries had returned.

My husband still refused to be alarmed. 'Give her time, love. She'll snap out of it.'

But would she? Suppose I let her go past the point of no return? I dreamed up a new strategy. I would phone up and give her three hours' notice and propose a shopping trip or a visit to a nearby garden centre or even a drive along the coast when the weather was nice. It worked once or twice but then she played me at my own game. She would say 'Yes' and then two hours later, ring me to say she was feeling tired and was going to potter in the garden for half an hour and then take a nap.

'The doctor says I have to rest,' she told me.

Had she even *been* to the doctor? I couldn't bring myself to pry. Checking up on her made me feel deceitful. The situation was beginning to cause arguments between me and my husband. He thought I was fussing and said I shouldn't bully her. *I* said I was simply concerned. *He* thought I was interfering.

'Look,' I told him. 'There's always a certain time when a mother stops caring for her child and the child starts caring for the mother. It's been going on for centuries. My grandmother struggled on, resisting Mum's efforts to help, until one day she slipped on the icy steps outside her back door. She could have died of cold.' I remembered it vividly. The frantic telephone call late at night from a neighbour and the terrified rush to the hospital. 'She was nearly eighty when she finally agreed to come and live with us.'

Suddenly he gave me a hug. 'I know you mean it for the best, dear, but I think she'll recognize that certain time when it comes. I don't think this is it. Give her a bit longer, dear. Everyone values their independence.'

I gave in reluctantly.

Then the time came for the flu jab. Mum had been having this for some years but she always dreaded it. She had a great fear of needles and tried every trick in the book to avoid it.

'Sitting in that waiting room is downright dangerous,' she insisted when I brought up the subject again. 'All those sick people. I could catch something. I might catch something *worse* than flu!'

'Flu kills!' I gave her a steely look.

'I don't care. If my time's up I'll go anyway.'

'I'll be here at quarter to two to collect you.'

She thought quickly. 'No need, love. I'll go with Marjorie when she goes.'

'Marjorie isn't old enough for a free flu jab, Mum. You know she's not.' I stood up before she could invent another excuse. 'I'll be back at quarter to two.'

'It's raining.' A last desperate attempt.

'We'll be in the car!'

She was waiting at the gate when I returned and climbed reproachfully into the passenger seat. I noticed the felt hat was missing. She made a big deal of fastening her seat belt, grumbling that she hated 'the blessed thing'.

'No hat today?' I asked cheerily, reversing carefully and heading towards Rye.

'No point, is there. I'm sure to faint and then it'll fall off and . . .'

'You won't faint, Mum. You never faint.' I smiled at her. 'You're not the fainting type.'

'I come over a bit faint, sometimes. One day I will. I'll just

141

drop like a stone. Probably break a wrist or a hip.' She gave me a quick look to see how I was enjoying this scenario.

I turned on the radio and found some soothing music.

'Nobody bothers with flu jabs,' she announced. 'Only vulnerable people need the jab and I'm hardly what you'd call vulnerable.'

You will be, I thought, if you don't pull yourself together. Saying nothing, I hummed along with the music until Mum reached across and turned it off. She was fussing with her handbag and I knew she was nervous.

'You'll have to come in with me – into the surgery.'

'Of course I will. I always do.'

'Well . . . On your own head be it!' she said crossly.

We drove the rest of the way in silence, parked and ran through the rain and into the clinic. The waiting room was almost empty. An elderly man and woman, possibly also waiting for flu jabs, sat together on one side of the room. A mother and toddler waited on the second side. I gave Mum's name to the receptionist, who smiled at Mum and said, 'Won't keep you long, Mrs Granger.' We settled ourselves on the third side and reached for magazines. Mum thumbed listlessly through a gardening monthly and I pretended to read *Hello!* magazine. I saw her studying an offer for gladioli bulbs and wondered if I might revive the interest she had once had in gardening. Perhaps if I bought her some bulbs and a gardening book . . .

The door to the car park burst open and a burly man came in. He was probably in his late seventies with a neat white beard and very blue eyes. Actually, that's an understatement. He erupted into the room, booming, 'Good morning! Good morning! What a lousy day!' With extravagant gestures he brushed rain from his coat and smoothed his hair.

Larger than life, he had everyone's attention and he was obviously loving it.

The young receptionist came to the desk and he turned to her with a beaming smile.

'Ah! There you are! My favourite receptionist!'

142

To everyone's surprise he reached across the desk and gave
her a resounding kiss on each cheek. Blushing to the roots of
her blond hair, the young woman checked his name on her
list and gave it a tick. Beside me, Mum was transfixed. She
suddenly straightened in her chair and tucked back a strand
of hair. Leaning towards me, she hissed, 'It's *him*! Those
devastating blue eyes!'

'Him? Who's "him"?'

She was staring at him with shining eyes. 'It's Bernard
Brent! I'd know him anywhere!'

I stared at him as he stood in the middle of the room, deciding
where he would sit. Bernard Brent had been Mum's idol for
as long as I could remember. She'd seen all his films more
than once and had once kept a scrapbook containing clippings
from the newspapers about his career.

'Are you sure?' I whispered. 'I thought he was dead.'

'Well, you were wrong. He isn't, is he?' Her eyes were
shining. 'He's much older now but I'd recognize him
anywhere.'

She caught his eye and smiled radiantly. Thus encouraged,
he sat down beside her. Now, I thought, she really *might* faint!
She kept a signed photograph of Bernard Brent on the sideboard along with those of the family. Mum's unrequited
passion for him had been a family joke for years and Dad
claimed he had spent his married life trying to compete with
BB, as he called him. Not that he minded, he added. It was
something to live up to.

Mum and her idol – together at last, I thought and wished
Dad had been around to hear the news. He would have had a
good laugh. Maybe he was looking down even now and chuck-
ling to himself. I have to admit that even I was a little bit
thrilled. It's not every day you get to sit next but one to a film
star and he certainly was a charmer. Mum was chatting and
laughing away and looking years younger with every passing
minute. She told him about our daughter, Verity, and he told
her about his grandson, Tom.

At last a nurse came out and called Mum's name. I rose to

143

go with her as promised but to my surprise she pushed me back down in my seat.

'I can manage *perfectly* well, dear!' She turned to Bernard Brent. 'My daughter looks after me a little *too* well!' she said. 'I'm not decrepit yet!' She gave me a look which dared me to say anything about fainting and tripped airily after the nurse. Bernard Brent turned to me and I now experienced the full power of the devastating blue eyes.

'My mother's been a bit depressed lately,' I told him. 'Seeing you has cheered her up no end.'

'Glad to hear it, my dear. My good deed for the day.' His booming voice rang out but at that moment the nurse called for a Mr Robinson – and Bernard Brent stood up and disappeared through the swing doors.

Mr Robinson? I thought it rather odd. Maybe that was his real name and he'd reverted to it when he gave up his film career. Film stars often used stage names. I was intrigued. I crossed to the desk where the receptionist was busy with her files.

'Excuse me but was that the film star, Bernard Brent?'

She smiled. 'I'm afraid not. He's dead, so I'm told. That was George Robinson. Apparently he's a dead ringer for the other one – and he knows it! Same deep voice, too. Plays up to it no end but there's no harm in it.' She regarded me hopefully.

I said, 'Of course not.'

'It's just his fun. He's a lovely old boy! Used to run the pub until last year. Even now he plays cricket if they're a man short.'

I hurried back to my seat just as Mum appeared, looking none the worse for the dreaded jab. A moment later Mr Robinson followed her out.

Mum turned to him. 'Well, that's done for another year.' She tucked away a stray lock of hair.

George Robinson rolled his eyes at her. 'We're survivors, you and I!' he said in a melodramatic tone. 'We suffered and we survived!'

Nodding, Mum smiled up at him and then remembered me. 'Just a pinprick, dear. I don't know what all the fuss is about.'

The three of us walked out into the car park, where the rain was easing. George Robinson climbed into an ancient Bentley. A young man was sitting in the driver's seat reading the *Daily Mirror*.

Mum nudged me. 'His chauffeur!'

I thought it was probably Tom, his grandson. Two black labradors were in the back, breathing heavily and misting up the windows. Mum fastenend her seat belt without giving it a second thought. There was a hint of pink in her cheeks, she looked alert and a long sigh of pure happiness escaped her.

'Fancy meeting Bernard Brent after waiting all my life! Your father used to say, "Everything comes to he who waits".'

'He's certainly dishy.'

So what if she hadn't seen her old heart-throb? She *thought* she had and that's what mattered. I was going to keep George Robinson's secret.

She chattered on as I turned the corner into the main road and headed back to her bungalow. 'I suppose he's a bit of a recluse now . . . After the sort of life he's led he must appreciate a bit of privacy now that he's retired.'

I said, 'The receptionist was telling me how active he is. Still plays cricket apparently.'

'Really? Isn't that wonderful. Maybe I'll find out where and when and watch him play. Cheer him on.' She smiled. 'He still has that funny little smile. Humorous, I suppose that's what you'd call it . . . He called us survivors – and we are!'

'Of course you are.'

She looked at me. 'I've always loved him. I daresay you think I'm daft.'

'I do not! I rather fancy him myself!' I pulled up outside the bungalow and reached out to unfasten her seat belt.

Mum held up a hand. 'No need to help me out. I can manage.' She unfastened it and sat for a moment longer. Then she said, 'I think I'll phone Marjorie and ask her round for a cup of tea. Haven't seen her for days – not to speak to. Wait until she knows who I saw today!' Still she made no effort to get out of the car. 'I'm out of biscuits but I could whip up a few fairy cakes.'

I waited curiously, enjoying this new version of my mother. She said, 'When's the best-kept garden competition?'

'About seven weeks from now, I believe.'

'I may go in for it this year. A bit of pruning and a few bedding plants. I've let it go a bit and your father always worked so hard on it . . .'

Minutes later she almost ran into the house to make her phone call to Marjorie. Probably going to find some polish for Bernard Brent's photo frame! Ah! The power of love. I drove off, grinning with relief. Flu jabs have their place but the NHS is missing something vital, I thought. They should run a 'love jab' campaign. That way we would all be much healthier.

# Unforgiven

I put down the telephone and turned to Kate. I was trembling. 'What?' she looked up from the sofa, immediately alarmed. 'Who was it?'

'It was . . . Flora!' I stammered, sitting down heavily on the nearest chair and squashing one of the cats. I stood up and the ginger tom sprang from the chair to the window sill, where it sat, flicking its tail reproachfully. Sitting again, I took three or four deep breaths because I could hardly speak.

Kate blinked. 'Flora? That was *Flora*?'

I nodded and Kate closed her eyes. We stared at each other, shocked. Thirty years had passed since we had last seen her. Thirty long years since that terrible day. We were both silent, remembering Flora as she left the house in her wedding dress. I could still hear the soft swish, swish as the white silk hem brushed the floor, and the scent of the freesias she was carrying. Flora had been radiant. On her way to the church to marry *him*. So unbelievably *happy* to be leaving us. We had never seen her again because we didn't go to the ceremony and Flora had gone away straight after the wedding, back to her new home in Scotland, leaving us stunned by the betrayal. She didn't come to Father's funeral because she was ill with pleurisy and she didn't come later to Mother's because we didn't tell them until it was all over. We knew she'd want to bring *him*.

The three of us were born together, christened together, in the same class at school. Bishop Bailey confirmed us together when we were twelve.

Kate was recovering. 'What did she say?'

'She wants to visit. To come here and see us. *To stay overnight.*' I was as frightened as Kate.

Her fingers twisted nervously. 'As long as it's only –'

'– Flora? No, it's him as well. I'm sorry, Kate.' Guilt washed through me. Desperate to see Flora again I had said 'Yes' without conferring. I shook my head. 'Flora said it was both of them –'

'– or neither?'

'Yes. Did I do wrong?'

Nervously I waited for her answer. *I* answer the telephone but Kate makes the decisions. That's the way it is. When we were still three Flora made the decisions, so when she left we were quite lost for a while but we've worked it out over the years. Nowadays Kate does the shopping. I cook. She does the washing, I fetch the coal in. That's how it is without Flora.

'We do *want* to see her, Kate, don't we?' I asked.

'Of course. We *must* see her.'

'But could we bear it – having him in the house?' It was difficult to imagine. I wondered how Flora had dared to suggest it to us but perhaps she was under his influence after all this time. Or maybe she was desperate to see us.

'We don't have to speak to him,' Kate said at last.

She's clever like that, Kate. Straight to the heart of the matter.

'That's true.' We would pretend he wasn't there the way we did before they were married. It made Mother and Father cross but it had to be done. Kate and I always blamed them – Mother and Father I mean. They should have spoken up instead of encouraging her. Not that it would have made much difference. Flora was determined to marry him and couldn't understand what a terrible mistake she was making.

Kate nodded. 'They can both come but we won't speak to him. Not a single word.'

So it was settled but at once I felt a rush of anxiety. Flora was coming back home. Kate and I still live in the house where the three of us were born. Kate and I survive on the

148

money Mother left us. It's a frugal existence but we're content. It means we don't have to find jobs, which means we never have to be parted from one another.

I said, 'We're going to see Flora again!' We were so thrilled, we clung together, almost unable to believe it.

I sat back, imagining how it would be. 'I wonder what Flora will look like after all these years. Will we recognize her?'

'She'll look just like us, of course! Three peas in a pod, remember?'

Clever Kate. So we *would* know her. I felt better.

'Except for her clothes,' I said. She would be wearing different clothes and that was a shame. Mother had always dressed us alike as children and Kate and I had never seen any reason to change. But Flora would be dressing in a Scottish way. She'd be the odd one out. Kate and I would wear the matching print dresses which Mother had made the year before she died – the spotted cotton with the white collars and cuffs. Perhaps seeing us in them would remind Flora of all that she gave up for him.

Kate looked round the kitchen. 'We'll have to spring-clean –'

'– the house.'

'Yes.'

Flora was coming and the house must be welcoming. She would remember it as it was when Mother was alive. Clean and bright, warm in winter and cool in summer. With bowls full of flowers from the garden.

I frowned. 'What about the garden?' Father had loved it but we had never felt drawn to it. I glanced out at the waist-high weeds, overgrown herbs and tumbledown shed. The lawn had disappeared under a succession of rotting autumn leaves.

'I think not,' Kate decided. 'Flora won't think about the garden. With any luck it'll rain.'

The next day we started the housework. It was really quite exciting. We banished all the cats to the conservatory and made them comfortable with old blankets and rugs. Kate covered their chair in the parlour with an old bedspread to hide the stains and I tucked sprigs of rosemary down the sides to make it smell better.

'Rosemary for remembrance!' said Kate, smiling.

She looks quite pretty when she smiles. I suppose I do.

A terrible thought struck me. 'Flora won't know the cats!' I cried. 'They're different cats.' I stopped polishing the table and Kate looked up from blackleading the grate.

'None of them?'

'It is thirty years. Moggy was the last one she would remember.' Moggy, the old tortoiseshell, had been run over years ago.

'It won't matter. We'll introduce the new cats.'

We talked about Flora all the time – and sometimes about him.

Kate said, 'I expect he's put on a lot of weight. Probably eats too much. That's the sort of man he is. You can tell.'

We never use his name.

'And drinks too much.' I was sure of it. 'Probably got broken veins in his nose.'

I scrubbed the kitchen floor several times and it came up well. I'd forgotten the tiles were almost red. Kate wiped over the lino in the hall and tacked the edges down again. She washed the front-room curtains very gently and rehung them, and we made the spare bedroom as comfortable as we could.

I found the wedding photograph at the back of a drawer. Flora had sent it in a silver frame for us to keep on the kitchen mantelpiece with the rest of the photographs but *he* was in it, so Kate said we couldn't. I looked at it for the first time in thirty years. Everyone looked happy. Even Mother and Father. I had forgotten there was a bridesmaid. From his side of the family. She was in blue with a posy of forget-me-nots. *He* was dressed in a kilt and dark-green jacket and long socks and looked quite ridiculous. Trust him to dress up. He was flashy, but poor Flora could never see it. We refused to be bridesmaids and we didn't go the wedding even though it made poor Flora cry.

I showed Kate the photograph. 'We could cut him out of the photo,' I said doubtfully.

'Flora might be cross.'

'We needn't look –'

'– at him. I don't know . . .'

In the end Kate decided it might make Flora feel at home, so I put it on the table in their room.

Two days later Kate made another decision. 'We'll rent a television. Just for a few days. Flora won't know it's not ours.'

I was astonished. We have always agreed that there was no room in our lives for television – there are still dozens of Father's old books that we haven't read. But Flora was coming and that made a difference.

I tried to imagine the three of us sitting together on the sofa watching it.

'Suppose he wants to watch it,' I said. 'We couldn't. Not all of us together.'

'We'll say it's broken.'

We took a bus into town and found a shop that sold televisions and the man was very helpful. He seemed to like us at first. He showed us lots of televisions and demonstrated them. Black and white, colour and something called digital. In the end Kate chose a really big colour set but then the man told us the rental price and Kate changed her mind. She told him we'd be too busy talking to Flora to watch it. He changed then and grumbled that we'd wasted his time but Kate said afterwards that some men are like that – unreliable – and not to let it bother me.

I made a cake with caraway seeds in it and wrapped it in greaseproof paper to keep it moist. Flora loves caraway cake. We all do. We were going to have a chicken instead of stew because Kate thought we could be extravagant once in a while. 'Let's be daring!' she laughed and it was good to see her so happy.

'We could have parsnips and potatoes with it,' I suggested and set to with some steel wool to get the grease out of the oven.

The day before Flora was due to arrive she rang again. Five minutes later I found Kate on her knees in the conservatory, breaking bread into a dish of milk for the cats.

'Flora's . . .' It seemed impossible to say. I swallowed and tried again. 'Flora's not coming!'

Kate closed her eyes. The hurt was unbelievable.

'She says he's got bad stomach pains and the doctor's rather worried. Flora said she's terribly sorry but she daren't leave him on his own.'

After a long despairing moment Kate stood up and put her arms round me.

'Don't cry,' she said but she was crying too.

That evening we took the bedspread off the chair and let the cats back into the parlour. I put the photograph back in the drawer. The clean house seemed to mock us. We hardly spoke for the rest of the day.

Next morning at breakfast Kate said, 'Do you believe Flora – about the stomach pains? Could it have been –'

'– an excuse? I was wondering the same thing.' I spread margarine on my bread. 'It didn't have that ring of truth now that I think back. Do you think –'

'– he was really ill?' Her eyes widened. 'Or did he pretend to have pains so that Flora would cancel the visit?'

I nodded. 'I think he might have done. He's that type. Because Flora would want to come. She wanted to see us again. I'm sure she did.'

Thoughtfully Kate sipped hot water and lemon. 'My guess is he always blamed us for spoiling the wedding. He's probably been bearing a grudge ever since and he's been poisoning her mind against us. Or trying to . . . but he didn't succeed because she did write to us five times. Now he's got a guilty conscience and doesn't want to –'

'– accept our hospitality.' I sighed. 'Perhaps he was afraid to show his face. That's the sort of man he is.' I rubbed a small blob of marmalade into the tabletop and watched it blend into the wood. 'Or else . . . *maybe* he didn't want to miss the golf on the television. Do you remember what Flora said in her fourth letter – that he's a golf fanatic? That when he isn't playing golf he's watching it "on the box"?' I looked at her triumphantly. 'That's about it! It didn't occur to him that we might have hired a set especially for their visit!'

'But we haven't.' Kate pressed the lemon slice with a spoon.

'No . . . But we nearly did. He's so selfish. I'm sure that's it. He thought he'd be missing his wretched golf!' Another idea struck me. '*May*be they had a better offer. Maybe some friends invited them to stay with *them* and he thought it would be more exciting than if they came to *us*. More –'

'– fun?'

'Exactly.'

I glanced across at our photographs. The three of us as babies – Mother holding me and Flora, and Father holding Kate. We had identical gowns, white with silver smocking. Then the three of us as toddlers with buckets and spades and sun hats at Margate. Mother always called that photograph 'three peas in a pod'! School photographs and confirmation . . . I sighed. 'We've still got the chicken,' I reminded her. 'At least we won't have to share it with him.'

Kate said, 'Do you think we *should* have gone to the wedding?'

My heart began to race as it always did. We had debated this point over and over again for the past thirty years.

'But we . . . we don't like crowds,' I reminded her.

That had been our excuse – not that anyone believed it. But if we *had* gone . . . Naturally we would have been polite to his parents because it wasn't their fault, but we would never have said a word to him. Not a word. We never have and never will.

I brushed crumbs off the table on to the floor. 'They've probably been invited to a party and he didn't –'

'– want to miss it. Very likely. Flora did say he's always the life and soul of the party.'

'A party animal.' I rolled my eyes. 'That's what Flora called him. He wouldn't mind disappointing Flora if there was a party to go to.'

At the sink, rinsing everything under the tap, Kate said, 'I think he made Flora lie to us about the stomach pains. That's the sort of man he is.'

\*    \*    \*

153

Three days later Flora rang to say he was in hospital having tests.

'Exploratory tests,' I told Kate. 'Something about an ulcer. A stomach ulcer.'

'How did Flora sound?'

I thought about it. 'Worried,' I said at last. 'I think she was crying.'

'Worried about *him*?'

'He is her husband.'

Kate tossed her head. 'She never should have married him. All this worry. All these exploratory tests. Poor Flora!'

Six days later in the early hours of the morning Flora rang to say he was dead. Died in the hospital soon after he'd been admitted. Just before midnight. I put down the telephone and went up to the bedroom to tell Kate. He was dead and I was glad.

I sat on the end of Kate's bed. 'Flora sounded terribly upset. It was a something ulcer – septic or peptic – and something set in. Complications. We're invited to the funeral next Wednesday at three o'clock.'

'Up there?'

'Yes. She said come on the train and she sent us a map to find the house.' I knew it was impossible. We would never find our way to Scotland even with a map. A pity because I'd like to have seen him buried.

'We won't go,' Kate decided. 'We'd get lost and anyway it would be too expensive but we'll send flowers instead.'

The Interflora shop was quite an adventure. It smelled wonderful and there were pretty vases and huge spools of coloured ribbon and flowers everywhere. A woman gave us a big book to look through and Kate decided to send a bouquet instead of a wreath.

The woman opened an order book and found a pen. 'And the flowers?'

Kate hesitated. 'Ten yellow roses.' She glanced at me.

'And ten of those blue flowers.' I pointed.

154

'Irises.' The woman scribbled again in her book. 'Any greenery?'

Kate wasn't listening. She was looking round the shop. 'Ten carnations . . .'

'And ten of those big daisy things . . .'

The woman hesitated, her pen poised. 'The bouquet is going to get a bit unwieldy, if you don't mind me saying so. If it gets too big it can look a bit . . . Well, flashy.'

Kate said, 'Flashy? *Flashy!* . . .' Her eyes widened. 'But that's –'

'– perfect!' I agreed.

The woman looked at us in surprise as we exchanged delighted smiles.

'Flashy.' I fished out our purse and counted out the money. 'That's just the sort of man –'

'– he was!'

# The Cheeseboard

Ending a relationship is never easy. Ros had read enough articles in *Cosmopolitan* to know that. Telling Doug that it was over was going to be one of the hardest things she had ever done because she loved the man. But not enough to spend her life with him. She was so afraid that by refusing him as a husband she would lose him as a friend.

'I want to keep him in my life,' she told Gina earnestly.

'Just tell him!' Gina insisted. 'It's the kindest thing. You think you'll break his heart but men are horribly resilient. You'll probably see him two weeks later arm in arm with another woman, happy as a sandboy!'

Ros shuddered. The idea held no appeal. Doug with another woman?

Gina went on. 'You don't want to settle for a humdrum existence with a man who manages an ironmonger's shop. Tell him you've changed your mind and then get on with your life.'

Gina was always ready to listen and give advice and Ros was grateful. Sitting on the floor in front of Gina's electric fire, sipping cheap sherry and putting the world to rights, Ros had finally admitted the problem. Gina was a friend as well as colleague – they both worked in the bookshop in the High Street – but she was older and wiser and married and Ros felt that with all that experience she should be able to help her.

But now Ros bridled as she always did when someone put down Doug. 'What's wrong with managing an ironmonger's shop? You're such a snob, Gina! Doug does very well. He's so good with the customers and he has a knack with the window display – he changes it every few weeks to tie in with the season or with something special. The jubilee display was mostly purple and gold with a big cardboard crown in the middle. It has to be eye-catching to keep people's attention. He's planning to buy the business when Mr Crewe retires in three years' time.'

'So he's always going to sell ironmongery! Why can't he sell books or antiques . . . or be a jeweller?' Gina's expression was mournful.

'Because he doesn't know anything about those things and he *does* know about ironmongery. He can repair lawnmowers and advise on all sorts of things . . .'

Gina rolled her eyes and with an effort Ros hid her irritation. 'Anyway you can't talk. *You* settled for humdrum. I wouldn't call Tony exciting.'

'Of course he's not but I *wanted* humdrum!' Gina's expression was triumphant. 'I went looking for it. With the life I've had, humdrum was positively *desirable*. For you it obviously isn't.'

Ros understood that argument. Gina's parents had fought like cat and dog for many years before settling for a highly acrimonious divorce and a long-drawn-out custody battle over Gina and her brother. Her uncle had been arrested for arson and falsifying an insurance claim and their mother had married again – a man both children hated. Gina's brother had eventually run away and was still on the missing persons list. For Gina, life with Tony was probably heaven.

Ros's parents, on the other hand, were a happy couple in their fifties. Her mother had given up work when Ros was born and her father, an English teacher, had remained at the same school for twenty-five years and had just made it as Deputy Head. There had been no alarums and Ros had secretly found their lifestyle rather boring. She had hoped for a whirlwind romance with an exciting man who would take her backpacking in Thailand or working for a charity in a mission station somewhere in Africa. Instead she had fallen in love with Doug, who reminded her of her father.

Ros shook her head. 'Doug's mother gave him some pyjamas for his birthday and they're miles too small but he won't take them back to change them. I shall have to do it for him.'

'Avoiding confrontation! Pathetic!'

'And he always wants me to make the decisions. He says, "I want what you want!" It's one of his mantras! The other one is "Whatever makes you happy!"'

Gina shook her head. 'Sounds wonderful but you need someone more decisive. Someone dynamic. Powerful. Write Doug off and start again. Isn't there anyone else in your life? The boy next door, perhaps?'

Ros shrugged. 'Just old Mr Parks.'

'Well, *think*, Ros! Sometimes women ignore the most obvious men. What about that chap you met at the garden centre? You said he hinted that he'd like to take you out for a drink. You see, now he *was* positive. He took the initiative. Seized the moment, as they say.'

'The garden centre? I don't even remember him.' By this time in the conversation Ros was beginning to feel disloyal. She had fallen in love with Doug and hadn't really looked seriously at anyone else since they'd moved in together. Doug was a quiet man with gentle ways. Softly spoken and slow to anger, he never raised his voice when they disagreed but he did have annoying habits. He believed in giving people the benefit of the doubt and seeing both sides of any argument and it drove Ros mad. He also chatted to strangers while they waited at the supermarket checkouts, explaining that he found people fascinating. *But* he loved cooking, which Ros hated, and could turn out a sparkling dinner for six or eight people and still be cheerful at the end of it. Ros, on the other hand, was hugely impatient, inclined to make rash judgements and often dissatisfied with her life and prospects. On the plus side she was fiercely loyal to family and friends, a hard worker and honest as the day is long but she was aware of her shortcomings and often wondered why Doug found her so attractive. They were definitely chalk and cheese.

Three days after her talk with Gina, Ros finally decided to break the news next time they ate out. They had a date arranged already. Unfortunately it was the anniversary of the day she and Doug had first met at a friend's birthday party but now that she had made up her mind, Ros couldn't bear to wait any longer. She wouldn't say that he was not the right man for her. Instead she would be diplomatic and point out that *she* was not the right woman to make *him* happy. If she put it in those words Doug wouldn't feel a failure. Ros wanted to save him hurt or humiliation and she had convinced herself that dealing with it in a public place would make both of them behave better. No tears and no recriminations.

Doug had made a booking for eight o'clock at a small restaurant in the nearby town. They had never dined there before and Ros was interested to see the venue Doug had chosen. It turned out to be a confused bistro-like place with French-style checked tablecloths and Country and Western music. As soon as they sat down Doug touched her hand and said, 'Happy anniversary, Ros!' and smiled the sweet smile that had touched her heart all those years ago.

She said, 'Ditto,' and returned the smile and then they waited for someone to take the order. It seemed so relaxed and natural to be with Doug that Ros's resolve was already beginning to weaken.

Watch it! she told herself. Gina had warned her: 'Whatever happens, make sure you say your piece!'

An unsmiling waitress brought the menus and they deliberated for a few minutes until she returned, notebook and biro in hand.

'So?' she demanded. She was probably nearing twenty, short and shapeless with brown eyes. Her dark hair was scraped back into an untidy mass which was held by double-toothed tortoiseshell comb. She seemed to be a girl of few words.

Ros guessed that Doug would choose tomato soup and watched with dismay as he did so. He always opted for soup of the day. The girl wrote carefully in her book. Ros chose spinach and red pepper roulade. 'Sounds exciting,' she told Doug.

He was grinning. 'I knew you'd go for the roulade. You never go for "tried and true". You're always wanting to try something new.'

Ros was startled. Had he started reading her mind? 'Why don't *you* try something different?' she asked. It sounded more challenging than she had intended.

Doug shrugged good-naturedly. 'I know exactly what I want, so why order something I might hate?'

It came promptly and they ate in silence. For a main course he had chosen pork chop with mashed potato and peas. To shame him, Ros had chosen goat's cheese in filo pastry with wild rice and some exotic mushrooms although she wasn't keen on rice. When it arrived it proved to be disappointing but when Doug asked her she said, 'Delicious!' because her mind was on other things and because she didn't want him to gloat. Tried and true, indeed! But back to the matter in hand. Get it over with, Ros! she told herself. There's going to be no good time to tell him.

Swallowing a mouthful of cheesy pastry, she laid a hand on Doug's arm.

'Doug, I have to tell you something,' she began gently. 'I've been thinking for some time now . . . about us, I mean . . .'

'So have I!' His smile broadenend.

'No, Doug. Please let me have my say. What I mean is that you and I—'

'Don't you want to know what I've decided?'

Ros counted to ten. Doug deciding something? Unlikely. She couldn't understand the gleam in his eyes. 'You're not listening, Doug,' she told him firmly. 'I'm trying to tell you *my* thoughts and . . . and I feel the time for—'

The waitress loomed up. 'OK?'

Ros snapped, 'Fine!'

'Only asking!' She tossed her head and walked away.

Two women on the next table pretended not to notice the exchange.

Doug gave Ros a mildly reproachful look. 'They have to ask.'

'I'm trying to talk to you, Doug. She's getting on my nerves.'

He lowered his voice. 'I think she might be pregnant.'

'So why the long face?'

He tapped his ring finger and whispered, 'No wedding ring!'

Reluctant to be sidetracked, Ros pressed on. 'Doug, I think when we were first together we were a little . . . star-struck. With each other I mean. Carried away by the excitement.'

'Exactly!'

'We weren't looking ahead but now . . . I think we have to ask ourselves where this is going and the answer . . .'

'I've been thinking the self-same thing!' he told her cheerfully.

The girl reappeared, notebook and biro at the ready. 'Didn't you want wine?'

Doug blinked. 'Wine? Of course!'

'You should have said.' Her tone was accusing.

Ros said, '*You* should have asked!'

Ignoring her contribution, the waitress looked pointedly at Doug, who looked at Ros and said, 'What do you fancy, Ros?'

What Ros fancied was to be able to finish her little speech and without even looking at the wine list she said, 'Mateus Rose,' because that was the one Doug liked.

While the girl wrote carefully, Doug said, 'This chop's great. Not everyone can cook a chop, especially pork. They can be very tough but this is perfect.'

He looked ridiculously happy.

When they were again alone, Ros put her knife and fork together. 'I'm so full up!' she lied. 'Look, Doug, what I'm trying to say is—'

Doug swallowed and smiled. 'I know what you're saying and I agree entirely. There comes a time when you have to take stock and this is it. We'll make it official. Tell all our friends.'

The waitress was back with the wine. She glared at the food which remained on Ros's plate.

'Didn't you like it?'

161

'I'm rather full.' After telling Doug it was delicious she could hardly admit that she hadn't enjoyed it but the small lie rankled. She was also appalled by Doug's lack of understanding of the situation.

'Chef makes it fresh every day.' The waitress snatched up the plate and stalked back to the kitchen.

Ros caught the eye of one of the women at the next table and said, 'No gold star for me, then!' and they both laughed. To Doug she said, 'I hope we're not going to give the waitress a tip. Pregnant or not she's awful.'

'Probably having a bad day. She must have worries like everyone else.'

Groaning inwardly, Ros tried again. Leaning forward she said, 'The point is, Doug, that I'm feeling very unsure about us. Very unhappy, if you must know. I'm not sure that I'm the right woman for you . . . or that you're the right man for me. We are so different . . .'

She stopped, distracted by Doug's puzzled expression. 'But that *is* the point! It's the attraction of opposites. It's what keeps relationships alive! Think how boring it would be if we were like two peas in a pod. Unthinkable!'

Ros closed her eyes. For heaven's sake! They were going round in circles. This was not how she had expected the discussion to develop. She had meant to be crisp and positive but the thought of breaking Doug's heart was making it difficult and here she was, still pussyfooting around.

She took a deep breath and said, 'Doug, this isn't easy to say but the truth is I don't want to mar—'

She was interrupted by the arrival of the cheeseboard. The waitress banged it down on the table and stood back. Ros and Doug looked at it with dismay. It contained two sticks of celery, a large wedge of Stilton, a very small slice of Brie and a piece of dried-up Cheddar. Six water biscuits had been spread out in a fan to fill the remaining space. The last of Ros's patience evaporated instantly.

As the waitress turned to go Ros said, 'One moment, please!' Doug would never forgive her, she thought, but this wretched woman was not going to get away with it. This was such a shoddy offering. She, Ros, was going to make a scene and Doug would have to put up with it. Perhaps it would finally make him realize that she was not his kind of woman. Her throat tightened in anticipation. She would put this dreadful girl in her place once and for all.

Ros began, 'I'm sorry but—'

The girl sighed theatrically. 'Now what?'

'I'm not satisfied with this cheeseboard. I think it's rather insulting to expect your diners . . .' She faltered.

She had expected the girl to be cowed by her authoritative tone but instead she put her hands on her hips and the button brown eyes flashed angrily.

'Not *satisfied*? It's *you* that's being insulting! The trouble with your sort is that—'

Shocked, Ros felt her face burn but immediately Doug's large hand, warm and reassuring, slid over hers.

To the waitress he said quietly, 'I'll ask you not to speak to my girlfriend like that. She is quite right. The cheeseboard *is* unsatisfactory. Unappealing, to say the least. Perhaps you would be kind enough—'

The girl swung round to her new tormentor, bristling like an angry dog. 'You in it as well, are you? Well, if you don't like it, don't blame me 'cos I didn't—'

'We're not blaming anyone but this is hardly a decent selection. There is very little choice . . .'

Ros, astonished, watched Doug as he battled on.

'. . . almost no Brie, the small piece of Cheddar is dry and—'

All heads were turning towards the argument and Ros was well aware of the agony this must be causing Doug. She imagined him cringing inwardly but he showed no sign of backing down. She sat back in her chair, soothed by the firm pressure of Doug's hand.

The waitress now folded her arms like a belligerent washerwoman in an early *Punch* cartoon. 'No selection? There's three bits of cheese. That's a selection, isn't it? You're the gentleman, so let the lady choose first.'

Doug's hand trembled slightly but he held the girl's stare. 'And if she chooses the Brie and the Cheddar?'

'Then you can have the Stilton. There's plenty of that one.'

'And if I don't like Stilton?'

'*If*,' she pounced. 'Do you or don't you?'

'I do, as it happens, but I should have a choice.' Doug gave her a patient smile. 'One piece of Stilton, however large, is not a choice. There should be enough cheese so that we can both choose something we like. That is the idea of a cheese-board.'

Ros held her breath. How could he remain so calm? She would have throttled the girl by this time. Perhaps he *was* wasted on ironmongery, she reflected. He would make a wonderful teacher.

The waitress had flushed angrily and now tossed her head. 'My God, you lot really are—'

With a thud Doug brought his fist down on to the table so that the cutlery jangled and the waitress jumped back in alarm. The room was suddenly silent as everyone waited for the outcome of the battle.

Doug picked up the cheeseboard and handed it to the wait-ress. With admirable restraint he said, 'Please take this to the chef and suggest that he might improve the selection. I'm sure he'll be understanding.'

The waitress was tightlipped and furious. Doug appeared calm but a fine perspiration had broken out on his forehead. Ros resisted the urge to fly to his defence. This was his battle and somehow she knew that it was important to him. The room waited.

The waitress broke first. Snatching the cheeseboard from Doug's hand, she muttered something, fortunately inaudible, flounced off between the tables and retreated into the kitchen. A low ripple of applause swept through the room and Doug half stood to make a humorous bow.

Laughing, he reached for his handkerchief and wiped his forehead.

Awed, Ros said, 'You were fantastic, Doug!'

164

He swallowed hard. 'Don't cheer too soon. We haven't got the Mark Two cheeseboard yet. In fact we might not get any cheese at all! But while we still live in hope . . .' He pulled a small red box from his pocket and held it out to Ros. 'I do love you, Ros.'

She opened it with trembling fingers. The ring was set with alternate rubies and diamonds on a chased gold band.

'They can alter it if it doesn't fit.'

She looked at him with shining eyes. 'I take it you're proposing to me.'

He nodded. 'I believe I can make you happy.'

Briefly Ros closed her eyes. Thank God for the awful cheeseboard! If she had finished her sentence . . .

'I'd love to marry you, Doug. And this is beautiful. Will you . . . ?' She handed the ring to him and with a minimum of trouble, he eased it on to her finger.

'Chef says to say he's sorry.' The girl was back clutching the renewed cheeseboard. 'He hopes this will—'

She broke off, startled, as Ros stood up and moved round the table to kiss Doug. Catching sight of the empty ring box, her eyes widened. She said, 'Are you two . . . ?' and Ros, nodding, held out her hand to show off her ring.

'Ooh! That's lovely!'

Doug took the cheeseboard from her and said, 'So is this! Thank you for going to so much trouble for us. Look Ros! Chef's given you your favourite – Dolcelatte!'

So gracious in victory, thought Ros, regarding him with growing admiration. She felt incredibly lucky to be marrying such a man.

There were two other fresh cheeses on the board and a small bunch of black grapes. The biscuits were in a small basket.

Taking a leaf from Doug's book, Ros smiled at the waitress. 'A special cheeseboard for a special evening. Thank you.'

'Did he propose? In here?'

Ros laughed. 'At this very table!'

A beaming smile transformed the girl's face. 'I must tell Chef!' she cried and rushed back to the kitchen.

As Ros helped herself to cheese and biscuits the coffee arrived and the rest of the meal passed in a delightful whirl of plans for the future, but Ros secretly acknowledged that she had come perilously close to making a serious mistake. First thing in the morning she would telephone Gina and ask her to be a bridesmaid.

# The Morning After

Annie woke and stretched, a broad smile on her face. This was the morning she'd been looking forward to for months. The morning after her son's wedding. It was all over – 'bar the shouting', as her mother would have said if she'd lived long enough to see her grandson married. Not that she would have approved entirely of the bride. Leila was training to be a solicitor and would have been deemed 'too clever by half'. Annie's mother had been hopelessly old-fashioned and thought wives ought to stay at home and cook and sew and look after her man. As Annie had done.

Her gaze settled on her wedding outfit – pale-blue lace – which hung from the picture rail and moved on to Edmund's suit laid carefully across the armchair. Her delicately strapped shoes might never be worn again because Patrick was their only child and there would be no more weddings. Unless she were to be invited to a garden party at Buckingham Palace, when the shoes would come into their own. Edmund's joke. Smiling, she slid from the bed.

Padding across to the mirror, Annie surveyed her plump radiant face with satisfaction. Their son was happily married (or one hoped so!) and she and Edmund were free to enjoy their retirement. Squinting shortsightedly at her reflection, she remembered that she hadn't even bothered to remove her make-up when she finally fell into bed in the early hours of the morning.

'Mucky pup!' she told herself and found cream and cotton wool and did a quick repair job. She could hear Edmund downstairs grinding coffee for the first jug of the day. Today, she decided, she would treat herself to a spoonful of sugar. She deserved a treat after the hours of frantic preparation she had invested in the wedding. Patrick's announcement that he was going to make an honest woman of his girlfriend had taken them by surprise and it had been a terrific scramble. Leila had wanted a white wedding in church complete with bridesmaids, photographers, a hundred guests, a romantic honeymoon in Spain . . .

Edmund at the bottom of the stairs shouted, 'Coffee!' and she could hear weariness in his tone. A holiday would do them both good but for some reason Edmund had resisted the idea. Maybe not resisted, exactly, but had shown a surprising lack of interest. Probably his age. They were both in their early sixties, having met and married late.

Pulling on her fluffy pink housecoat, Annie made her way down to the kitchen, where Edmund sat slumped at the table, both hands round his coffee as though for warmth. But this was mid June.

She dropped a quick kiss on the back of her husband's head and settled in her own chair. 'You OK, Ed?'

'Not particularly.'

Too much to drink the day before, she thought but said nothing. He and Patrick had been close. He was probably aware that with the wedding over their own lives were going to change. Edmund had always feared change.

She said, 'It's not going to be that different, Ed. Patrick flew the nest two years ago. He only slept here occasionally . . . and we shall see them. They're not a million miles away. More like seven.'

He grunted by way of reply.

Leila had sold her flat and she and Patrick had bought a bungalow, which they had redecorated together. Annie and Edmund had helped on a few occasions but the paint gave Edmund a headache, so they gave that up and Annie made the curtains for the lounge windows while Edmund seeded the tiny lawn and bedded down primulas.

Now she said, 'The best man's speech went down well,

don't you think? Considering how nervous he was. Poor old Leo!' She smiled. 'And Leila's mother looked very nice.'

'Stepmother.'

'Oh yes. I always forget.'

And the two little bridesmaids in their frilly dresses and mob caps . . . 'I can't wait to see the photographs. The photographer was everywhere. I couldn't fault him. Whatever he charged, it was worth it.'

She glanced at Edmund, disappointed by his silence. Had he overdone it yesterday, dancing until nearly one, refusing to give up and leave it to the youngsters? She had only just averted a disaster by dragging him off to bed. He'd behaved very badly, flirting outrageously with Margot and trying to pick a quarrel with Luke. Poor Patrick was furious. Humiliating to have your father making a spectacle of himself. Edmund wasn't good with alcohol and never had been but this time she had promised herself 'no recriminations'. The morning after was a time to be cherished. The chances are Edmund wouldn't remember his behaviour and she was feeling magnanimous. If you couldn't get a little drunk at your son's wedding it was a sad affair.

'Did you take your Andrews?' she asked, blowing on the coffee. 'That usually settles—'

He looked up. 'Does it really matter, Annie? In the scheme of things? For heaven's sake!'

She blinked. Had she missed something? 'Which scheme of things?'

'Please, Annie! All I ask is a few minutes peace and quiet!'

Annie looked at him carefully. Was he spoiling for a fight? Lately he had been so irritable but that was to be expected with so much to think about. He had hated all the fuss. Lists and more lists. Invitations. Meeting Leila's parents for dinner. Choosing a florist. Seating arrangements. Hiring a disco for the evening. Annie had thrived on the excitement but Edmund had complained, refusing to enter into the spirit of the event. Even whingeing about the cost although they were comfortably off. Perhaps he needed to eat something after all that wine.

'Shall I make some toast?'

'No thanks.'

'A toasted teacake?'

'No!'

Count to ten, she told herself. Allowing a few moments to pass, Annie walked with her coffee into the conservatory and stared across the immaculate garden. Most of it was hidden by the large marquee which had housed the wedding. It had been so pretty. Fairyland. She smiled at the notion. She had taken so many photographs of the marquee from inside and out. The weather had been perfect and inside, the pale green silk panels and yellow ribbons had made it magical. 'Mystical!' Margot had called it. Annie's face softened. Margot and Luke had paid for the flights to Malaga for the bride and groom. Their wedding present. They had no family of their own and had volunteered to be godparents the moment Patrick was born.

Annie took several deep breaths and decided not to let Edmund's mood affect her own. Instead she focused on the wedding. The meal had been a great success. Cold meats including wonderfully tender beef, pork and turkey. Salmon and huge seafood platters with salads followed by various ice creams, gateaux, strawberries, chocolate torte and lashings of cream.

'I ate too much,' she murmured, 'but it was heaven.' Her diet had lasted for five months.

'High Days', the caterers from Canterbury, had been recommended by a friend of Luke's. And all at a very reasonable price. Thank goodness for a spacious lawn. The marquee had been large enough to seat everyone comfortably with no cramped elbows to make eating difficult.

Turning, Ann glanced back into the kitchen. Edmund hadn't moved. A sudden thought occurred. Had he really overdone it? Was he ill? He'd been complaining about headaches for weeks but refused to see the doctor. His usual reaction to any form of ailment was to ignore it until it went away.

'Probably stress,' he'd told her. 'I've got a lot on my mind.'

But stress was inevitable because he owned a small iron-monger's shop and hated to delegate the work to his staff – two full-timers and a school-leaver on Saturdays. She went back inside and poured herself a second coffee. Start again, she told herself.

'Well, it went off very well, didn't it, dear? Everyone enjoyed themselves.'

'I should hope so. It cost enough.'

'Patrick looked wonderfully happy . . . and Leila. She's a very sweet girl.'

'Look, Annie, I have to say something . . .'

Surprised and pleased, she sat down. He was going to apologize. So he *had* remembered. Maybe he was turning over a new leaf. She put a hand over his.

'It doesn't matter,' she said. 'Forgiven and forgotten. Let's talk about a holiday. We both need a break. I went into Thomas Cook's last week and—'

'I've told you, Annie. No holiday.'

She stood up, partly to hide her annoyance. Their first official day on their own and they mustn't quarrel. 'I'm having some toast. D'you—'

'For heaven's sake, Ann!' He never called her anything but Annie and she felt a frisson of alarm. 'I do not want any toast or teacakes or cheese biscuits or . . . or anything else you have to offer!'

'Anything else I . . . What's that supposed to mean?'

'Nothing. Can't you see I'm . . . I'm so bloody . . . sorry!'

Annie's hands shook as she unwrapped the loaf and slid two slices into the toaster. He *was* ill. She closed her eyes. A spectre from the past raised its ugly head. His grandfather had been a manic depressive. Edmund's boyhood had been filled with alarming whispers and hints about the condition. Was this irritability a symptom? Was it hereditary? How cruel of fate to choose this moment . . . but whatever it was they would survive it. Had he been to the doctor without telling her? Maybe he had put off telling her because of the wedding? That would be so like him. All those headaches . . . a brain disorder? Or maybe his heart. Her father had been very irritable before his heart condition was diagnosed and his own sweet self again after the operation. Oh God! She would stay calm and be reassuring and help Edmund to face whatever was around the corner.

He was looking at her with a peculiar expression.

'Tell me, Edmund,' she said softly. 'Everything. You're ill, I can tell.'

'I'm not ill.' He rewrapped the loaf as the bread popped from the toaster.

Annie ignored it. 'Tell me, darling. Please.'

After a long silence he said, 'I don't know how. I want to spare you but . . .'

'Spare me from what? Edmund, the not knowing is the worst.'

'Do you really think so?' His mouth trembled. 'I can't go on holiday with you because I won't be around. I'm going to— I won't be with you, Annie.'

The room seemed to spin and she found it difficult to focus in the darkness which followed his words. It was worse than she had expected. He had only a few months to live. Or weeks.

She whispered, 'Oh darling! No!' and then she thought of Patrick. 'Does anyone else know? Patrick?' But that was impossible. Her son had been so happy yesterday. Thank goodness he had Leila now.

'Patrick knows. He saw us together. I asked him not to say anything.'

Annie frowned. Now she was really out of her depth. 'He knows you are dying? He *knows*? How could he have put on such a brave show?

'Dying? I'm not dying. I'm . . .'

Her mind was slowly replaying his previous sentence . . . 'saw us together'. She said 'Saw who?'

'Me and . . . Annie darling, I'm sorry but I'm leaving you.'

'What are you talking about, Ed? You're not making any sense.'

Edmund wasn't dying. Cling on to that, she told herself. It was a reprieve.

She watched as he twisted the wire tie to keep the loaf together, his familiar fingers trembling. He went on, 'I want you to know that I didn't want this to happen. Neither of us did. It just happened.'

Stricken, Annie clasped her hands so tightly that her knuckles were pale. 'You're *leaving* me? But why? Everything's fine. We're happy . . . aren't we?'

She had the feeling that she was watching this happen to someone else. 'Who is "neither of us"? Do you mean another woman?'

'It's Margot. I'm sorry.'

She stared, trying to understand. 'Margot? *Our* Margot? Luke's Margot? Oh no, Edmund! You couldn't!'

But the expression on his face said it all. He had. They had. The knowledge crushed all the breath from her lungs. For a moment she was unable to speak. Then she gasped, 'Does Luke know?'

Edmund glanced at his watch. 'Yes. He does now. Margot told him at eight o'clock. We agreed a time.'

She was appalled by this small detail. 'You agreed to tell us at a certain time?' She thought of Luke across the road at number 8. 'You synchronized your watches? For heaven's sake, Ed! It's not a military operation! For Christ's sake! You . . . you bastard! And Margot! How long has this been going on?' She was aware of a creeping anger. Shock, hurt, rage and above all fear – all mingling, sending the blood rushing round her body. Adrenaline pumping through her veins as the enormity of the crisis struck home. She snatched the loaf from Edmund's twitching fingers and threw it on to the floor.

She was trying to find some terrible words to hurl at her husband but she was unused to serious confrontation. She longed to cry but her eyes remained dry and her throat was tight with emotion. Her mind whirled. There must be a way out of this. There must surely be a way to resolve it. Edmund and Margot? No. And yet . . . Her eyes widened. No wonder Edmund had been flirting with Margot yesterday – and trying to quarrel with Luke. He knew it didn't matter any more. They

173

were going to break up both marriages anyway. He and Margot had been living the last few hours of their old lives. Today would be different.

She stammered, 'I thought . . . thought you were drunk. All that kissing and cuddling!'

How was Luke taking it? she wondered. Was he, too, shattered by the news? When had it all started? Annie couldn't believe she had missed the signs. The four of them had spent their holidays together each summer in a rented villa in Sorrento. Had Edmund and Margot been lovers there? Had they gone off together on some excuse or other? She tried to replay last year's holiday. And the summer before that? It was all so incredible.

She watched Edmund and the thought occurred that this might be, must be, a nightmare.

He muttered, 'For God's sake!' and retrieved the loaf. Set it on the table. 'There's no need for histrionics, Annie.'

No need? There was every need. If Annie stopped feeling angry she would die of misery. The thought of life without Edmund was impossible. They had plans. She didn't want to be alone. How would they manage? How could she bear it? The sympathy from her friends . . . And how many of those friends were already in on the secret? How many had been chatting to each other in shocked voices, sympathizing with her, but saying nothing to her face? Had anyone been different to her lately? Had Margot been different?

Edmund said, 'Don't you want the toast?' He hated waste.

'Damn the toast!' She leaped from her chair, snatched the toast from the toaster and threw it into the pedal bin. She sat down again, trembling. Edmund came round the table to put an arm round her shoulder but she pushed it away. 'Don't you dare touch me!'

Edmund backed away, leaning back against the sink. 'We want you to know that you'll never want for anything. We'll make proper provision.'

'How very sweet of you both!' She couldn't believe her ears. She thought of them, their heads together, making plans for poor Annie, the deserted wife. The betrayed friend. 'I don't believe Margot would do this to me,' she said. 'My closest friend. For more than twenty years. I trusted her.'

'Don't blame Margot,' he said quietly. 'This has been my doing from the start. She tried to stop it as soon as she realized how strongly I felt. She thought it was simply a holiday fling. A bit of madness. Margot didn't want us to break up – any of us. She even tried to persuade Luke that they should move right away to give us all a chance. She pretended she wanted to move to Cornwall to be nearer her mother.'

'I remember that. That was ages ago. So it's been going on for years!'

'I wouldn't let her go. I said that if she tried to leave me I would tell you and Luke about us. She's not a bad person. It was me. I have to be with her. She loves me, Annie, but she fought against it. She really did try to talk me out of it.'

'She didn't try hard enough!' Annie snapped. Nothing her husband said would restore Margot in her eyes.

'Annie, it wasn't my choice either. I didn't fall out of love with you. You've been a wonderful wife and mother. I simply fell hopelessly in love with her . . . It's been an agony all these years until I finally persuaded her that we were meant for each other. That it would be worth all the heartache.'

'And you think you'll be happy together after all this? After hurting us so badly?'

'We have to try. It's our decision.' He sat down again.

He looked haggard but Annie resisted the temptation to feel sorry for him. He could hardly feel worse than she did.

He said, 'Look Annie, it's not so bad. I'll get you a solicitor and—'

'I'll get my own solicitor, thank you, Edmund!'

'You can keep the house. And there's Luke. He'll be across the street. He'll help you. He'll—'

'When did Patrick see you and Margot?'

'Does it matter?'

'To me it does. Yes.'

'A few weeks ago. We were coming out of a pub in Brighton.

He was coming in with a group of chaps from his office. They went in and he came back out and found us getting into the car. He was furious. We had a stand-up row.'

She frowned. 'Was that when he went to stay with Leo for a few days? I thought that was odd.' Leo only lived a few streets away. 'He should have told me,' she muttered.

'He didn't want to ruin the wedding for you or Leila or anybody.'

Where had he said he was going? Annie tried to focus her confused thoughts. Ah! The medical check-up. Blood pressure and lungs. She'd protested mildly when he mentioned it, certain that it was a six-monthly check-up and that only four months had passed from the previous one. What had been Margot's excuse? Lunch with one of her girlfriends, probably. Luke wouldn't have questioned it.

'So where are *you* going to live?' she demanded. She must learn as much as possible before he left. If he was going to disappear she might never see him again – unless he appeared in court to contest something or other. She would insist on an address.

He hesitated. Annie tried to imagine him at breakfast with Margot. It wasn't difficult. They would be radiant. In love and so pleased with themselves. Margot was five years younger than Edmund and she was plumply pretty in a blowsy rose way. Margot and Edmund would smile at each other over the toast and cornflakes and congratulate themselves that they had finally shucked off the spouses.

'We're going to Sorrento. There's a small villa—'

'You've already bought a villa? Jesus Christ! I don't think I know you, Edmund. All this sneaking around. This secrecy. Treachery, I suppose it is. You're unbelievable. Both of you.' Had he gradually removed the money from their account? Had Margot done the same? Without warning, tears sprang into her eyes and rolled down her face. She searched for a handkerchief in the pocket of her housecoat but found it empty. Edmund handed her a handtowel but she waved it away and fled upstairs to the bathroom, where she locked the door. She snatched sheets of toilet paper from the roll and tried to stem the flow of tears but while she did so her mind was sharpening. Perhaps she should go across to Margot and beg her to change her mind. Or threaten them. No divorce. They would have to live in sin – but would they care? They may not even want to marry. A villa in Sorrento. That was what she and Edmund had talked about for years. A second home with a spare bedroom for Margot and Luke!

Was there a big argument going on in their kitchen? she wondered. Luke wouldn't be sitting in the bathroom with handfuls of loo rolls but he would be devastated.

'Perhaps I should get dressed and go over there.' Perhaps she would insist that she and Luke talk somewhere alone.

The telephone rang and she knew at once it would be Patrick. She rushed downstairs and snatched it from Edmund's hand.

'Mum? Are you all right?' He sounded so afraid. 'Dad and Margot!'

This must be awful for him. She mustn't let him know she'd been crying.

'I'm going to be fine,' she told him. 'It's been a terrible shock. I'm sorry you had to find out the way you did. But we'll sort something out. I'll get a good solicitor. You forget all about it, love. Enjoy your honeymoon. What's the weather like?'

'Hot and sunny. But you will be there, won't you, when we get back? At home. Nothing sudden is going to happen, is it? I'll help you all I can. I can't forgive him, Dad I mean, or Margot. Poor Luke. Leila's in a bit of a state. She blames Dad for spoiling everything for us.'

'Oh darling!' I closed my eyes. 'Tell her to put it all out of her mind. And you do the same. These things happen but people survive. It's not the end of the world. It's not even your problem and you must enjoy your honeymoon. Now don't waste any more money on this phone call, Patrick. We'll talk when you get home. And it will be OK. I mean it. You're not to worry. Give my love to Leila and thank you for phoning.' She put the phone down before he could notice the shake in her voice.

'It's not the end of the world,' she repeated bitterly. 'Well, it certainly feels a lot like it! Could the end of the world be any worse?' She went back upstairs and stood under the shower for twice as long as usual. Then she dressed carefully and did her hair, took great care with her make-up and added perfume. Regarding herself critically, she told herself she didn't look so bad in the circumstances. Not bad for a woman of fifty-nine whose life was falling apart. She wondered if Luke had had his suspicions before this morning. Was that why he and Edmund had been snarling at each other last night?

Feeling a little stronger, Annie went back to the kitchen where Edmund was wiping down the draining board as though nothing had happened.

Without meaning to she said, 'Is this truly what you want, Edmund? You're not going to regret it, are you?'

He turned slowly. 'I want it more than anything else in my whole life. I'm sorry but that's how it is. I adore her, Annie.'

'And you've stopped loving me?'

'I'm sorry but I have.'

'I want to be sure of that. I wouldn't want to fight for our marriage if you have no feelings for me. I have my pride, Edmund.'

There was a long silence. 'Annie, we've had a great marriage but it's over. I don't love you the way I love her and I don't want to live with you any more. I've been counting the days.'

'And Margot is a hundred per cent with you on this? She wants to leave Luke?'

He nodded. 'I can't expect you to understand or sympathize but we're like a couple of kids waiting for Christmas.'

'So there's no going back. I see.' She nodded, numb inside. 'I'm going over to speak to Margot and don't try and stop me, Ed. I'm entitled to have my say after all she and I have been to each other.'

'Not without me! I'm coming.'

'You're not dressed and I'm not waiting for you.' Gulping for air, Annie wondered frantically what she would actually say – and whether she would be able to say it. Her throat was

178

tight and her heart raced. How would Margot look? And Luke?

Edmund made a grab at her, clinging to her arm. With her free hand she slapped his face and he released her, shocked by her behaviour. Annie backed towards the front door. 'Margot doesn't need you to hold her hand! If I can deal with all this, so can she!'

He stared at her dumbly as she reached blindly for the door handle. As she closed the front door she caught a glimpse of Edmund taking the stairs two at a time, no doubt to shower and dress and hurry after her. Afraid of what she would say or do. Afraid she would upset his precious Margot. Afraid of coming face to face with Luke. As she ran down the steps she became aware of a commotion across the street. An ambulance and a police car were drawn up outside Margot and Luke's house and a small crowd had gathered. Hesitating, she turned back but she had locked herself out so called through the letterbox.

'Edmund! Something's wrong! Hurry!'

But she didn't wait. She ran across the wide grass verge Ed had mowed in preparation for the wedding, she crossed the road and caught sight of Luke dressed as usual in jeans and a turtleneck. He was staring into the rear of the ambulance beside a young police constable who was speaking into his walkie-talkie. She ran up to Luke. 'What's happened?' she cried. 'Is it Margot? Is she hurt?' Had he lost his temper with her? Struck her, maybe?

He was very pale, stunned. Without turning his head he said, 'An overdose.'

'Oh no!' An overdose. Not Margot. Not cheerful, bubbly Margot.

The medic slammed the ambulance doors shut, walked round to the front and climbed into the driving seat. Luke turned slowly to Annie and his grey eyes were dark with shock and grief. 'She told me last night, after we got home. She couldn't wait. About her and Ed. We had a row. I went to bed and she wouldn't sleep with me. She said she'd sleep on the sofa. I had no idea. When I woke up . . .'

Annie put an arm round his waist. 'Ed's only just told me.' Around them the spectators were drifting away, urged on by the policeman. Annie said, 'I don't know what to say. I was going to confront her. I wanted to – to shake some sense into her . . . Oh Luke, how *could* they?'

Luke shook his head. 'I was being to wonder about them. Little things that made me uneasy.'

'I had no idea. None at all . . . But she will be all right?'

'Margot? Of course she won't. She's dead. I told you. She took—'

Annie's heart almost stopped beating. 'Dead? She's *dead*? Oh my God, Luke!'

'I told you . . . She left a note saying she just couldn't do it. Couldn't hurt us. You and me. She was already dead when I found her. On the floor. She must have waited for me to fall asleep and then taken them.' Turning, he saw the anguish in Annie's eyes and put his arms round her in a brief hug. 'She said she didn't love me. Never could again.'

'Edmund said the same thing to me. Almost word for word. I was coming over . . . Oh Luke! What a mess everything is – and there's Edmund! He's looking over here. Poor man.'

Dully they watched the ambulance drive away. The police constable said, 'I'm afraid I'll have to trouble you for a statement, sir. Here or down at the station. Later today if you prefer it. It's been a shock for you.'

Luke looked at him blankly. Then he turned and stared back at his home. 'Not . . . not there,' he stammered. 'I can't go back in there. Not yet.'

Annie said, 'If you want to go to the police station and get it over with I'll come with you.' To the policeman she said, 'Is that allowed? I'm a family friend.'

'No problem. We'll run you both down and bring you back.' He indicated the police car and they stumbled towards it, her arm still round Luke's waist. Like walking wounded, Annie thought – which they were. She was aware of a rush of bitterness. As the car drew away she glanced back in time to see Edmund running across the road to three people still in a huddle outside number 10. One of them pointed at the police car.

Annie said, 'Someone's told him.'

Edmund stood frozen, his face a mask of horror and then he began to run after the car.

Luke turned to follow her gaze. 'I've nothing to say to him. Not ever.' His voice was harsh.

Annie still couldn't believe the speed of the disaster. The morning after the wedding had changed everything for all of them. Margot was gone. Edmund alone. She and Luke trying to come to turn with betrayal and loss.

'Poor Ed!' Annie whispered but already the stumbling figure, dwindling into the distance, looked sadly unfamiliar as if the events of the past hours had turned him into a stranger.

# A Real Gentleman

It's a nice-looking clock. One of those with no hands. The numbers are all in squares and different bits of the square glow so you can see which number it is. Very modern, I grant you. Digital. I think that's the word.

We all got a lecture on it when I turned up for work Tuesday afternoon.

'It's state of the art,' Mr Barnes told us. 'No one's to touch it except me. Cost an arm and a leg, if you must know.'

We all nodded except Evie. She's the secretary and a bit of a smart alec. She's pretty and she knows it. Dark hair cut in one of those styles where the hair keeps falling over one eye. I never did reckon it but it suits her in a funny way. She said, 'Looks expensive.' Meaning the clock.

She's a bit on the flirty side and I do wonder if she and Alan . . . but maybe not. Arthur, my husband, says I think too much and maybe he's right.

'It keeps split-second timing.'

Poor Mr Barnes. He was so proud of his clock, I could tell, but trying not to show it. You see, I know him through and through. I've been cleaning the office for nearly sixteen years – an hour a day several days a week, after they've all gone home – and I understand him. I think he understands me. Always a 'Good morning, Mrs Greaves'. Nice manners. Never uses bad language. Never tells smutty jokes. Old-fashioned, I suppose, in a way, but I like that.

Young Ben said, 'Split-second timing? Like they do in the Grand Prix? You know, pit stops and lap times and all that. A hundredth of a second.'

I make allowances for young Ben. He's seventeen and the
office junior, come straight from school. Funny-looking lad
with a weird hairdo. Cut very short with a bit at the front that
sticks up. His nose is turned up too which makes him look
even younger than he is and I do wonder somehow whether
Mr Barnes will ever make anything of him. He's too kind for
his own good, that man.

Evie said, 'We'll all have to be on time now then.' She's
got this silly smirk, grinning round at the others, but I can see
right through her. She's making fun of Mr Barnes and thinks
he can't see it.

Mr Barnes gave her a straight look. 'That would be nice,
Evie. Make a change for you, wouldn't it?'

It seems the clock came from Heathside's in the High Street.
A very posh shop. It does look good but not much like a clock.
Like something from another planet really. All silvery with
black buttons. It's electric and Mr Barnes made a great show
of plugging it in and setting it up on the shelf to one side of
his desk.

Alan said, 'My sister bought an electronic organizer from
Heathside's and had no end of trouble with it.'

Trust him to throw a damper on everything. Alan Deeds is
the junior partner since he passed his exam a few weeks ago.
His third attempt. He's shaved off his beard for some reason
but he looked better with it on.

I smiled. 'I shan't lay a finger on it, Mr Barnes,' I told him,
meaning the clock. I was trying to set an example and show
some respect. Young people these days don't know the
meaning of the word.

He gave me a quick smile and it always makes him look
years younger. Not that he's old – a few years younger than
me, I suppose – but his hair's going very thin and he wears
old-fashioned glasses.

After a bit more chat about the clock everyone drifted off
home and I was left to get on with the cleaning. It's a nice
little job – dusting, emptying the waste-paper bins and sometimes a bit of hoovering. Whenever I empty Evie's bin I see

lipsticky dog ends so I know she smokes the odd ciggie, as she calls it. Mr Barnes would go mad if he knew because a few months ago he put up a *No Smoking* sign and locked all the ashtrays in the bottom drawer of his desk.

Before I locked up I looked at the clock again and wagged a finger at it. 'You behave yourself!' I said. 'Don't let Mr Barnes down.'

Would you believe it, when I turned up two days later the clock had gone. I stared at where it had been on the shelf and Evie said, 'Don't ask!'

'You mean it's been pinched?' I gasped.

'Of course not. It's gone wrong, that's all.' The smirk was back on her face and I wanted to slap her. Poor Mr Barnes, I thought. His precious clock.

Alan came in and saw my expression. 'Ben had to take it back to Heathside's in his lunch hour. His lordship is not best pleased.'

'Not a happy bunny!' Evie giggled. 'Poor old Barnes. His state-of-the-art clock! The expensive get-what-you-pay-for clock! The clock *par excellence*!'

*Par excellence*, indeed! She talks like that sometimes. Her grandmother has a second home in France and she reckons she can speak the language.

Alan said, 'It lost ten minutes.'

I was so sorry I could have cried. When I passed Heathside's on my way home I felt like throwing a brick through the window. Poor Mr Barnes. Why did these things happen to him? A real gentleman if ever there was one. All right then. I do have a bit of a soft spot for the man. He's never married and I reckon he's lonely. Doesn't look after himself properly since his mother passed away. Crumpled shirts sometimes – has he *got* an iron? I wonder. And shoes that need a good polish. But always a coloured handkerchief in his breast pocket.

The next time I went in, the clock was back. Mr Barnes was admiring it and he turned, smiling all over his face like a dog with two tails.

'Teething troubles,' he told me without waiting for me to ask. 'It's been fine.'

'Oh Mr Barnes! That is good news.'

I was so pleased for him. Next Monday I was a few minutes late and Mr Barnes had left already and so had Evie.

'He's gone to murder the chap at Heathside's,' Ben told me with a cheeky grin. 'Barnes. He's livid. He'll have a heart attack if he's not careful.' When he grinned he looked about eleven. There were three lads after that job. There *must* have been someone better than Ben.

'What?' I said, not understanding. 'Murder who?'

'It's still losing,' he told me. 'Nearly fifteen minutes.'

Alan said, 'I could have told him. Avoid Heathside's like the plague. My sister's organizer was nothing but trouble.' He was stuffing papers into his briefcase. 'His lordship wants it returned to the maker but the shop's saying there's nothing wrong with it. They've checked it against a similar model and it keeps perfect time.'

'They should give him his money back,' I said indignantly. 'All this worry and it was an expensive clock.'

I looked from one to the other and suddenly an awful thought entered my head. Was it them? Had they altered it? I wouldn't put it past any of them, they're so silly at times. Before I could stop myself I blurted it out. 'It's you lot, isn't it? You've done something to it!'

They both stared at me. If they were acting innocent they were very good.

'Done something?' Alan was glaring at me. 'I can't believe you said that!'

Ben said, 'Why should we do anything to it? It's gone wrong all by itself.'

I swallowed hard, feeling very nervous and shaky. What had I said? But if it was true ... 'It ... it could have been Evie,' I stammered. 'She might ... She doesn't like him because he made her give up smoking. She could have fiddled with it. Moved the hands.'

Ben said, 'It hasn't got any hands!'

They were quiet then, and seemed to be thinking it over. A slow grin spread across Alan's face. 'You may well be right, Mrs Greaves. Maybe she did. Good old Evie!'

Ben's eyes widened. 'Suppose he finds out? She'll get the sack!'

'How can he find out unless we tell him? And we won't.' Alan turned to me. 'And you won't say anything, will you, Mrs Greaves? Because you might get her sacked.'

It was on the tip of my tongue to say she *deserved* to get the sack but I just shrugged. Didn't say yes or no.

'If it *is* her,' Alan said. He flicked sugar from the top of his desk with a hanky. He always does that last thing. I think he must have a doughnut every afternoon with his coffee.

Back home I brooded about it while I mashed potatoes and ladled out the casserole that had simmered all day in the slow cooker. Then when we were sitting down at the table I told Arthur. He laughed. Thought it a great joke.

'It's not funny,' I snapped. 'She's making a fool of her boss. That poor man. I think it's a shame and I'm thinking of telling him.'

Arthur gave me a quick look. He knows that tone of voice. 'You watch it,' he said. 'It's nothing to do with you, Ellen. Don't go poking your nose in.'

'It *is* something to do with me,' I told him. 'I work for him too and I think it's a spiteful thing to do. I don't see why she should get away with it. Nasty little piece!'

'But suppose it wasn't her? Maybe the clock's faulty. It happens. Then you'd look a right fool.'

He was right. I went in the next day and there was the clock. Mr Barnes said, 'They agreed to replace it. Hardly with a good grace but they did agree.' He was gathering up his belongings – umbrella, briefcase and the rolled newspaper which he always pushed into the pocket of his gaberdine mac.

I said how pleased I was. Maybe now it didn't matter what Evie had done. Unless she did it again with this second clock, but surely not. The joke was over. I was almost disappointed. I had been longing to see her get her comeuppance.

He said, 'I have a favour to ask you, Mrs Greaves. I have

to meet someone and I've forgotten to collect the liver for my dinner tonight. Would you be a dear and pop along to Bristows?'

Would I? Of course I would. He'd never asked a favour before. 'But where will you be?' I asked.

'I'll come back for it in half an hour.'

I only hesitated because I do another office and I hate being late. He must have read my thoughts.

'You can skimp the cleaning for one night,' he said. 'Just empty the bins.'

I rushed off to Bristows and sure enough when I mentioned Mr Barnes, the butcher reached under the counter and handed me a package. I paid for it and hurried back to the office. I was just finishing when Mr Barnes came up the stairs to collect the liver and settle up for it.

Next day the clock was still there, still keeping perfect time. Great relief all round. So maybe I had misjudged Evie. I began to feel rather guilty.

They had all gone except Alan and he was still at his computer but I got on with my work. I reached his chair with the hoover and said, 'Feet up, please, Mr Deeds.' I hate disturbing him when he's at the computer because they're funny things and can crash, which could be dangerous. He lifted his feet, still staring at the screen, and I worked round him.

Suddenly he stopped what he was doing and said, 'Oh my God!'

It gave me quite a shock. 'What?' I asked. I thought he'd hurt himself or something. He was staring at the hoover.

'That's it!' he whispered. 'The hoover! Oh God! That's priceless!' He began to laugh.

'What's *it*?' I looked at the hoover, which didn't seem at all funny.

Alan couldn't stop laughing. Soon tears were streaming down his face. He's hysterical, I thought, getting a bit panicky. I hoped I wouldn't have to slap his face. That's what they do on the telly but I didn't feel quite up to it.

He spluttered to a stop and took a breath. 'Every time you plug in the hoover . . .' he began and then off he went again.

'Stop that, Mr Deeds!' I said as sternly as I could. 'Pull yourself together.'

It did the trick and he started to calm down.

He said, 'You pull out the plug when you use the hoover, so the clock stops working. Then you plug it in again and it carries on . . . but it's lost time.'

'I don't get it,' I said crossly.

'Think about it!' he said, wiping his eyes.

Well! I nearly died of shame because when I thought about it, he was right. It was all my fault. I felt hot and cold and I had to sit down. After what I'd said about Evie and it was me. I'd let poor Mr Barnes down. Not Evie but *me*!

I cried when I got home that night and told Arthur. He was very kind but I could see he was trying to keep a straight face. Why did everyone think it was funny? I wanted to throw myself under a bus. That's how bad I felt. I knew it would be all round the office and they'd all be laughing at Mr Barnes behind his back – and I was to blame.

As soon as I set foot in the office there was a shriek from Evie and she started telling me about how Alan had broken the glad tidings to Mr Barnes.

'His face! It creased me! All the wind knocked out of him. I wish you'd been here.'

I was glad I hadn't. I felt my face getting redder and redder. 'Where . . . where is Mr Barnes?' I stammered, dreading coming face to face with him. I was sure he'd never forgive me. Every time I'd hoovered round I'd messed up the clock. It hadn't gone wrong the night before last because I'd popped out for the liver and hadn't done any hoovering.

Evie said, 'You're not flavour of the month, Mrs Greaves. "That bloody woman!" That's what he called you.'

*That bloody woman!* I couldn't bear to think of it. I could feel tears coming, so I just turned and ran out of the office. Alan shouted after me but I took no notice. I went home and wondered what to do. He was such a gentleman – and yet he'd called me that. He never swears, so he must have been so mad at me and I deserved it and I couldn't blame him at all. How could I have been so daft? So stupid. *Stupid.*

Well, I had my pride. The next day when Arthur was in the garden, I wrote my resignation letter.

*Dear Mr Barnes,*
*I am so sorry about the clock and me hoovering. It was my fault for not thinking about it being electrical as well as digital. I don't feel I can go on working for you, having let you down. I will work a month's notice if you want and I shall miss you.*
*Yours faithfully,*
*Mrs E Greaves'*

When I read it through I crossed out the bit about me missing him because he wouldn't want to know that now. I copied it out again and I was pleased with my efforts. I must say I do write a good letter. It was dignified.

I went in to the office first thing next morning and marched straight into his office before I could change my mind. I was pulling the letter out of my handbag when I saw that he was smiling.

'A little token, Mrs Greaves,' he said, taking a box of chocolates from his desk drawer. A big box with a ribbon. Those special chocolates that look like seashells. 'To show there's no hard feeling.'

'Oh, but I can't . . .' I began. The letter was in my hand.

'It was entirely my fault,' he told me. 'Apparently I should have plugged it into a sealed plug – a permanent plug that can't be used for anything else. I don't want you to worry about it. You couldn't have realized.'

He was looking at me so kindly I couldn't find any words, just stared at him as he pushed the chocolates into my hands. 'We'll say nothing more about it, Mrs Greaves.'

Then he winked. He actually winked at me. I had to laugh and then I knew we were friends again. He didn't apologize for calling me what he did because he didn't know that I knew. *If* he ever did call me that. Evie might have made it all up . . . And if he *did* say it, I know he was upset and he didn't mean it. I know Mr Barnes and he's a real gentleman.

# What Goes Around Comes Around

When the doorbell rang I muttered a small oath and glanced at the clock. Ten to eight in the morning? Even Jehovah's Witnesses don't call that early.

'What d'you want at this hour?' I muttered irritably.

I hate it when people turn up unannounced. They usually catch me looking like an unmade bed and this time was no exception. I had just pulled on a pair of ancient jeans and a sweater in preparation for my most unfavourite job – unblocking the gutters. Thank God I lived in a bungalow or I'd have broken my neck long before. I'm not good with ladders but there was no one else to do it and my pride doesn't allow me to ask for help.

'Whoever you are, I'm out!' I grumbled, shoving my feet into a pair of trainers.

Scowling, I made my way along the passage, but abruptly I stopped and my pulse began to speed up. Through the patterned glass of the front door I thought I recognized the outline.

'Don't be such a fool,' I told myself. 'He's thousands of miles away!'

I closed my eyes briefly before I opened the door.

'Oh it's you!' I said although my heart almost stopped beating.

He grinned. 'What sort of welcome is that, Maggie?'

The same husky voice but with a trace of South *Ef*rica in it. The same humorous glint in the brown eyes. I hadn't seen him for seven long years. I tried to steady my voice. 'You'd better come in.'

What goes around comes around, I thought. My husband used to say that, although neither of us knew what it meant.

Alan stepped into the hall and immediately the house seemed smaller. My daughter Emma's ex-husband was built like a tree, tall and broad-shouldered and he hadn't changed much. There was a little less of the silky blond hair and South Africa had given him a tan to die for. Last time I'd seen them together, Emma was crazy for him but I'd been less than pleased. Then she was not quite twenty, a bright, pretty young woman with a promising career ahead of her. Of course I could see why she found him so attractive – any woman would – but she was halfway through her medical training and intended to specialize in pediatrics. She had always wanted to be a doctor and we had shared her enthusiasm. Even after my husband Carl died, I had struggled to find the fees, determined that she should qualify and find her dream.

Instead she found Alan. He was forty-eight and divorced – a senior doctor with a bedside manner that effortlessly won the hearts of all his patients and, of course, his staff. Not to mention his students. And the mother of one of them! Me. But I kept that to myself.

I led the way into the kitchen, although he could have found the way blindfolded. I had no idea why he'd come back to the UK or why he'd called in on me. We had parted with bitterness and I had never expected to see him again.

'No red carpet?' he asked.

I shook my head, no longer trusting my voice. The kitchen was not looking its best – a page from *Homes & Gardens* it was not!

He hesitated beside a chair by the table and I wished I had cleared away the breakfast things. Crumbs, a carton of Olio, a packet of sliced bread, more crumbs and a jar of marmalade.

'What time d'you call this?' I smiled to soften the accusing tone.

'I know. I'm sorry. I should have rung first but I didn't dare. I thought you'd say "No".'

I always loved his voice but now, hearing it again almost

reduced me to tears. It was rough but warm with a hint of tenderness. To hide my feeling I said briskly, 'You'd better sit down now you're here.'

Obeying, he grinned. 'You look great, Maggie.'

'You always were a smoothie! The famous bedside manner.' If only I hadn't been headed for the gutters I might have worn something more glamorous and a dab of lipstick would help. Too late.

'I could kill for a slice of toast.'

My smile wavered as I pointed to the loaf and then to the toaster. 'Help yourself.' I wasn't going to treat him like visiting royalty but how should I treat him? I had no idea. Not a friend in the true sense of the word nor a long-lost lover. Simply a ghost from the past.

I had a sudden vision of Alan and Emma together at the table, squabbling over the last of the lemon curd, eyes only for each other. She had kept him a secret for months, simply telling me that his name was Alan and he wasn't married. Later she referred to him as her tutor and alarm bells rang. A tutor could be any age over thirty, I thought. Maybe not too terrible – but anyway, it wouldn't last. All young students had crushes on their tutors. I understood that. Even when I realized how deeply in love *he* was, I crossed my fingers that they would be sensible and that he appreciated the need for her to finish her training.

I was sadly misguided. Emma had other ideas and a few months after I was allowed to meet Alan she was pregnant.

'And don't blame Alan,' she'd insisted. 'It was quite a shock for him.'

'And for you, I expect.'

'No.' She looked at me defiantly. 'I wanted his child. I know Alan. He'll never leave me if he has a child.'

I gasped. 'Did you think he might leave you? You must be mad. He's crazy about you.'

'Now he is, Mum, but there are so many available women, Mum. You've no idea. He's so terribly fanciable!'

She laughed but I couldn't join her. It seemed she was

already having doubts and this was her solution. I was horrified and angry that she had been so manipulative. She saw my disapproval but brushed it aside, refusing further discussion and with indecent haste they were married. A dreadful rushed affair in a registry office, Photocall outside the Town Hall, nibbles and drinks in a room over The Grey Owl pub. At least it was cheap but my poor dead husband had probably turned in his grave! We had always promised her a wonderful day, white dress, bridesmaids, big reception. Had she wanted a white wedding I'd have borrowed the money even if it meant being in debt for the rest of my life, but she couldn't wait, so anxious was she to secure what she saw as her future happiness with Alan.

I was thankful Carl was not alive to see the impending catastrophe. Emma immediately dropped out of medical school. She claimed to be feeling sick all the time but I think she had simply lost interest in her studies. I lost my temper and told her what a fool she was, which wasn't the cleverest thing to do. I should have kept my mouth shut but I didn't and we quarrelled. Then, out of the blue, Alan was offered a job in South Africa. He wasn't particularly keen but Emma leaped at the chance to move and positively badgered him to accept. I told myself that she wanted to make a fresh start but secretly I knew she wanted to punish me for my lack of enthusiasm. Or perhaps she wanted to get away from me! I begged her to stay until the child was born but she refused.

'It's a wonderful opportunity for us,' she insisted.

'But at least give Alan a chance to think it over,' I suggested. 'He doesn't seem too keen and you're rushing him into it.'

'You just don't understand,' she shouted. 'I'm not a child. It's my life and I don't want your advice. Mind your own damn business!'

After yet another bitter argument the real truth emerged. Emma thought he was seeing another student – a girl called Kelly. Someone, a woman, had phoned several times, asking to speak to him.

'I don't believe it,' I told her. 'Alan adores you. Ask him

about her. Tell him how upset you are. It's called communication, Emma. Let him put your mind at rest. All this worrying won't do you any good – or the baby.'

She wouldn't even consider it.

'Then let me talk to him.'

With hindsight it was a fatal mistake but then I thought it might clear the air. Emma panicked and two weeks later she and Alan flew to South Africa, where little Virginia was born. My granddaughter. My first grandchild but I wasn't invited to the christening. Alan wrote apologizing, saying that Emma was adamant. Eighteen months later he wrote again to say Emma had left him, taking little Ginnie with her. Two years after that they were divorced. I hoped she'd come back to England but she didn't. I tried to resign myself to the fact that I'd lost her but I still kept hoping for a miracle.

I spooned instant coffee into a mug. 'So how's Emma? Have you kept in touch?'

He was standing by the toaster with his back to me. 'She's met someone else. I thought you might know.'

'She never writes.' I blinked back tears.

'His name is Charles Stopes. Nice chap actually. More her age. Something to do with land clearance. I met him at their wedding. I was invited – don't ask me why – and I went because I knew I'd see Ginnie. She was bridesmaid.'

'They're *married*?' I was shocked. Perhaps I'm old-fashioned but I hadn't expected my beloved daughter to be on her second husband before she was twenty-eight. Should I have seen it coming? Were there signs as she grew up that I had missed?

'Charles insisted, apparently.' Alan shrugged. 'Emma's pregnant again and the baby's due in October. They're coming back to the UK in June for his brother's wedding.'

The toaster popped and I jumped. Alan spread Olio and marmalade. As I set coffee in front of him my hands shook. Another grandchild I would never see.

He said, 'Don't worry about Emms, Maggie. She's a survivor. We all make mistakes.'

194

'You were her first!'

I regretted the words as soon as they were out – I had never blamed Emma for falling in love with him because he was irresistible. Sometimes I think that being desirable has its drawbacks. I *did* blame Emma for the indecent haste with which she threw up her well-ordered life and secure future. She would never finish her training. Would never have a career or independence.

Alan found milk in the fridge and I took deep breaths when he wasn't looking.

He said, 'So how're things with you? A new man on the horizon?'

'No. I've given up on men.' I wanted it to sound flippant but it came out as bitter. Bitter and twisted, I thought. That's probably how he sees me. 'But I'm a survivor too.' I'd been a widow since Emma was thirteen. I'd hoped to fall in love again but when eventually I did, it was with Alan, which was impossible. 'I started up a mother and baby group at the village hall. There was a need for something like that.' I omitted to say that the need was mine. 'I booked the local hall and leafletted the neighbouring streets. It grew from small beginnings and we have thirty-five children on the roll. We even have a small grant from the council.' I smiled cheerfully. I was proud of what we had achieved and I wanted him to know it. What he would never know was the ache of loss which had never left me. My own child and her children were not a part of my life and nothing could fill the void.

'Sounds wonderful! But it doesn't surprise me. I always knew you had hidden depths! Emma told me.' He was watching me closely. 'I've brought you some snaps of Ginnie. She's so like Emma.'

I took the small album with shaking fingers. Alan's child. My granddaughter. I stared at the cherubic face beneath the floppy sun hat. Ginnie paddling in the sea, holding Emma's hand . . . My eyes filled with tears but I blinked them away. Ginnie blowing out birthday candles. Ginnie sitting on Emma's lap, listening to a story. And there she was, still a toddler,

riding on Alan's shoulders, her little face alive with excitement. There were several photos of her with a strange man.
'Is that Charles?' I studied his face, praying that he was good
to Emma and Ginnie.

Alan nodded.

I whispered, 'Ginnie is Emma all over again!'

At that moment hope suddenly blossomed as my mind made
a connection with something Alan had said – that they were
coming to the UK. If so, Charles might be persuaded to bring
Emma and Ginnie to visit me. Even if Emma had still not
forgiven me, she might at least allow me to see my grandchild. Charles might persuade her. I would think of ways and
means before I spoke of it to anyone.

I looked up. 'Ginnie's wonderful! You must miss her terribly.'

He nodded and swallowed hard. Lost for words. I wanted
to comfort him but didn't dare. Had he ever guessed how I
felt about him? I hoped not. Time had moved on for both of
us. Life had come between us.

He finished a mouthful of toast and washed it down with
coffee. 'You were right, Maggie. I was much too old for her.
I realized that she wasn't the woman for me . . . but by then
she was pregnant.'

'It was Kelly!' I whispered. 'Emma was afraid . . .'

He regarded me blankly. 'Who's Kelly, for God's sake?'

So maybe it wasn't. 'Sorry . . .' I stammered. 'Forget it!
Nobody . . . that is, I'm getting a bit confused.'

My voice shook, my eyes filled with tears and I grabbed
for a sheet of kitchen roll. After a painful silence I asked the
crucial question. 'And you?'

He hesitated. 'I'm still alone . . .'

'I thought perhaps by now . . .'

'Who'd have a selfish bastard like me? No . . . But I'm
hoping – that is, I've been wondering lately . . .' He stopped.

I waited, curious.

He had stopped eating. 'I've been looking for a way to put
things right, Maggie. I've been such a fool. I made Emma
unhappy, you've lost your daughter – and I've lost my little

Ginnie.' But at the thought of the child his face brightened. 'She's a very bright kid. We talk on the phone. Emma's not creating difficulties between us. She's quite happy for me to see her but they live seven hundred miles away.' He shrugged. 'It's been tough.'

Tell me about it, I thought.

He sighed. 'Life gets so bloody complicated, and we can't untangle the past but maybe we could do something about the future . . . Look, don't jump down my throat but . . . At least think about it . . .'

'About what?'

'I want to take you back with me to South Africa. For good.'

Stunned, I stared at him, my heart racing. 'South Africa? I don't know . . .' I began, shocked. I had made a life for myself. Did he expect me to toss it all away on a whim?

'Maggie, listen. Live dangerously before it's too late. Sell your house and live with me. I've got this sprawling old house – six bedrooms, would you believe! You could have your own separate flat . . . at first.'

'At first? What does that mean?'

'It means that, if later on, we found we could get along . . . then we could share the whole house. Sort ourslves out at last. I think you know, Maggie.' His eyes were no longer humorous but dark and intense. 'I think we both know . . . we made a mistake back then. We knew what was happening between us but neither of us said a word. We went through the whole charade because of Emma.'

His words echoed in my mind but I couldn't find anything to say. Alan *loved* me? Was that it? Could it be that simple?

'I'm right, Maggie, aren't I?'

At last I nodded.

He went on. 'And we'd both be able to see Ginnie. She could come and stay. And the new baby, of course, later on. Emma would be reasonable. What do you say, Maggie?'

We stared at each other.

He said, 'We could make it work, Maggie. We'd be happy. We'd forget the past.'

197

My heart was racing. Could we really salvage something from the wreckage? I felt faint with longing.

'I want to say "Yes" but . . .' Suppose it didn't work out. It was a risk. Torn between fear and hope, I covered my face with my hands and sat very still, hearing the clock tick, while Alan waited silently.

I came to a sudden decision. Everything I wanted was being offered to me, so why was I hesitating? I would take the risk. Slowly I looked up into Alan's familiar face and saw how much he wanted me to agree. I nodded and his face lit up. The next moment we were hugging each other, both talking at once and stopping occasionally to kiss and at that moment I thought of my husband. I would be leaving the home he and I had shared and all the memories – and his grave nearby in the churchyard. But if he were looking down on me, I was sure he would approve.

What goes around comes around! I thought, and at last I knew what it meant.

# Compromise

I knocked at the door promptly at 10 a.m and stood there, huddled in my anorak, trying to shelter from the cold east wind. I'd hated November ever since my husband died on the seventh of that miserable month. I shivered, looking round the neglected garden. Withered plants in pots stood in a row on the flagstones and a gnome lay face down in a puddle, which suited me fine. Presumably drowning, but I was not about to rescue him. I've never liked gnomes. In fact I've always worried about people who *do* like them.

How did I feel? I was nervous. I admit it. But brisk, cheerful and impersonal – that was what they advised and that was how I intended to play it. The home help. Underneath my anorak I wore a new floral apron and in my pocket I had a new pair of rubber gloves. I was going to look the part. When the door finally opened I saw a frail old man with a thatch of white hair, faded blue eyes and a bad-tempered expression. A half-smoked cigarette was clutched between two fingers of his right hand. He was dressed in shapeless corduroy trousers, a collarless shirt and sleeveless pullover. His spectacles needed cleaning and he peered through them shortsightedly.

'Are you her?' he demanded.

'Yes. Good morning.'

No reply. That figures, I thought, trying to remember 'brisk, cheerful and impersonal'. It was probably a no-win situation, the doctor had warned me. Don't hope for too much, he warned. I told him I wouldn't.

'I suppose you'd better come in then.' Grudgingly, he held open the door and, crossing my fingers, I stepped inside.

199

Without another word the old man led the way down a narrow passage and into a dismal kitchen. Dr Phillips was already there, bless him. Tall and thin, he wore a suit that he had bought when he was fatter but his lined face was creased with kindly concern as always. He had promised to prepare the ground, so to speak. He smiled and I knew by his expression that he had recognized my dismay. He turned to the old man.

'Mr Willerby, this is Mrs Forde, your new home help. I told you she would be starting today.'

'Today? Is it Monday?'

'Yes.'

The old man stared at me until I began to feel uneasy. I must remember to call him Mr Willerby, I told myself. And I would be Mrs Forde. No Christian names. It was a job of work.

The doctor said, 'Mrs Forde will do a bit of tidying up for you and some shopping and will make you a bit of lunch.'

'I can make my own lunch. I'm not helpless.'

'You do find cooking a bit difficult. You don't see very well. You burned your hand on—'

'I can manage!'

I pretended not to notice this exchange. The doctor had told me bluntly that Reg Willerby was a problem. 'His sight's going. Reads with a magnifying glass. Memory's bad. Some loss of motor control, too. He's also very cantankerous. The last woman only stayed for ten days. She said that if she had to stay another day she'd probably murder him!'

'In other words, old and crochety! Tell me about it!' I'd laughed. 'At least I'm prepared.'

The alternative to a new home help, the doctor told him, was to find a room for him in a local care home, where he'd be looked after twenty-four hours a day and might have to share a room. Mr Willerby had refused outright.

'He was furious.' The doctor shrugged. 'His exact words were "You're not stuffing me into any bloody care home! I can look after myself!" There was more along those lines and I think the phrase "Piss off!" came into it somewhere!'

Looking at Mr Willerby, I could quite believe it. I said, 'I'm sure we'll get along fine,' in what I hoped was an impersonal but brisk tone of voice.

'Do you? We'll see about that,' he muttered, glaring at me.

The doctor gave me a reassuring smile and said he must be going as he'd to get back for the surgery. He let himself out.

After he'd gone, Mr Willerby stared at me for a long time and then said, 'What's your name again?'

'Mrs Forde. With a final *e*.'

'Hmm . . . So what's this job then, for you, I mean. A bit of pin money? The last one was saving up to take her kids to Disneyland.'

'Something like that.' Quickly I pointed to a framed photograph of a young man in army uniform. 'Is this you?'

His eyes brightened. 'Lance Corporal Reginald Willerby, Royal Engineers. REs, they called us. Couldn't have won the war without us. The Jerries blew up the bridges and we had to build new ones. Pontoon bridges mostly. They were good, too. Take the weight of a tank, they would.' He gave a shaky salute to an imaginary officer.

'You look very smart!' I smiled. 'I see you had stripes?'

'I made sergeant in forty-one.' He picked up the photograph and peered closely at it. 'Course I was younger then. Hmm . . .' He put it back and turned to me. 'Well, you'd better get cracking, Mrs Whatever-your-name-is. Earn your money.'

Cheeky old devil! 'You've taken the words right out of my mouth!' I told him.

He lit another cigarette and watched me as I wondered where to start. There were cups and plates piled in the sink, so I ran some hot water and searched for the detergent. Alternatively puffing and coughing, he chuckled, waiting for me to ask for help. I didn't and at last he said, 'Try under the sink!'

'Thank you!' I began the washing-up, which meant I could keep my back to him but there was a small cracked mirror on the window sill in front of me and I kept an eye on him. Rather at a loss, he fiddled with a hole in the sleeve of his pullover.

'You're making it worse!' I told him.

'Mind your own business!'

He had a point. I said nothing. When I had a draining board full of washed crockery he handed me a tea towel. As I dried the dishes I asked about the previous home help.

'Useless!' he told me. 'Called herself Mrs Watson. Called herself a cook, too, but her pastry was like cardboard. My old dog could have cooked better than you, I told her!'

According to Mr Willerby, poor Mrs Watson was nosy, interfering, sharp-tongued, lazy, tried to diddle him out of his pension and dyed her hair. My heart went out to her. I found the right cupboard and stowed most of the crockery.

He gave me a sly look. 'You want to watch out. There's a mouse in that cupboard sometimes. Might run up your arm!' He chuckled, spluttered and began to cough again.

'I'm not scared of mice.' I wiped over the table and emptied the washing-up water. 'I'll pop to the corner shop later and get you a bit of shopping. D'you want to make a list?'

'No, I don't. I don't need anything. Or anybody. I can do my own washing-up, too. Always have done.'

Not recently, I thought. As I wiped round the sink and work-tops I stole another glance at him. His collarless shirt was stained, the moths had been at his pullover and the designer stubble didn't suit him.

'My husband used an electric shaver,' I said. 'They're very good.'

'Got one! It's bloody useless. Mostly I don't bother.'

'Not even when you have visitors?'

He scowled. 'Visitors? Huh!' He stubbed out his cigarette, his hands shaking. 'Don't smoke these things,' he warned. 'They'll kill you.'

'So I've heard.' I took off my apron. 'Dr Phillips says you've a daughter. Doesn't she visit you?'

'He talks too much!' He scowled.

I said, 'My daughter Emma used to play me up terribly when she was in her teens. They do at that age. But now she's twenty-two she's different again. Great company. We're more like mates.' When this provoked no comment I added, 'You should invite your daughter to visit you.'

The scowl deepened. 'Invite her to . . .? I haven't seen her for more than twenty years.'

'Too far away, perhaps?'

'I don't know where she is and I don't care!'

'Oh dear! Like that, is it? Dr Phillips was hoping . . .'

'He thinks too much, that one! Always poking his nose in. Always sending people round to help me. Sent round a Mrs Brooks before Christmas. She never stopped talking. Gabble, gabble! Jaw the hind legs off a donkey, she would. Get rid of her, I told him or I will.' He drew on another cigarette and I wondered if you really could die of passive smoking. 'As for my daughter, if she ever shows her face round here she'll get a flea in her ear!'

'No other children?'

'One was enough!'

He stood up and headed for the stairs. Shuffle, shuffle. The big toe was through in both slippers.

While he was gone I had a quick snoop. Nothing in the freezer compartment. Evaporated milk, margarine and a tomato in the fridge. Digestive biscuits, a packet of Sugarpops and an opened tin of grapefruit with a spoon sticking out of it.

'Mr Willerby,' I muttered. 'You're starving yourself.'

I emptied the pedal bin, washed it out and relined it with a plastic carrier bag while the old man stumped around upstairs, doing goodness knows what. I was making a shopping list when he reappeared. He'd exchanged the pullover for an ancient waistcoat and I wondered why.

'Nice,' I said. 'My husband used to love waistcoats.'

'Dead, is he?'

'Yes.'

He fidgeted with the waistcoat buttons. 'My daughter made me this. Years ago.'

'That was nice of her. She's made it very—'

'I didn't ask her to make it. I don't like waistcoats. They're poncy things but they're warm. I'll grant you that.' He sat down again. 'So your hubby's dead?'

'Died a few years ago. Harry John Forde. I still miss him.' That was true, anyway.

At the corner shop I bought ham, bread, baked beans, eggs, apples and fresh milk. I didn't get any thanks when I unpacked.

'We'll settle up at the end of the week,' I said.

'Will we?' he growled.

Ignoring the comment, I laid the table, made him an omelette and left him to it. The next day I took him a pot of orange primulas, pretending I'd dug the plant from my garden.

'I hate house plants.'

Ignoring the comment, I put it on the window sill behind the sink. Upstairs I changed the bed and gathered up some dirty clothes. I put it all in the rusting washing machine and Mr Willerby glanced up from his newspaper.

'Doesn't work. The washing machine. Hasn't worked for months.'

I hesitated. I certainly didn't fancy doing his washing by hand. 'How doesn't it work?' I asked. 'Maybe it's the fuse. I can fix a fuse.'

'It leaks like a bloody sieve.'

'Much?'

'How should I know? All I know is it leaks. I don't use it any more.'

I crossed my fingers and turned it on. It leaked a bit but not too much so I spread a copy of the *Daily Mail* on the floor to soak up the trickle of water and the machine did the job. Mr Willerby trailed after me into the garden and hung about while I pegged out the washing.

'Give it a bit of a blow,' I suggested.

'I dry stuff indoors. Hang it all over the chairbacks.'

Inside I made a pot of tea and as we sipped I told him about my daughter – how she'd stayed out late and worried me and Harry half to death. When I mentioned his daughter his face darkened.

'Seventeen, she was, our Sandra. Seventeen and thought she knew it all! Met this lad – twenty-two *he* was – and thought he was God's gift. Know what I mean?'

I nodded. We all make mistakes, I thought.

'Me and her mother – we could see at once he was no good. Flash. A bit dodgy. Alan Cobbett. That was his name. No job. No prospects. Nothing. But Sandra couldn't see it. Then she started staying out all night. Round at his place when his folks were away. Look, I told her, you're heading for trouble! If he gets you in the family way it'll be your own fault and you're out of here. "Oh but he'd marry me!" she said. "Will he, hell!" I told her.'

'There's a lot of it about!'

He sucked on his cigarette and blew an unsuccessful smoke ring. 'Sure as eggs is eggs she's pregnant and lover-boy's nowhere to be seen. Done a runner. Big row, I throw her out, council gets her a flat, my wife leaves me. Said I was too hard on her. Women always stick together.'

I murmured something non-committal.

'That was years ago,' he went on. 'Mucked up my life properly, that girl did. Never set eyes on her since and don't want to.'

'So she had the baby. Girl or boy?'

'Girl, so my wife told me. Ex-wife, I should say. Went on and on about the kid. Wanted me to see it. Said it had my eyes. That sort of stuff.' He swallowed. 'I heard she finally married some bloke. I wouldn't go to the wedding. Why should I, after what she did to me?' He shrugged.

I sighed. 'Water under the bridge.'

'You could say that.'

'Has she ever been in touch?'

We went indoors and I started to peel potatoes for his lunch. He was staring at me again.

'Oh, she'd come crawling back if I let her! Wants "to look after me", according to my ex.' He pointed to the mantelpiece. 'That's her last letter. Didn't even open it.'

'How d'you know it was her from her if—'

''Cos I recognize her writing.'
I hadn't thought of that.

The following Monday I called in at the surgery to pick up
Mr Willerby's medication. High blood pressure, apparently.
Dr Phillips came into the waiting room and caught sight of
me waiting in the queue at the dispensary.

'How're you doing with our Mr Willerby?' he asked.
'Heavy-going, I imagine.'

'You could say that. Not exactly chums but we get along.
Mind you, it's early days yet!'

'Are you getting some food down him? The neighbour was
worried about that. Lives on air, she told me. Frightened to
use the cooker after that burn.'

'I cook for him when I'm there and sometimes leave him
a flask of hot soup for him to eat later.'

'And he hasn't twigged?'

'I don't think so. Once or twice I saw him weighing me up
with his eyes half-closed and I thought he was on to me. But
if he has guessed, he hasn't let on.'

'Maybe his pride won't let him admit that he's recognized
you. Or maybe that's his way of being one up on the pair of
us. If he had to admit who you are, he'd have to throw you
out so as not to lose face. This way he keeps a cheerful home
help and has the last laugh!'

'Maybe he likes me being around. I suspect we shall never
know. He told me all about his dreadful daughter.'

We both laughed but I remembered the photo album I had
found pushed to the back of his sideboard. Photos of me on
Dad's knee. The proud look on his face made me want to cry.
He'd loved me once. I couldn't tell Dr Phillips that.

I said, 'I wrote to tell my mother and she rang to say how
pleased she was. I did hope she'd come over, but Canada's a
long way and they can't afford it.'

'Will you ever tell him the truth?' he asked.

'I don't think so. If he hasn't already guessed he'd be
furious.'

'I warned you he was cantankerous.'

'He always was.'

And he recognizes his daughter's handwriting, I reminded myself. I'll have to be careful he never sees one of my shopping lists.

# Fallout

I had no way of knowing as I left the the churchyard that Monday morning and headed for the post office that my life was about to change yet again. I walked with my head held high and a smile ready if I should be challenged by one of my neighbours. Five months earlier my life had undergone one change when John died unexpectedly and I was suddenly alone and only the kindness of friends helped me through dark days. Now I was learning a different way of living and finding ways to hide my continued desperation. When well-meaning people ask, 'How are you coping these days?' they are hoping for a cheerful, positive answer. They do not want the truth.

Mrs Barnett on the other side of the High Street raised a hand in greeting but said nothing. I returned the salute. She had been one of the first to offer help. Village people are like that, I discovered, and thanked God that John and I had already left London. Mrs Barnett had offered to walk our dog when she went out with hers. It was a real blessing in those first few dreadful days before the funeral. Afterwards I resumed the dog-walking and made an effort to face life without John.

I saw the woman, a stranger, stepping out of an old Volkswagen which was parked halfway between the church and the post office. She was clutching something in a plastic carrier bag and I thought she looked ill at ease. Very thin, with a dark bob, she was wearing the ubiqitous jeans with a yellow T-shirt with something written across it and she had a large raffia bag slung over one shoulder. But it was her face that caught my attention – pale with large brown eyes. I only glanced at her as we passed and she didn't see me, but in that moment I was aware of a frisson of unease followed by a jolt of recognition. Unwillingly I turned to watch her and at once my suspicions were confirmed. She turned into the church-yard and out of sight.

At once I knew why she seemed familiar. I had last seen her at John's funeral, sitting alone at the back of the church. No one knew who she was and by the time we returned to the cottage for some refreshments there was no sign of her. Edith from next door called her 'the mystery woman' and her presence at the funeral had never been explained. I hadn't exactly forgotten about her but I had pushed her to the back of my mind.

Without knowing why, I quickly followed her into the churchyard, keeping a discreet distance between us in case she turned round. I saw her hurrying, head bent, the yellow T-shirt bright against the dark shrubs. Suddenly I knew where she was going and felt a rush of anxiety. She stopped at John's grave and bent down. I had left the grave only minutes earlier and my crimson carnations, carefully set in oasis, blazed against the grey marble of the headstone in the heavy stoneware vase. John would have been sixty-four if he had lived and we would have been celebrating our twentieth wedding anniversary in July. John loved red carnations and always gave them to me on my birthday. I didn't like to tell him that freesias were *my* favourites.

The woman opened the carrier bag and I caught my breath, shocked to the core. She was holding a flower arrangement. Red carnations. I rushed forward.

'Can I help you?' I blurted out the words, my voice rising angrily. A stupid question in the circumstances but I was shaking with indignation. How dare this woman bring flowers to my husband's grave? I was outraged. If she laid a finger on *my* flowers . . .

She glanced up. 'No, thank you.'

I waited beside her, my heart thudding. Nothing in the world would persuade me to leave her there alone with my husband. It was ridiculous but I felt absurdly threatened by her. She set her posy at the other end of the grave and slowly stood up. There were tears in her eyes and I already knew and didn't want to hear – and yet I couldn't bring myself to go. I couldn't do anything except stare at her.

She said, 'I suppose you're Lynn.'

'That's my husband's grave!'

'I know that. I'm Cathy.'

'You have no right . . .' I began but I didn't know what I was saying. My legs shook and I felt a sheen of perspiration break out on my skin.

'You look different,' she said.

'Cathy who?'

'John's Cathy, of course!' Her tone had sharpened.

She was – had been – his secretary! My throat felt dry. This was the woman who had given him a book of love poems one Christmas. I said, 'His secretary. You gave him that book!' We'd had such an argument that day. It had ruined our Christmas. I could still see John unwrapping it with that foolish smile playing at the corner of his mouth. Enjoying my fear.

'I wasn't his secretary!' She looked puzzled. 'What book?'

'An anthology of love poems. He said his secretary gave it to him.'

'His secretary was called Anthea.'

'And the leather gloves?'

She shook her head and I saw a flicker of doubt.

She fussed with the plastic carrier, folding it smaller and smaller until she was able to slip it into the shoulder bag. At last she said, 'What did he give her?'

'I didn't ask.'

With a defiant gesture she thrust out her left hand and I saw the ring – three diamonds. 'He gave me *this*!'

I was hurt but more than that I was astonished that for all those months or years John had led a double life. I wondered just how much money he had spent on this wretched woman while he was pleading poverty at home. We didn't attend my cousin's wedding because John claimed he'd had a bad year with an almost non-existent bonus. Scotland was too far, he said. We'd need an overnight stay and it wasn't worth it. Perhaps he'd spent the bonus on the ring. I wouldn't lower myself to ask. I was torn between needing to know and losing what happy memories I had been able to cling to.

I looked down at the flowers Cathy had brought and felt a fierce need to trample them underfoot. 'John's Cathy'! Now at last the truth was coming out and I wondered if I could bear it. I swallowed hard and said, 'Why are you putting flowers on John's grave?' I tried to sound strong but my voice wavered treacherously.

She was equally determined not to be browbeaten. 'For the same reason as you – it's John's birthday and he loved red carnations!'

I wished then that I had resisted the urge to follow her. If only I had walked on to the post office. I could have found a 'Get Well' card for my brother and known nothing about this Cathy person.

'Were you a friend of his?'

'I was more than a friend, Lynn, and you know it. Much more than a friend. I was the one he loved.'

The words seemed to beat at my mind. I told myself she was mad – or lying. I stared past her to the wording on the headstone.

*John Farrar*
*1944–1999*
*Remembered Always*

My mother had been shocked and had called it a 'minimalist headstone' but at the time I was too angry to want to put more. I was angry with John for killing himself. For driving too fast and carelessly ending our marriage. No other vehicle had been involved and the driving conditions were good. We had argued often about his style of driving. I thought it dangerous. He called it 'driving with a bit of flair'! When at last I was proved right it gave me no satisfaction.

I said, 'I saw you at the funeral.'

Finally I was facing up to the unwelcome realization that this awful Cathy was the other woman whose existence John had always denied. He had called me suspicious and paranoid and had continued to come home late from the office with only the flimsiest excuses. He had made me doubt myself. I felt a wave of faintness and looked around for somewhere to sit. I didn't want to faint in front of this woman. There was a wooden seat and I started to walk towards it. Somehow I made it and sank down with a gasp of relief. I had put a distance between us but she followed me and stood, arms folded defensively, glaring down at me.

She said, 'I suppose you're pleased in a way. Now you'll never lose him.'

'I *have* lost him!'

'To me, I mean.'

'I don't know what you're talking about,' I told her. 'I thought there was someone else but John always denied it. Now it seems that "someone" was you. So now I know he lied. Charming! I hope you're satisfied.'

She shook her head.'You're really something else! How can you sit there pretending after all that happened. First you said you would divorce him and then you wouldn't. I never knew where I was – and it drove John crazy!' She took a step closer and I could see the anger in her eyes. 'You no longer loved him but you—'

'What? That's a lie!'

Perhaps something in my face convinced her, because she hesitated, drawing back. Blinking, she stammered, 'He ... He said you didn't. That it was all over between you but ...' She made her way to the other end of the seat and sat down.

So John had been lying to her as well as to me. I said, 'I swear to you that he never told me about you. Not one word. I asked more than once but he denied it. Not that it matters. He's dead now. I just wish I'd known the truth.'

I wondered at that point what I would have done if John had admitted an affair and asked for a divorce. Could I have gone on living with him? Suppose he had promised that it was over and begged me to stay with him . . . Would I ever have trusted him again? I would never know the answer.

She sat hunched up, her face hidden in her hands, and I felt a surge of pity which I quickly fought down. This woman had been prepared to wreck our marriage. She didn't deserve any sympathy and she certainly wasn't to going to get any from me.

She looked up frowning. 'But you *are* a Roman Catholic.'

'No, I'm not.'

'He loved me,' she said and I had the feeling she was trying to convince herself rather than me. 'He wanted to marry me but you refused him a divorce. Don't deny it because he told me how many times he tried to discuss it with you.'

'I do deny it because John didn't ask for a divorce. Why should he? He was too busy pretending that there was no one else. I'm sorry if you don't—'

Two angry spots of colour had now appeared in her cheeks. 'He begged you to let him go – time and again – it used to upset him so much. In the end he gave up because of the children. I understood. Children need their father. But when they were older . . .'

She said, 'And now I've got nothing. My mother was right. I should have kept it. Even though she didn't approve of him she wanted me to keep the baby. I would have managed somehow. At least I would have his child. A part of him.' She began to cry.

I watched her with growing horror. There had been a child! John had fathered a child. I let her cry, resisting the urge to offer comfort. When she finally stopped she said, 'I gave him the Mickey Mouse tie!'

I remembered that tie. It was the thing that had first alerted me to the fact that something odd was going on. John was very much a plain-stripe man. When I saw it he said he'd an hour to wait for his train and had killed the time in the Tie Rack. A young assistant had dared him to buy it! I dared him to wear it but he never did. At least not to my knowledge.

Maybe he had taken it up to town with him and swapped the plain stripe when he met Cathy for lunch.

My mind went into overdrive and I imagined them visiting museums and art galleries together . . . or visiting friends as a couple! All those 'late nights at the office'. John had insisted that he liked to work without constant interruptions from colleagues. Why had I believed him? Perhaps I believed what I wanted to believe – that he was faithful. I was beginning to recover from the initial shock and anger was creeping in.

I said, 'Was the child adopted?'

'No. It didn't . . . It was never born. *He* was never born. I waited as long as I dared but John was adamant. John didn't want it. He talked me into a termination. If you must know, he said it wouldn't be fair to your two. I had to respect him for that.' Her face crumpled again.

I was surprised to feel the beginnings of sympathy for her. She and I had both been deceived. John was good-looking, funny, affectionate and we had both fallen in love with him. Cathy had suffered too in her own way. Parting with a child must have been agony – of mind as well as body. We had both trusted him and we had both been betrayed.

'Look,' I said. 'I live quite near. I could make a pot of coffee.'

'No, thanks!' She tossed her head. 'I don't want anything from you. I'll be getting back.'

What to? I wondered. A small flat? A room in her parents' house. She didn't look old enough to have earned much. No doubt she had been expecting to move in with John at some stage.

'Please yourself!' I snapped, stung by her rejection of my small olive branch. 'I don't know why you're feeling so sorry for yourself. You're young enough to start again. You'll meet somebody else. It's not so easy for me at my age.'

Abruptly she stood up. 'You had him for years. You should have made him happier. He said that—'

I jumped to my feet and slapped her face. 'Don't you dare

to criticize me. Whatever John told you is a pack of lies! I never wanted any other man but John, and until you came along he—'

'Or until the secretary came along!'

We faced each other furiously. Up until that moment I had meant to hold back the most damning evidence of John's duplicity but my patience snapped.

'For your information, *John's Cathy*, we didn't have any children. John didn't want any. So his reason for not leaving me was that he didn't want to. Try to get your head round that!'

It was a low, spiteful blow but I watched her expression change with a malicious pleasure that I had never experienced before. I knew it was the truth but Cathy hesitated, the word 'liar' almost visible on her lips.

Without a word she fumbled in her bag and drew out a photograph. John was sitting on the grass with his arms round two children.

'John, I believe!' she said.

'Yes.'

'And two children!'

'Yes. My sister's children. Sarah and Tom with Uncle John.'

'You're lying! They're John's!'

'I think I'd have noticed giving birth twice!'

If John had been present at that moment I think I would have throttled him with my bare hands. 'We had no children!'

I closed my eyes then to shut out her anguished expression but was swept by a wave of dizziness. As I staggered to stay upright I heard her say, 'No! *No!* Oh God!'

Swaying, I fell back on to the seat and thought I was going to be sick. Shock, I told myself. That's all it is. For a moment I sat with my eyes closed and let the world spin around me.

Cathy said, 'Are you all right? You're white as a sheet.' She looked frightened.

'Yes ... at least ... No. Not really. Just the shock and everything.' I tried to smile. 'I'll be fine.'

215

She sat beside me, still clutching the photograph. I said, 'If you don't believe me I can give you my sister's address. John didn't want children. It wasn't just your child, Cathy, that he didn't want. He made that clear from the start of our marriage, although I did hope he'd come round to the idea. He never did.'

I was trying to find some comfort in the knowledge that John could have left me if he'd wanted to. He had the perfect excuse. Cathy was expecting a child. So maybe in spite of everything that had happened, he had wanted to stay with me. It *was* reassuring in a way but the problem remained. If I had known about the affair, would *I* have wanted us to stay together?

Cathy's face had lost some of its charm. She looked pinched and miserable. Very much the way I feel, I thought. Two pathetic women.

I said, 'If John could see us now!' and smiled shakily.

The smile was not returned. Instead she said, 'It was my fault he died.'

'Of course it wasn't. It was an accident. He was on his way—'

'On his way to see me. It was my birthday and he'd promised to spend it with me. He'd *promised*! We were going to have a meal out at our favourite restaurant and I sat there at the bar like a lemon, waiting . . . When he didn't turn up I asked them and they said he'd never made a booking. I rushed outside to phone him and he said he couldn't come because he'd forgotten he had company coming. I'd bought this new dress with a sequinned top . . .' She stopped, needing to take a breath.

I remembered the occasion. We had invited two close friends to dinner. We both loved entertaining but there was an added bonus for John. He prided himself on being 'a bit of a wine buff' and loved to share his latest discoveries. Ellen and Mitch had already arrived and the starters were on the table beneath their cling film. I was about to announce dinner with the little gong John had bought me as a joke when we were in Morocco.

He always teased me about my love of formality.

I smiled.

Cathy was still talking. 'I screamed at him down the phone that if he didn't spend time with me on my birthday then he didn't really care about me and we were finished!'

John had answered the phone in the bedroom and when he came back he said he had to go because his boss had been rushed to hospital with a heart attack and wasn't expected to live. He dashed out and drove away. I shouted, 'Don't drive too fast!' That was what I always said, knowing him and his 'flair' for driving.

'I booked a table for later and went home. My parents were away on holiday and I just sat there. Of course he didn't turn up. Eventually I rang the police but by then he was already dead.'

The three of us had eaten the meal in an atmosphere of forced gaiety and our friends had left around twelve. I hadn't expected John to return that night because I imagined him sitting beside his boss in the intensive care unit. I *did* expect him to ring me but he didn't and I woke the next day to find two policemen on the doorstep with the news that he was dead. When I didn't hear from his partner's wife I assumed the emergency was over and that he'd recovered.

Cathy said, 'Damn him!' Then she leaped to her feet and darted over to the grave and snatched up her floral tribute. With an enviable overhand swing she hurled it into the shrubbery and burst into tears. This time she sobbed uncontrollably, large hopeless tears for a lover now lost to her in more ways than one.

I was recovering from my dizzy spell and walked over to retrieve the carnations. I fiddled them back into shape and held them out to her. 'For all the happy times,' I suggested.

After a moment she smiled through the tears and took the flowers. I watched her replace them. She stood staring at the headstone. Then she came back to me and said, 'I wondered about the wording. It's a bit mean, isn't it?'

'I was angry. It was all I could manage.'

'Ah!' Her smile was a bit crooked.

I said, 'I could make that pot of coffee ... or we could have something stronger. We could raid John's cellar.'

She took my hands in hers and said, 'Why not!'